# THE NATURALIST

# MARK SUMNER

*Word Posse*

Dedication
*For my son John, at a time of both joy and difficulty.*


Acknowledgements
*Many thanks to John O'Neill at Black Gate Magazine,*
*without whom this book would not exist.*
*Additional thanks to Marella Sands, Sharon Shinn, Rett MacPherson,*
*Thomas Drennan, Deborah Millitello, and Laurell K. Hamilton,*
*who, taken together, make up the best writer's group in all the world.*


From Word Posse
*The Naturalist,* Mark Sumner
*Sleeping the Churchyard Sleep,* Rett MacPherson
*Pandora's Mirror,* Marella Sands

Visit us at www.wordposse.com

This book has been typeset in Fanwood. Titles and headers are in Alien League. Cover design by Word Posse. Cover photo by Golden Mean Photography. Portions of this book previously appeared in Black Gate Magazine.

ISBN-10: 0990839249
ISBN-13: 978-0-9908392-4-8

*Editor's Note*

This journal has been modified only slightly. Some of the most archaic passages have been altered to improve clarity for the modern reader and slang terms of the period have been removed where the meaning is less than clear, so that only rarely is the reader faced with terms such as *balbutiate* rather than *stuttering*, or *hoddypeak* rather than *fool*. In a few places, an effort has been made to fill in brief portions of the text where weather and time had rendered the original pages problematic. In several instances, the Latinate names for plants and animals have been updated to more current taxonomic standards to avoid confusion. Place names have generally been left as they were at the time of the British Central Lumber Company rather than updated to those terms used today, in order to better capture the tone of the original account.

Otherwise, the journal entries stand as originally written.

# I

*Central Selvanos*
*6 August 1832*

By the third day of the expedition, my socks were no longer dry. Nor was any territory or portion of other piece of clothing or gear which I possessed.

Starting from St. George at the deepest incision on Amatique Bay, we had been charged to follow the gently twisting path of the River Sarstoon and to discover the source of wild tales coming from a logging village far in the interior of company lands. It was not, perhaps, the sort of errand which would have normally required the presence of a medical man, but the task had piqued my interest as a chance to collect creatures and improve my knowledge of the deep forest. However, I cannot say that the rest of our party appeared to have any enthusiasm for making a difficult journey in the season of rain.

Our total number amounted to six. In addition to myself and Captain Valamont, we were joined by three other soldiers of the West Indian Regiment under the Captain's command. All of them were men that I knew passing well. Sergeant Harness was an exceedingly large man with a head roughly the size of a milking bucket and shoulders that would have done credit to an ox. The other soldiers were privates: one a balding Scotsman named Donnel, and the other a dark-haired young man two years my junior. The young soldier's name was Sherman, and he had a cheerful disposition that served as a counter to the rest, who were a generally ill-tempered crew.

But if the soldiers were sour, the sixth member of the expedition seemed near to despair. A settler called Richardson—one of those who had fled the settlement of Applewash in the last week—had been forced to join

with us. The intent was that he serve as our guide, since among the rest of
the group was no one who had ranged so far inland as Applewash in a
number of years. However, having escaped his home and made it intact to
St. George, it was clear that Richardson looked on reversing this path with
all the favor generally accorded the thirteen stairs leading to a hangman's
noose. Even so, whether he relished the prospect or not, we were all put on
horses and pointed west.

With foul weather dogging us through every hour, and the path we
followed more wallow than way, we were three days making our way to
the Sarstoon Ferry. We crossed the ferry at night, making a journey that to
me seemed tinged with no little peril, though the ferrymen pulled along
without comment and Private Donnel spent most of the voyage sleeping.
We halted late that evening on the wild north bank. Captain Valamont
was extremely vexed by our poor progress and declared that we should
have completed the whole trip in half the time. How we might have done
so without breaking the horse's legs and the rider's necks he did not say,
but when the fourth morning dawned bright and warm, he forced us along
at a pace that would have put us in good standing for a Derby.

We were fortunate that our travel at that point carried us over firm,
sandy ground and we made good progress for several hours. However, as
if to make up for our progress under the morning sun, fresh torrents of rain
fell through the afternoon. The narrow road momentarily left behind the
savannas and moved back among the huge trunks of the forest. Guanacasta
trees with boles some eight feet in diameter loomed on all sides. Some of
these shot up as single straight trunks. Others split into two, three, or more
very near the base. All of the trees were festooned with heavy coats of
bromeliads, along with airborne ferns and orchids. They were beautiful to
see, but the rain which slipped from their overlapping leaves by the pints
and gallons made it difficult to find much pleasure in even the most sylvan
of surroundings.

We were still some ten miles short of Applewash when night came
and we were forced to reign in our tired mounts. Our little band camped
that night in a narrow clearing at the side of the road where a fallen giant
had cleared away the lesser trees. Captain Valamont took his grey and
scouted off through the woods in the company of tall Sergeant Harness,
leaving me with Richardson and the other two soldiers. Together we

gathered and stacked a good mass of fallen branches, and I even offered to sacrifice some dry pages from the center of my folio, but neither flint nor sulphur match could prevail against the rain. After an hour of trying, the soldiers gave up. I could do no more than lay under my oilskin and shiver, more chilled than I could ever remember.

One of the soldiers, the old Scot named Donnel, leaned against a massive kapok tree and tried to fashion a shelter from a system of overlapping leaves. "Damn, me boys," he said in that way that soldiers will, "I have served this army two decades and then some, but seeing all this water, I believe I must have been pressed into the navy while I wasn't watching."

The younger soldier laughed a bit at this. "I been in the navy," said Sherman.

"When was you ever in the navy?" said Donnel. He gave the younger man an eye sharp with skepticism. "Never is when."

"I was so." Sherman pulled his cloak up around his face and shook off a shower of water very like a dog coming from a lake. He walked around the stack of dank wood and sat down next to me. "Sir," he said, "I was pressed in at Bristol when I was fourteen, you see? We come here straight off, and I got pressed out just as quick." He inserted his thumb into his mouth, and pulled it free again, producing a popping sound like the drawing of a cork from a bottle. "Selvanos was short of soldiering types, because of that there plague, that you know so well, sir, so they took off my grey coat and give me a new red one."

"Aye, I recall well enough that coat we gave you," said Donnel. "It weren't new. Man who had it before you died of yellowjack." He paused in his work and scratched at his head. "Come to think of it, don't know that we chanced to wash the coat before handing it to you, neither. After all, one short sailor more or less makes little difference."

"A sailor makes a fine soldier," Sherman answered him, "though not one of you boys would stand a day on the decks. I expect you'd be wishing for the plague after you rode out a little weather."

"There's nothing a pigtailed sailor can do that a soldier can't do better." Donnel hooked his thumbs into his jacket and raised his chin. "No discipline among tars, and that's the truth of it."

"That right?" Sherman shook off another spray of water. "I'll tell you one thing that sailors do right well. They take their roofs and their beds with them. Weather like this on any ship and I'd still have hot supper and a dry sleep."

"I came from England, myself," I said, mostly as a means of ending their argument. "My parents came into a claim on some land here, so we left Hampshire when I was twelve."

"You're a landowner then?" asked Sherman. "A holder in the company?" He seemed impressed by the idea.

"Not yet," I replied.

"But you will be when your parents are gone."

I shook my head. "My parents are dead already."

Donnel peeked out from his shelter of leaves. "Then why haven't you gone off to your own place?"

The truth was embarrassing enough that I regretted beginning this conversation, but it would get no less embarrassing if I lied. "My parents borrowed heavily against their land," I said. "I indentured myself to the company until those debts are paid."

Sherman thought this over for a moment, but seemed unbothered by the idea. "Still, one day you'll be a landowner," he said. "An honest member of the company."

From his place beneath the leaves, the Scot let out a hard laugh. "Company debts have a way of getting bigger as time goes by, not smaller," he said. "Young Mr. Brown here is likely to find that they won't be paid off this side of his dotage. It's the same with you and the army. You'll never be set loose while you can still hold a musket."

Sherman resumed his argument, but I was too tired and too chilled to pay much attention. I stared at the dripping mass of firewood in the center of the clearing, willing it to dryness. The horses were tied up to a pair of smaller trees at the edge of the clearing, but they seemed as tired and miserable as the rest of us.

Across from me, Gerald Richardson looked neither tired nor cold. He looked absent. Richardson had spoken clearly enough back in St. George when he described his flight from Applewash, and for the first two days on the road he had been talkative, if resentful of his own temporary impressment into our expedition. But from the time we had crossed to the north bank of the Sarstoon and moved on inland, Richardson's eyes and thoughts had wandered off. Sometimes, he would speak a word or two, but often as not what he said had little to do with what was around him. I had seen men caught in nightmares of delirium when they were dying of fever or injury, but I had never seen a fit, healthy man such as Richardson whose mind just drifted away. It was quite unnerving.

I fished into the depths of my rucksack and drew out a specimen jar. There was a pair of insects inside whose feet were broadened into leaf-shaped protrusions and whose bodies were so patterned in shares of lilac and orange as to be riotous compared to the muddy ground beneath us. I had taken the pair from a large example of Brassavola while we were at one of our rest stops. The colors of the insects that seemed so odd now had made them a perfect match for the orchid's interior. I turned the jar slowly, peering at my captives. I expected that they would prove to be not only a new species, but perhaps a new genus as well. I wondered if I might name them after my good friend, Miss Morgan, and whether such a gift might please her. I started to open my folio, but the failing light was far too weak to allow me to describe the insects adequately and the rain such that any effort at depiction would have been swiftly reduced to a blur. I had trouble enough seeing the jar, much less the contents.

With a sigh, I put the specimens back. Too wet to sleep, too dark to do anything else. It was apt to be a very long night.

Donnel and Sherman were still trading barbs when I heard horses slowly approaching, their hooves splashing carefully on the slippery ground. A few moments later, I saw two vague shapes emerge from the forest. Captain Valamont and Sergeant Harness were leading their horses instead of riding them. They did not seem happy about our situation.

"Where's that fire?" said Captain Valamont.

"Sir! Pardon, sir. Too wet by half, sir," said Donnel. He got to his feet and raised his hand in salute. "We gave her a good effort, but there's not so much dry wood in this forest to make a match."

The captain made a noise that was very like a growl. "You men cannot be trusted with the simplest task. It's a good thing I came along on this trip, or you would have wandered halfway to join the Spanish in Mexico by now." Valamont did not mention that he, like the rest of us, had been made to come along on the trip by direct orders and would not otherwise have chosen to leave his pleasant home in St. George. He turned to the other figure in the darkness. "Sergeant, get us a blaze."

"Right you are, sir." Sergeant Harness tied up his horse and the captain's. Then he leaned over the mass of wood and went straight to work. I watched with no small degree of interest as he first opened a pouch and produced thin curls of shaved cedar and pinches of dried moss. Flashes of light came from flint and steel, glaring in the little clearing like miniature lightning. Harness was a hard man, with a knife-sharp nose, eyes as dark as the openings on a pair of muskets, and a narrow face flanked by thick side-whiskers. So far, he had all but ignored me on this journey, and I decided it was the best situation I could hope for with the man.

The rain had begun to slack, and with his dry kit, Harness had more success with his sparks than Donnel. In a few minutes, the Sergeant had coaxed out a dull red glow and not long after that, he fed damp twigs into a small fire that steamed as much as smoked. In the red light, I could see Donnel staring toward the sergeant with obvious resentment. Harness was the younger man, and had been in service only a few years, but already he held a rank greater than the old Scot. It was natural that there should be some tension between the two soldiers. Of course, Captain Valamont was of an age with Donnel and held a much more elevated post, but Valamont was the second son of a prominent landowner. It had long been the army's habit, in both Selvanos and back home in England, to sell commissions. No one would question Valamont's position as an officer.

Not long after the fire was started, there was a crashing from the forest. Freshly dazzled by the flames, we all turned and stared toward the darkness as the sound came rapidly closer. The horses snorted and shuffled around nervously. I struggled to get to my feet and the soldiers searched up their guns, but none of them was prepared when a shaggy grey form burst from the trees.

What followed was a scene of absolute confusion. Captain Valamont shouted orders. Horses reared and kicked. Donnel cursed. Richardson laughed. Men ran after the creature and around the growing fire. The creature threw a long snout back and forth, rising momentarily on its rear legs than coming back down with a splash. Knives glinted in the fire light, and a single pistol shot cracked out. During all this, I kept myself pressed back against a kapok tree and hoped that I did not get shot, stabbed, or trampled.

After leading all on a merry chase, the creature loosed a sharp whistling sound and vanished back into the woods.

"Did you hit it?" asked Sherman, his breath coming out as steam.

"No," said Captain Valamont. "I think not."

Donnel went over to calm the horses. All of the other men stood closer to the fire now and I moved to join them. "Is anyone hurt?" I asked.

"No," said Donnel, "but that was a hell of a big pig."

"Anteater," I replied. Having seen the elongate head and sharply marked form of the intruder, it was clear to me that it had been no escaped domestic animal.

"What?"

"It was a giant anteater," I said. "Myrmecophaga. They're sometimes called ant bears, but they're not related to bears at all. I'm told they're fairly common further south, though it's not so common that you should see them in—"

"Looked like a pig," said the Scot.

Before there was any additional discussion of the nature of our visitor, there was another disturbance in the forest. All of us looked into the dark trunks north of our little clearing, waiting to see what might emerge next. Then the sounds started up to the south of us. And again to the north. And again and again everywhere to our west. Something flashed past us at the dim limits of the light cast by our fire.

"That was a panther!" shouted Donnel. He looked my way with a scowl. "And don't go telling me it was something else, because I know what a panther looks like."

A red brocket deer dashed past, its rusty hide seeming to glow in the firelight. Two more came right behind.

The noise around us grew steadily in volume. We crowded together around the slowly growing fire. Donnel made a last attempt to calm the horses before abandoning them to kick and tug at their ropes. The Scot crowded in with the rest of us. All of us were standing so close to the fire that our damp clothing steamed in the heat. Sherman so close that I could smell the leather of his boots browning in the flame. There was a crashing of branches overhead, and I caught a glimpse of a monkey troop hurrying past. Something very large went blundering along just out of sight. Parrots whipped past, squawking by our heads. There were cries and shouts from the darkness, most of them completely strange and a few all too human.

"There must be a fire," said Sherman, yelling to be heard over the commotion. "A fire in the wood could have set them all running."

Captain Valamont removed a second pistol from his waistband and discharged it toward a shaggy form that momentarily appeared in the shadows, then quickly fled. "Don't be a fool. No fire would spread far in weather like this."

The incredible mayhem reached such a pitch that I could feel the soggy ground dancing under my feet. I stood with my heart beating well up in my throat. Some deep part of my mind told me to run, get away from this place, follow the same course as all the departing animals. Then, almost as quickly as they began, the noises passed on to the east and went out of our hearing. There was nothing left but the slowing patter of the rain falling through the canopy of leaves and the nervous stamping of our horses.

As the sound faded, the soldiers began to gradually ease away from the comfort of the fire.

"What on God's earth was that?" said Donnel.

Sherman pulled back his fire-scorched boots and stared hard to the west. "I still say there must be fire," he said. "Maybe lightning started something. Maybe..."

"Indians," said Captain Valamont. He examined his pistols and began to methodically clean them. "Indians," he repeated with a nod. "Gentlemen, this is all the work of the savages. It has been from the start."

"It is?" I asked, somewhat confused by his statement.

The captain nodded. "That's been clear enough from before we left St. George. Think." He tapped the barrel of a gun against his temple. "Whatever is going on in this place, the savages are behind it. Mark my words." His words did make a certain sense, and I could see the soldiers quickly accept the idea.

Sergeant Harness gave the woods a wary glance. "We need to set a watch."

"Yes," agreed Valamont. "Very good, Sergeant. With the way these animals are acting, those godless natives must be very close. We'll put two to a watch. I'll take the first watch with young Mr. Brown. Then Donnel and Sherman can have the second watch. The sergeant and Mr. Richardson can guard our morning."

With this matter decided, the soldiers seemed to relax. Even though they had just been told there were malicious Indians close by, having orders had clearly calmed their nerves and put them into action. I was considerably less reassured.

I cleared my throat. "Sir...that is, Captain. There's one problem with that plan, sir," I said.

Captain Valamont looked at me with irritation. Having put his men in motion, he clearly didn't appreciate having his actions criticized. "And what is that?"

"Where's Richardson?" I said.

The soldiers spun around and Captain Valamont gave a hard curse. Now that the fire was finally burning brightly, it only made the woods seem more dark and menacing. And it left no doubt that the settler was nowhere in sight.

"Richardson!" shouted Donnel. He took a step toward the shadow choked woods. "Richardson, are you there?"

There was no reply from the darkness.

"He must have run off," said Harness. "While all them animals was going by."

Donnel shook his head. "Out here in the forest, in the middle of all that ruckus?"

It fell to Sherman to say what all of us were thinking. "They took him," he said. "The Indians took Mr. Richardson. By now he's probably dead— or wishes he was."

# 2

*Near Applewash*
*7 August 1832*

Captain Valamont had us moving well before first light. With the dark limbs overhead and the muddy road beneath, we were forced to lead our horses along the path, but at least we were making progress. At every step, the captain expected to be overrun by hordes of Indians armed with spears, poison darts, and every sort of infernal weapon.

All of which was quite a surprise, because in my years on company land, I had seen only a few natives, and those I had seen had been far more interested in how they might get out of my proximity than in doing me any harm. Certainly, we had come across ruins of dwellings and other structures that suggested there had been a substantial number of savages within the area of Selvanos at some point in the past, but all indications were that these settlements had last been occupied decades, if not centuries, in the past. So far as could be told, the native population of the area was sparse, and the threat they posed insubstantial.

A suggestion had been made by Sherman that we might search for Mr. Richardson, but this was quickly dismissed by the captain, who did not want to separate our forces in such proximity to the enemy. Despite the amount of time I had spent in the forest, and even though I had no real thought that violent savages were near, I found myself weighted with fear that pre-dawn. So much so that even breathing seemed an effort.

After what might have been weeks of darkness, the sky finally turned to grey and then to watery pink. Even with the dawn, things did not feel as they should. The forest was far too silent. There were the clicks and whistles of geckos, but few birds. Even the morning chorus of howler monkeys was muted and distant.

As the light grew brighter, the tension that had tightened my chest all through the hours of darkness began to relax notch by notch like the loosening of a belt. The tall grey trunks of the great forest became visible around us; provision tree, raintree, and kapok rising up high while smaller cacao filled in the spaces between. All of the trees were well freighted with vines, bromeliads, and other aerial plants. Far up in the branches of a toboros tree, I even saw a miniature garden of cacti clinging to the boughs. The road passed up through an area of dense thorny undergrowth, and I could see all the soldiers scanning the brush for any sign of marauding savages. But we encountered no sign of Indians that morning.

Soon enough, the road passed out of the forest and into an area where old logwood works had cleared a wide swath right up to the brown foamy waters of the Sarstoon. The path here was drier, and with the trees cleared back we were able to climb onto our saddles. Mounted, with the sun rising up over the eastern hills, and the road clear ahead, the events in the wood seemed more something sourced from nightmare than reality.

At mid-morning, we reached a course that cut from the main road toward a largish plantation known at Grey's Works, which controlled both timber lands, a grain mill, and fields whose main product was molasses shipped out of St. George. The residents of this middling remote household were clearly aware of our approach, and obviously excited by the prospect of visitors. A pair of servants met us at the crossroads and urged us to journey up the lane to the house. Captain Valamont's features narrowed in impatience, but he assented to bring our force up the lane until we were all standing in the muddy way just a hundred yards or so short of the main house.

On the steps of the house the landowners had arrayed themselves, their children, and their considerable household to provide a greeting, and I heard Donnel and Sherman exchange speculation about being allowed to stop for a meal. However, this was not to be. Captain Valamont rode ahead, dismounted, and carried on a brief conversation with the owners of the works, before favoring them with a deep bow, remounting, and returning to the rest of us. Once there, he steered us back to the main road.

Captain Valamont consulted his map. "Caney Creek is only a short way," he said, "and Applewash no more than two hours ride beyond. Once the situation there is settled, there will be ample opportunity to pay calls on the locals."

As predicted, only a mile or two passed before we rode over a low hill and saw a stream snaking across the valley below. The land here was cultivated, with well-planted fields of barley and cotton. The road brought us down to a bridge that was new and well-built, and quite a serious structural undertaking for something so deep into the wilderness, with supports of placed stone and a deck of wide, thick planks. The heavy rains of the last few days had broadened Caney Creek until it looked near as wide as the Sarstoon, but the feet of the bridge stood well back from the banks. The fields on the other side appeared lush and pleasant under the morning sun. A solid farmhouse was visible in the middle distance along with a cluster of barns, sheds, and smaller buildings.

Captain Valamont rode up to the bridge and looked across the foaming brown waters of the stream. "The Bracewaithe lands are just ahead," he called back. "If the road stays dry, we'll be in Applewash while the savages are still buttering their toast for breakfast." He pressed his heels to the big grey and started over the bridge.

I was none too sure that Indians ate a proper English breakfast, and was still quite unconvinced about the existence of any savages at all, but I was not about to say anything that might dampen the captain's mood. Sergeant Harness followed across the bridge. I rode across next, followed by Sherman. Donnel trailed the group, with Mr. Richardson's riderless horse in tow.

The Bracewaithe home, like Grey's Works, was actually a series of servants dwellings, barns, and sheds that were scattered in the fields around a great central house as large as any back in St. George—quite a little settlement in its own right, though we were still some miles from Applewash proper. It would have been a fine thing to stop and pay a call, just for the chance of some fresh bread and warm tea, but Captain Valamont was clearly eager to reach the primary settlement. He passed the first small, well-built house without a glance and seemed ready to ignore the second, as well. As we trotted on, I noticed that there was no smoke at the chimney of either house, not even from the stacks on the kitchen houses.

"They're not baking any bread this morning," I said to Sherman.

The soldier pointed at the field beside the road. "They'll not be making bread for a year less they get out 'ere and scythe that barley."

I looked at the yellow and green stalks. The grain was sometimes reluctant in the near continuous warmth of Selvanos, but it was clear that the Bracewaithes at least had enjoyed fine yields this season. "It's ripe?"

"A week and more past ready," said Sherman. "I cut barley some back in England. See 'ow them grass heads is all bent over? Another week in this rain, and this'll all be rotting on the ground."

A wind swept over the fields, and I saw then how the heavy stalks bent and swayed. If what Sherman said was right, it could mean trouble for more than just the farmers that owned these fields. Most people in Selvanos worked at the lumber business. Landowners kept house gardens, but the people in St. George and the larger settlements were depending on the few large interior farms for food. Goods were, of course, available through the sea trade, but the barley rotting in this field might mean a shortage of bread in St. George come next month.

And then there was the more immediate concern—where were the people who should have counted this harvest? Why did all these farms seem so quiet? So...abandoned?

With these unpleasant thoughts in mind, we moved by the second house and its cluster of out buildings. I was nearing the last of these structures when I saw something white in a bare patch of earth next to a small shed. The thing on the ground was too far away to see clearly, but there was a feel to it—a certain color, a particular texture—that made me rein in my horse smartly.

"Captain Valamont," I called. "I think you should have a look at this." Without waiting for the soldiers, I guided my horse off the side of the road and up through thick, damp barley that grew tall enough to brush against the belly of my mount. I passed into a circle of shorter grass in front of the white painted shed, and stopped next to the object I had seen shining on the ground. The horse snorted, and I had some difficulty getting down without being toppled. Once on the ground, I tugged my reluctant mount forward and knelt down for a closer inspection.

The rest of the expedition came up behind me while I was still kneeling in the dirt. "Mr. Brown," said Captain Valamont. His exasperated tone gave me to understand that he thought I had stopped to

THE NATURALIST ✸ 19

point out some natural wonder. "We have to move on. There is no time for capturing fleas or looking at flowers."

I stood up. "What about skeletons?"

"Skeletons?" asked Sherman. The young soldier's voice jumped upward two octaves. "What do you mean skeletons?"

Sergeant Harness hopped down from his horse and stomped over to where I was standing. "This is no skeleton," he said. "Just animal bones."

"It is the skeleton of an animal," I said.

The soldiers pushed in closer. Sherman laughed. "It's a sheep, see? Only a sheep."

"Aye," agreed Donnel. "I've seen plenty of sheep butchered from here to Perth. Looks like someone's had a feast."

Captain Valamont drove his grey in amongst the other horses. "Mr. Brown, we did not come to this place to examine the remains of someone's lunch. Get back on your mount and let us get on with this pointless journey."

I examined the remains a moment longer then shook my head. "Something odd happened here. This animal wasn't butchered."

"What do you mean?" asked the captain.

"Look here, sir." I ran my finger along the smooth curve of a rib and around the protruding axial process of a vertebra. "The bones are not broken. Do you see? The skeleton is all together, and without any knife marks on the bones."

"A skilled butcher—"

"No, Captain," I said. "That's not it. I've seen skeletons flensed for display in museum, but none were prepared anything so cleanly as this."

Sergeant Harness took another step forward and pushed away a polished femur with the toe of his boot. "So no one cut it up," he said. "What does it matter? It's clear enough what happened."

I looked up at him. "It is?"

Harness pointed toward the nearby house. "This here farm is empty. Maybe the Indians got them. Maybe they went to St. George with all them what came from Applewash. Wherever they went, they left this sheep behind to starve."

This answer seemed to satisfy the soldiers. The Sergeant went to get back on his horse, while Captain Valamont and the others turned their mounts away.

"Wait!" I shouted. "This animal did not starve. There's still grass and barley in reach of the rope. And see how this grass has only been cropped a little? This sheep wasn't staked here more than a day or two before it died."

"Died of thirst, then," said Harness. He slipped one boot into the stirrups and heaved himself up onto his big bay horse. "Sheep die, boy. Who cares why? We wasn't sent after sheep." Behind him, the others trotted through the barley back toward the road.

I released my own horse and grabbed the side of the Sergeant's saddle. "Sergeant Harness, this wasn't thirst and it wasn't hunger." I pointed to the ground. "Look at this grass. It's been raining for five days, but the grass scarce reflects a fringe of new growth. Something happened to this sheep, and it happened fast. This animal was alive only a very short time ago."

Sergeant Harness shook off my hand. "You're a fool, Brown. That animal's been dead a month or more, look at those bones." He put his heels to the bay and pulled away from me.

"I am looking at the bones, Sergeant," I called after him. "That's what worries me." My own horse had wandered off a few steps, and was giving a series of low, nervous whickers, but thankfully it did not seek to flee when I approached. I managed to snag the dangling reins and struggled back onto the saddle. From the ground, the white skull of the sheep gave me a broad ruminant smile as I turned my mount and followed after the soldiers.

The first three soldiers had crossed the field of barley and reached the road, with Sergeant Harness not far behind. I glanced back at the shed and the skeleton one last time, reluctant to leave. When I looked around only seconds later, both Sergeant Harness and his tall horse were gone.

For a moment, I could only stare in confusion. It seemed as if the sergeant had vanished from the world between one heartbeat and the next. Then I saw that a patch of the barley was twisting and boiling. My first thought was that the sergeant's horse must have stepped on some uneven ground and fallen in the mud. I urged my own mount forward, but the chestnut shied away, sidestepping and tossing its head. There was a sharp and unmistakable scent in the air. A mixture of lemons and bright, peppery spice.

A dark patch of horsehide was visible for a moment among the barley, a brown leg kicked at the sky. Then it was gone again. A man's arm popped up, scarlet in the light, and I was puzzled, because Sergeant Harness had not worn his red dress coat. Then I saw that the red did not come from a coat.

"Captain!" I screamed. At the same moment, Harness himself gave a great, outraged bellow that brought the three riders on the road around sharply. I tried again to force my horse toward the fallen man, but the animal only added a scream of its own to the bedlam and sidestepped again.

The barley was moving now, and not solely around the site where Harness had fallen. The stems of grass rippled along a hundred yard line, though not as they would have done under the influence of a sudden breeze. Instead the stalks jiggled and bounced as if the ground itself were moving. There was a sound as well, a soft shuffling, a peculiar creaking whisper that seemed to come from everywhere.

I had a passing thought that the entire field had been transmogrified into some huge and fabulous sundew—an insect catching plant grown to a size where men and horses were its prey. Then a dark, lumpy liquid spilled forth from around the stalks and poured into the short grass surrounding the dead sheep.

The liquid glistened like tar in the morning sun, black with glints of deepest red. As soon as it appeared, my horse gave another scream, reared up, and pawed at the sky. I pressed my knees hard against its ribs, but my horsemanship was not up to the challenge of the animal's thrashing. In a moment, both I and my rucksack were on the ground. The horse turned and sped away before I could regain even my hands and knees, darting out of sight between the scattered buildings.

The fall from the horse left me winded and addled. In the distance, I could hear men shouting, and heard two pistols fired in quick succession, but from my seated position, I could not see past the trembling grass heads. I got to one knee and started to search along the road for my companions, but before I could spot them a situation much nearer to hand caught my attention—the liquid was surging closer. And it wasn't liquid.

It was a boiling mass of insects, black and red chitinous shells scraping together to produce the whispering sigh I had heard moments before. I could see little detail in this advancing swarm, but many of the creatures were surely quite large, the size of my thumb or better, and they were coming toward me with nightmarish speed.

I snatched up my rucksack from the ground and sprinted off along the path my horse had blazed. Before I could even reach the other side of the clearing, more of the insects came rushing from the grass along that margin. They blanketed the ground completely, cutting off my escape.

There was a small shed off to my right, the sort of place where tools might be stored safely away from the incessant rain. I turned toward this shed in desperation. The roofline of the building swept down to perhaps six feet off the ground and was covered in wooden shakes cut from durable monkeypod. With a quick flip of my arm, I sent my rucksack sailing toward the roof then I grasped the edge and tried to pull myself up. Wood shakes came loose in my hands and I fell back into the dirt. I made one look over my shoulder and saw that the wave of insects was no more than a yard to my rear. I jumped again. The wood shifted under my fingers, but the next line of shakes did not fall. My feet kicked against the painted boards at the side of the shed. Then I was up and gasping on the roof.

It took me a second to recover and turn over so that my back was to the roof. The rafters groaned dangerously beneath me, but for the moment the shed bore my weight. Out across the fields I saw one figure on horseback spinning around and around in the road. The horse was brown, not grey, so it couldn't have been Captain Valamont. I could not be sure, but I thought it was Sherman. Where Sergeant Harness had fallen, I could see now the movement of red and black swarms within the barley, but there was no motion that suggested either man or horse was still alive. Most disturbing was a glimpse of something glittering white in the midst of the insect mass.

My eyes began to water and the smell of lemons in the air was so thick that each breath seared my lungs. I eased forward and looked over the ragged edge of the roof.

The insects were climbing toward me. Their speed up the boards was not as frantic as they had been on the ground, but they were coming with alacrity. Despite my evident peril, I could not help but be transfixed by this sight. From only four feet away, I could see the creatures much more clearly, but could make but little sense of what I was seeing. The mass of them was confusing. There were too many legs, too many segments. The things coming up the wall didn't look like any insect I had collected or seen in books.

Then I saw that each of what I had taken for individuals among this advancing horde was not one insect, but two. The first was a fairly conventional creature in all but size, not too different from a great dark ant some two inches in length. It had a smooth carapace of shiny black, a shortened thorax, and a narrow elongate abdomen. Fierce hooked mandibles were spread wide at the front of its dark head. Mounted on this large insect's back was a second creature of much odder configuration. In that brief glimpse, it appeared to be a tiny man in crimson armor, with a finger-length lance in one hand.

And at once, my mouth flew open and I croaked a single word. "Antriders."

Though there had been few natives in the region of Selvanos, and still less sociable contact between these forest inhabitants and the members of the company, there were still some few fragments of local folklore which had passed into our knowledge. Chief among these were warnings of the antriders. In the retold tales which had reached my ears, antriders were diminutive knights who went about the forest on insect-back, tackling foes of all sizes. A clear impossibility. An amusing amalgam of English garden fairy and native myth. Precisely the sort of capilotade that might be expected from such a blend of fancies. Except that now this myth was rapidly climbing toward my face, and from what I had seen, there was nothing either amusingly chivalrous or safely imaginary in its actions.

I pushed back from the wall and carefully stood. The roof sagged under my feet and a half-dozen monkeypod shakes went skittering off the side of the shed, but I managed to pick up my rucksack and step across the low peak of the roof to the other side of the building. There was no escape there. The ground on that side was already blanketed with glistening black and red. There was another shed perhaps eight feet away, but the thought of leaping that gulf seemed as unlikely as learning to fly.

Another look across the fields showed no one else in sight. The horseman on the road had vanished and what I could see of the road was transformed into a river of glistening insects; a shining torrent of tarry bodies on the march. Their numbers seemed impossible. In that one glimpse, I was seeing what were surely millions of these antriders. I, on the other hand, was quite alone.

Behind me, I heard a hissing sound and the clatter as a fresh shake fell from the roof. Looking back, I saw that the first wave of antriders had joined me on top of the shed. On this gentler slope, the insects seemed to have regained the rushing speed they had demonstrated in the fields below. Inspired by this sight, I took two quick steps down the sloping roof, swung the rucksack, and flew. My arms pin-wheeled through the air and my feet kept moving as if I might run across the space. Still, it was immediately obvious that my boots would not clear the void. Instead, the awning of the next building struck me at the waist hard enough to drive all the air from my lungs. My feet sagged toward the ground even as I clawed at the roof, using my hand and the weight of the rucksack to secure a purchase. The sighing, creaking sound behind me grew louder. It sounded eager.

Gasping, I dragged myself onto the next roof. This building was larger, a barn of some sort, and the roof pitched up at a considerably steeper angle. I couldn't manage to stand. Instead, I crawled up the slope with my chest heaving and arms aching with the effort. At the peak, I glimpsed back. The antriders had gained this roof and were following close behind.

The ground on the other side of the barn appeared to be clear, but I was not about to take that chance. The summer kitchen was only a short hop away, and beyond that, the house itself was connected by a roofed-over breezeway. I slid down the side of the barn, stood at the edge, and made the short jump to the kitchen roof.

The roof collapsed under me, and I came down in a shower of broken beams, dust, and splintered wood. I caught myself part way down, grabbed a sagging board, and slowed my fall enough to keep the final drop from being a deadly one. Still, I hit the ground hard enough to send pain shooting along my limbs and up my spine. I groaned and closed my eyes. Distantly, I knew that I should get up and continue my flight, but the brick walls of the kitchen were surely safe against these creatures. Besides, I hurt too much to run more. I opened my eyes and rolled over on my side.

THE NATURALIST ✳ 25

I found myself face to face, or at least face to former face, with a clean white skull. Despite the pain I was feeling, this grisly reminder of the situation was enough to propel me to my feet. There was a tattered and bloodstained dress still stretched across the bones on the floor and an iron pan near a skeletal hand. The antriders had clearly taken this woman in the middle of her daily chores, sweeping into the kitchen like a blaze.

There was a soft pop in the still kitchen, then another right after it. I looked up and saw antriders raining down through the hole in the roof. There was no chance of getting back up through the torn roof and little time to make any other decision. I went to the front door and shoved it open. There were antriders on the ground, but they were not yet an unbroken sea.

I dashed out through the insects, turned to the right, and kept running. Soft snaps and explosions of insect bodies came from under my heels as I ran. Twice there were sharp pains at my ankle that nearly caused me to stumble, but I kept moving.

The back door of the house was hanging open. It was enticing to think that I might find shelter inside, but the terrible form on the floor of the kitchen had proved to me that doors and walls would not provide an adequate barrier. Instead, I looked to the east and kept running as quickly as I could. Within a hundred yards, my heart was beating in my head and my breath was ragged. The smell of lemons was still with me and that hissing noise of the insectile army's movement never left my ears. By the time I passed the house nearest the bridge, I was staggering. I began to angle my path, hoping to get back to the road, but as I moved that way I could see more of the insects following along the line of the road. With the pike out of reach, I turned and aimed myself straight for the muddy banks of Caney Creek.

The distance to the creek seemed like leagues, though I knew it to be no more than a quarter of a mile. Each step across the sodden fields only added more weight to feet that already seemed to be ten stone each. Finally, in a fugue of exhaustion, I stumbled past the trees along the side of the stream and plunged into the water. Fortunately for me, a dry morning had begun to reduce the flow, and the creek had lost some of the volume that we had seen when riding the other way. Still, the water was brown, foamy, and soon grew deep enough to sweep me from my tired feet.

I got my rucksack slung over my shoulder and paddled toward the far bank. The water spun me around more than once, and my wet clothing and heavy, muddy boots weighed down my movements. Bits of passing driftwood hammered at my face and shoulders.

Something touched my wrist, and I confess my immediate response was to scream. I tried to pull back my arm, but the grip on my wrist grew tighter. An inexorable force began to tug me forward. I looked up, expecting to see some horrid mass of glistening insects. Instead, I saw the frightened face of Gerald Richardson.

"Don't fight me," he said, "unless you want to end up swimming down the Sarstoon."

I put down my feet and was surprised to find that I was in water only a bit over knee deep. With a few shoves of my legs, and Richardson pulling on my arm, I pushed myself free of Caney Creek. Behind me, the antriders raised a howl of insect frustration.

# 3

*Caney Creek Bridge*
*7 August 1832*

For several minutes I could only lie on the cool mud of the bank and gasp. I could hear Richardson talking and knew that he was talking to me, but I was too far gone in a haze of shock to understand a word. The muscles of my arms and legs trembled, and I ached from crown to heel. Even here, with the rich organic mud of the stream close against my face, my throat burned with the acrid smell of peppered lemons.

Improbably, my rucksack was still looped over my shoulder and its contents seemed more or less intact. I dragged the canvas bag around and used it to pillow my aching head. I closed my eyes and did my best to sink into the mud.

There was a sharp pain in my side. After a moment's respite, it came again and this time I recognized it as the toe of someone's boot prodding me in the ribs. I rolled over and opened a single eye. Richardson stood over me with an expression of mingled fear and determination.

"Get up," he said. The toe of his boot swung into my side, and I felt another burst of pain. "Get up now."

He swung his foot back for another blow, but I raised my hand in defense. "I'm getting up."

Richardson hesitated with his foot in the air then he planted his foot, bent, and offered me his hand instead. With a painful effort, I eased to my feet. "We have to go," he said. "They've stopped at the water, but I don't think they'll be stopped for long."

I turned and looked back across the stream. The antriders were there, massed in a wave of shining red and black that swelled up in waist-deep mounds and lapped at the brown edge of the stream. I saw dozens of the creatures drop into the flow, but the water swiftly carried away the miniature riders and their thumb-sized steeds. The greater mass of antriders held back, evidently afraid of the swift-flowing water.

"Is this what you saw in Applewash?" I asked.

The settler ran a hand across his sweaty face. "I never saw anything like this in Applewash. It was too dark. Thank the Great Lord for that much. If I had seen what these things did to my farm—to my family—I..." He voice choked off and he shook his head. "This is the first time I've truly seen them."

"Where are the others?" I asked.

"Others?" Richardson jumped as if pinched from behind. "You mean there's more of them things?"

"I meant the other men." Beyond the antriders I saw the wind moving over the rows of barley, but of our expedition to Applewash, there was no sign. "Have you seen Captain Valamont or the other soldiers?"

Richardson shook his head. "I barely saw you. I..." He hesitated and wiped sweat away from his forehead. "I ran off when all those animals came. I thought it was those...I was afraid."

I took a quick glance across the stream. "Yes, well, it's hard to blame you for that," I told him. "I was close to running myself, and I'd not lived through what happened in Applewash."

The settler nodded, but his expression was unchanged. "After that," he said, "I got lost walking through the woods, see, at a daver, heading plum from the direction I'd thought I was walking, 'til at last I cast up against the creek. I was by the bridge, deciding which way I ought to walk, when I saw you in the water."

"No one else?"

"No."

I stood up fully and scanned the fields on the other side. Antriders were visible in every bare space across a span that must have been better than a quarter of a mile. There were more than millions. There were thousands of millions. A possibility remained that the captain and his men had passed beyond the insect threat in the other direction, but I held little hope for this idea. Looking along the road, the ground was blackened by the little beasts all the way from the abandoned houses to within a hundred yards of the bridge.

"The bridge!" I cried. I looked around me and found my damp rucksack. With a twist of the canvas strap in hand, I half carried, half dragged the sack toward the bridge. "Do you have any matches?" I asked Richardson.

"Matches? What for?"

"The antriders are stopped by the creek, which means they haven't found the bridge yet. We have to stop them before they do."

He pointed across the river. "There's more of them things than there are stars. How can we stop them?"

"I mean to burn the bridge."

By the time we reached the stone footings of the bridge, the antriders were closer, no more than fifty yards away. I was unsure that insect sight allowed them to detect us from the far side of the water, but it was clear that in some way they were following our movements. From my pack I produced flint and steel. There was a sleeve of sulfur matches as well, in a container that had been well impregnated with beeswax, but I could only look at them in despair. The trip across the stream had left them well and truly soaked.

"Gather wood," I instructed. "Grass. Anything you can find that might burn."

Richardson nodded and began snatching debris from the side of the road and the stream. I left the tools of fire making at the edge of the bridge and quickly gathered stalks of barley that had made their home on this side of the creek. Without looking for more fuel, I carried the armload of grass back to the bridge.

The front edge of the antriders had spread out, and I could see that the leaders of the swarm were no more than a dozen yards from the other end of the bridge as I crouched and began to strike sparks into the barley. If it had not been for the morning's bright sun, I would never had been able to generate a blaze, but at least a few handfuls among the grass were by now quite dry and the stalks were past their prime. With only a few blows of the steel wedge, a tendril of smoke emerged from the center of the mass.

I bent down to breathe life into the fire and found myself with a very close view of a tiny knight charging directly toward my face. I fell back with a shout. At this range, the mounted creature no longer looked so much like a shrunken man. It had the dark glittering eyes of an insect, and the suit of armor was its own chitinous skin. There were cornaceous protrusions about the head, and a ridge of small spines around the "shoulders." What I had taken for a lance was actually the left forelimb of the animal, which was extended into a serrated blade fully twice the length of the creature's body.

While I was making these observations, the antrider dodged around the smoldering grass and charged straight at me.

Richardson's shoe came down on the antrider with an authoritative crunch. "There's more coming," he said. "If you're to burn this 'ere bridge, you better get to the burning." He raised his boot and drove it down again. "I can't stomp them all."

Even without my help, the barley had bloomed into flame. I tossed more grass onto the growing fire and scrambled for the kindling that Richardson had carried. While I worked, I heard the sound of boot heel striking board at least a dozen times, and a fair stream of cursing to accompany the sounds. By the time I looked up, the fire had spread across the pile of grass and twigs, blocking most of the bridge. The wood of the bridge was not burning itself, and the grass would soon be reduced to ash, but it was a start.

Richardson came jumping back around the fire and landed beside me. "Too many," he said. "There's too many by half."

The mass of antriders was pouring onto the bridge in a stream that seemed as unstoppable as the rushing water passing below the boards. I gave a kick to one edge of the fire, spilling a drift of burning sticks across the remaining gap. The fire was now a complete curtain across the bridge, but it was a thin and temporary barrier. Seconds later, the red black horde came racing up to the fire. I stepped back in surprise and fear as the first antriders went plowing straight into the flames. The lemon smell turned suddenly bitter. Antriders popped in the flames like cedar knots. A few of the things emerged from the fire, but they were seared, smoking, and unable to advance more than a foot or so from the flames.

"More grass!" I shouted. I dashed to the roadside and jerked out an armload of barley and weeds. The fresh fuel joined the fire. Seconds later, Richardson contributed a collection of driftwood and flotsam from the stream's edge. For the next five minutes, we ran back and forth like stokers laboring at a forge. The fire on the bridge grew smoky with green wood and greener weeds, but it also grew in size and heat. By the time Richardson dragged up a long fallen branch and added this to the blaze, the antriders had stopped trying to best the fire and the boards of the bridge had begun to blacken and crack.

Richardson sat down at the end of the bridge with his head in his hands. Sweat ran through his thin brown hair in rivulets. "They'll come through that, won't anything stop them."

I nodded, but I kept my eyes on the front of the antrider swarm. They had pulled back, leaving a good yard of space around the flames. As the bridge began to burn, the insects retreated again. I watched to make sure the fire didn't require additional fuel, but the bridge top was by now well engaged. There was a crack followed by a hiss as a pair of boards fell from the bridge into the water. The antriders gave up the last stretch of bridge and returned to the far bank.

"Shame," said Richardson. "Real shame."

The statement left me puzzled. "You're upset that we stopped them?"

"I wasn't talking about the bugs," he replied. "I was talking about the bridge. Folks from all over these parts worked on that bridge—setting the stones, cutting wood." He shook his head. "I put on a goodly share of that deck myself. Finest bridge in Selvanos."

"Oh," I said. "Yes, I suppose it is a shame. All of it."

With the antriders blocked by the burning bridge, I was seized by a feeling of absolute exhaustion. It was all I could do to stagger a few steps away from the bridge footings and sit down on the stream bank in the shade of a young gum tree. Across the river the overripe barley stirred under the influence of a warm breeze and the white walls of the farmhouses flashed in the sun. It would have all looked quite splendid had I not known that the houses were empty and that a black and red terror lurked in the grass.

I must have drowsed then, because I was startled back to wakefulness by the crashing of the principal bridge beams into the stream. I sat up quickly, feeling somewhat rested, though still aching from the morning's events. From the position of the sun, it was noon, or not far past. Richardson was gone from his spot in the road, but when I stood I spotted him crouching on the stream bank perhaps a hundred yards away. There was still no sign of Captain Valamont and the other soldiers.

During my nap, the stream had fallen alarmingly. Without the daily feeding of the local rains, Caney Creek no longer looked like a brother to the Sarstoon. In a few hours, it had been reduced from a river wide and deep enough to be a challenging swim, to a brook that could be forded without wetting the knee. The reduction of the stream made me fear that the antriders might be close to breaching this barrier, but an examination of the opposite bank showed only a few spots of dark red moving over the mud. The mass of the creatures had moved elsewhere.

This immediately made me feel more hopeful. If the antriders had reversed their movement around Applewash, then perhaps they would return to the deep forests inland and quit company lands completely. It might now be possible to wade the creek back to the other side and locate the Captain and his men. After all, if I had managed to find refuge against the antriders; there was no reason to think that the others had not been equally fortunate.

It was with these somewhat more happy thoughts in mind that I walked down the bank to see what Richardson was about. The stream banks were steeper at the place where he waited, and the opposite bank was closer. A copse of small bookut trees, grown up since the loggers had cleared the area, clung to both sides of the water. As I grew closer, I saw that the trees on the other side were splotched by patches of red and black, and the ground below was dark as spilt blood. The antriders were here.

My momentary optimism receded as I ran the remaining distance to meet Richardson. "Are they crossing?" I asked.

The settler shook his head. "Not so as I can see, but these wee bastards are up to something. See if they're not."

It didn't require much study to tell that the antrider swarm in front of the trees was even larger than it had been that morning. The gap between where we stood and the insects was no more than twenty feet, giving a disturbingly good view of their activities. The creatures spread back into the grass like a glittering black and crimson carpet. They stirred and probed the edge of the falling water. They ascended and descended the trees in twisting ropes.

Had this been some harmless display, it would have been exhilarating, and it was no less fascinating for all the danger it implied. I watched their massing and shifting in a state not so different from hypnosis, my mind running more to the nature of social insects in general rather than the specific threat we were facing. Bees, wasps and other members of their order might demonstrate remarkable degrees of cooperation, but none could match the extraordinary complexity of the societies formed by ants. It was not until I began noticing flecks of a bright golden yellow among the red and black mass that I broke free of my reverie.

"What's that?"

Richardson shook his head. "Those lemony ones started showing up a while back. Going up into the tree. Never seen one come down."

Another yellowish spot appeared in the streams moving up one of the Bookut trees. It moved more slowly than the red and black riders around it, and I thought there was something a bit clumsy about its movements, but from where we stood, I could not be sure. Another yellow antrider labored up the tree, and another after that. As Richardson had said, I saw none coming down.

I hurried back to where I had left my rucksack lying on the ground and fished around inside until I found a spyglass. I pulled the instrument from the bag with some trepidation, sure that the lenses had been shattered in my escape. But miraculously, except for some water in the tube that partially obscured and distorted the image, the spyglass was free from damage. With the brass tube in hand, I ran back to the bookut grove, pulled open the glass, and trained the instrument on the insects.

The distance was too small to bring the antriders into perfect focus, but I could see well enough tell that these yellow insects enjoyed a structure considerably different from that of those I had seen earlier. They were as large as the red 'horses' for the black antrider knights, but they were more bulbous, with large glistening abdomens. And like the antrider horses, they carried some smaller, darker creature. In this case, the passenger was not carried comfortably on the insect's back, but was held in the grip of the mandibles. I watched several of these animals ascend into the cover of the dark green leaves before I could hazard a good guess at what it was they held. And even then, it took more minutes of watching before I was confident enough to announce my opinion.

"Spiders," I said.

Richardson moved over close to me. "The yellow ones are spiders?"

I lowered the glass and shook my head. "No, they're the same sort of creature as the rest, only a different color."

"But you said—"

"They're carrying spiders." I took another look to confirm my assessment. "I can't hazard the actual species, but from the way they hold themselves, I suspect some member of the Araneidae, that is, some type of orb-weaver."

"I thought spiders ate other bugs," said Richardson. "Why would these things go toting them about?"

Before I could reply, a sizable pile of leaves came tumbling from the top of the nearest bookut. Only this was not some unorganized mass of leaves. The pile was oddly uniform and coherent, with pale streaks of something stretched between the leaves. Moments later, another such pile fell from the treetops, and another right on its heels. No sooner did each of these collections of leaves strike the ground than the antriders swarmed over them. In seconds it was clear that they were dragging these leaves toward the water.

A tight, sick feeling seized my stomach. "Find some rocks," I said.

Richardson looked at me with puzzlement. "We going to pelt them from here?" He waved a hand toward the uncountable swarm. "Can't see that it will do much good."

"Not the ones on the bank." I bent over and began searching for pebbles among the twisted roots and fallen leaves. "The ones on the bridge."

"The bridge is burnt," said the settler. "There's none of these creatures on that."

But it was not a human bridge I was concerned about. Instead, I was fixed on the construction already unfolding in front of us. The antriders had tugged, pushed, and urged the mat of greenery out into the water. The pale streaks I had seen before were clearly thick cords of webbing that linked the leaves together. Another group of antriders rushed forward, bearing a second mat. They marched straight over the first section of floating bridge and out into the stream. The lead insects in this engineering team were pulled loose from the leaves and swept away downstream, but there was no hesitation on the part of the rest. In the space of a few heartbeats, the gap from one side of the stream to the other had been cut in half.

I dug along the bank and found some pebbles of feldspathic stone. I let lose my first handful of missiles. Several bounced from the interwoven surface of the leaf bridge. Even those that penetrated the green span only poked small, local holes, leaving most of the structure intact. When I bent for more stones, Richardson followed my example, desperately rooting on the ground for something that would disrupt the intruder's design.

Now the yellow antriders came down. They didn't descend by climbing along the trees. Instead, they rained down onto the fledgling bridge, some of them trailing threads of spider silk, others falling straight to the leaves with a soft plop. If they had been clumsy moving up the trees, they were not clumsy now. The yellow builders hurried about the mats with a near impossible velocity, mending and strengthening the works.

I hurled a fist-sized cobble that missed the bridge, but which swept an armload of wriggling insects into the water with the splash it threw up. Richardson had more luck with a broken limb. His throw made a rent that threatened to tear the intruder's construction in half.

The yellow builders fixed it in a moment. A third mat left the bank and was pushed out onto the bridge. The stream was beginning to distort the floating construction, dragging the front of the bridge downstream, but as the third mat was moved past the second, the remaining gap was no more than a good hop. A fourth mat was on the move. A fifth fell down from the trees.

More stones rained on the construction. More branches. I knelt by the edge of the stream and sent handfuls of water across the bridge. Hundreds of antriders went into the water. Thousands. And a thousand million more kept coming.

Richardson grabbed me by the collar and pulled me back. "We have to run," he said. "Or they'll have us."

I pushed him off. The antrider bridge had not yet made it across the stream. There was still some chance. With a heavy length of wood in hand, I prepared to deliver a shattering blow to the green bridge.

A fierce pain struck at my foot. I looked down and saw one of the red and black pairs sitting on top of my boot. The long lance-shaped forelimb of the rider was sticking straight into my foot. The development was so surprising, that I was momentarily in a state of complete detachment. I wondered if this set of antriders had come across the burning bridge, or if they had swum the stream straight out. Small as the stream was to me, it would still be quite a feat for anything so small; Like taking your horse across a mile of sea. I stood there, very still, in contemplation while the creature slowly withdrew its weapon, held up the long blade, then drove it through the boot leather a second time.

The fresh pain reminded me that I was really there, actually standing under the noon sun with an army of insects moments from stripping the flesh from my hide, and not reviewing this creature in some catalog of abnormities. The clean white bones of the woman in the kitchen were suddenly very clear in my mind. I rubbed the antrider from my boot clumsily with my other foot, almost falling in the process. I staggered back and saw that the insects had now all but completed their bridge. Scores of the yellow builders were working to secure the eastern end of the work with threads coaxed from their captive spiders. A much larger mass of the riders was not waiting. They were pouring up the stream bank like an ink spill flowing incongruously uphill.

I turned to look for Richardson and found the settler already a hundred yards away and sprinting hard. I followed.

At first Richardson followed the road, and I began to wonder if we might run all the way to St. George with this black and blood-colored horde in tow. But after a sprint of perhaps two hundred yards, the settler darted off the road to the left and plunged in among the thick boles of giant monkey-ear trees. I came after him, following the trail he had beaten through the undergrowth of ferns and bromeliads. Dodging between the trunks and avoiding the ensnarement of dangling vines kept me well occupied so that I nearly collided with Richardson.

"What are we doing down here?" I asked him between gasps for air. "Shouldn't we stay on the road?"

"I don't know about you," he said, "but I've run about as far as I can. We need to find some other way to travel."

In front of us, the Sarstoon cut its way through the thick forest. The banks here were slick with moss and the water grey and rippled by an irregular bottom. The width of the river was already great, and I was struck by how much this broad stream must look to us as little Caney Creek had to the antriders. Only we had no clever caste of engineers standing by to construct an instant bridge.

I looked around, half expecting to see the antriders closing on us. "Why did you run this way? Now we're trapped between the creatures and the river."

"I know."

"How will we cross the stream?" I asked. "It's too broad to swim and little but swamp on the other side if we did."

"Don't mean to cross it," said Richardson.

He inclined his chin toward a point upstream. Following this gesture, I looked and saw the trunk of a huge mahogany tree floating in the water. It was a giant, at least eighty feet long and a good six feet in diameter. From the marks of an ax at the severed end of the trunk, it was clear this was no natural fall, but the product of some works upstream. As it drifted closer, the log rolled far enough to reveal a circled brand burned into the wood, marking the tree as property of some landowner. Before I could think to ask how this affected our situation, Richardson had propelled himself down the muddy bank and was waist deep in the swift-flowing river.

"You better hurry," he called up to me, "or it'll be past us." He dived and began stroking strongly toward the drifting tree.

I looked at the water with distaste. Though I had made my way across Caney Creek at flood, I had not done so joyfully. Swimming had never been one of my principal skills, and I knew all too well that the river could contain many unpleasant occupants—from crocodiles a good deal bigger than a man, to voracious piranha and leeches near as long as my arm.

From behind me, a soft whispering sound drifted through the forest. There was a faint smell of peppered lemons.

In less than two seconds I was down the bank and in the river. The water was surprising cold. The current seemed to pull the log downstream more rapidly than it did me, and I had to make several adjustments to my path to have some chance of reaching this makeshift raft. Richardson was well aboard by the time my clumsy strokes brought me close, and he reached down and helped me up. I revised my initial estimate as I climbed aboard; the great tree was at least eight feet across. The trunk barely dipped at our added weight.

Back on the shore, the antriders came spilling through the woods. Red and black they coated the bank, and for the second time that day it was only the water that kept me from becoming their meal.

"We have to go back," I said.

"Yes," agreed Richardson. "Back to St. George."

"I didn't mean that." I pulled my feet out of the water to prevent offering any temptation to a passing crocodilian, and scanned the bank for good points of egress. "Captain Valamont might be there. And Donnel and Sherman, besides." I remembered the way that Sergeant Harness had fallen at the beginning of the affair, and did not add him to my list.

"They might be alive," said Richardson, "but unless they're in full gallop toward St. George, I don't expect I'll ever see them again. Soon as we get to town, I'm taking what little funds I've left and finding a ship out of here."

"I thought you owned two thousand feet along the Tamini Branch."

He nodded. "I do. I did. You're welcome to it if you want. I'll write you out the deed myself."

Even then, if I had thought him serious, I might have taken up the offer, but the thought of coming into land did not excite me as it normally would. "We should go back. The soldiers—"

"Are dead," said Richardson. He shifted his place on the log, bringing his feet further from the water. "Buck up, Mr. Brown. This is a passing freck river from here to the ferry and some ways beyond. It would have taken you a week to walk back to town, nearly as long to ride. If we stay in the center stream, you'll be there tomorrow."

I clung to the wet mahogany and thought about it. Traveling along the river would bring me home sooner. I would be able to get word of the antriders to the capital. There was some worth in this escape, thought it did feel cowardly.

Richardson flashed his teeth in an expression that had little to do with humor. "This time tomorrow, you can talk to your company men and get a whole new troop of soldiers. You burn enough bridges, maybe you'll even stop them from eating everyone in Selvanos. Not that I intend to stay around and see it out."

Behind us, the red stain on the riverbank grew small and finally vanished around a bend.

# 4

*River Sarstoon, Near St. George*
*9 August 1832*

It was after midnight on our second day of travel when the massive log drifted into the briny marshes south of St. George and became hopelessly wedged above a narrow point in the channel. Still, as Mr. Richardson had indicated, we had cleared the ferry sometime in previous night, and even though the Sarstoon slowed as it wallowed the final miles to the bay, our total passage was still a good deal faster than might have been achieved had we made the full trip on foot.

"Looks like we're walking now," said Richardson. The settler stepped across the floating mass with the skill of a man who had spent years sending trees down river. My own journey to shore was much more tentative, and I twice went up to my knee in the bog before putting a boot on more solid ground.

It was two hours more walking before I saw lanterns hanging at the corners of the old fort in St. George. As we neared the bridge, I noted that someone was still awake in the yellow house where I kept my rooms, and I was very tempted to go in and sleep till morning, but I felt it was my duty to go straight on to Company House.

As we crossed the center of town, Richardson plodded on at my side. We had exchanged few words on all the long, unpleasant journey, there being only so many observations that could be made of passing reptiles or vine-festooned trees.

As we crossed the center of St. George, Richardson suddenly turned off down Water Street. I stopped and turned to watch him.

"Where are you going?"

"The inn," he said.

"I doubt you'll find a room."

"Not looking for a room," the settler replied without bothering to look my way. "If there's a ship leaving this harbor tomorrow, I want to know it. And if there's one leaving tonight, I sure as hell don't want to miss it." He walked on down the slope and vanished around a corner without another glance or word. I continued on up the rutted street.

A single sleepy guard blocked my way at the door to Company House. This soldier was a stout man with a thick black mustache and muttonchops that made a thicket of his cheeks. I recognized him as Sergeant Norris, and addressed him by name, but he would not allow me to pass. Apparently, my malodorous coating of mud and general high level of grime did not recommend me for an audience with Lord Haverset. However, he eventually allowed me past the front gate, and I took this as permission to hurry through the corridors straight to the secretary's quarters.

The company secretary studied me as if men covered in stinking river mud breaking into his quarters after midnight was a common—if unpleasant—part of his daily affairs. "Whatever do you think you are doing, Mr. Brown?" he asked. "You're absolutely filthy."

I blinked away the exhaustion that threatened to close my eyes and tried to hold myself with as much dignity as my circumstances would allow. "Mr. Secretary, I need to see the director," I said.

"Sir, you will find that he's asleep, and wants to stay that way for some hours." The secretary's powdered wig was sitting somewhat askance on his bald head and his brown coat was pulled snug over a threadbare robe, but that did not seem to dent his normal air of superiority.

"Wake the director," I replied. "The settlers are under attack."

I expected some action at these words, but the secretary only folded his arms across his narrow chest and laced his bony fingers together. "I know of no attack," he said, "beyond the assault by the stench coming from you, Brown." He craned his skinny neck as if expecting to find someone else in the room. "Where is Captain Valamont? As I recall, you departed St. George in his company."

"I don't know," I said. "Near Applewash when I saw him last."

"Applewash. So, you became separated from the soldiers?"

"Yes, I suppose, but..."

"And after getting lost, you abandoned your companions and ran back here."

"I didn't run anywhere," I said. "And I wasn't lost." I pulled in a deep breath and tried to throw off my exhaustion. "Captain Valamont is the one who's lost, dead, I suspect, he and all his men—like everyone else within ten miles of Applewash."

"Dead?" For the first time, the secretary seemed to be giving some thought to more than just the amount of mud I was leaving on the good hooked rugs. "What makes you think that Captain Valamont has fallen?"

The sound of screaming horses drifted through my tired mind. And the smell of lemons. "I saw Sergeant Harness go down. And one of the other men, though I couldn't tell you if it was Donnel or Sherman." Dizziness overcame me, and I had to lean more heavily on the bench to stay upright. "I didn't see the captain lost, but I don't believe he could have survived."

My words clearly had an impact on the secretary. He stood for some time, staring at me with his lips pressed into a hard, bloodless line. "And what was the cause of this calamity?" he asked after a time of uncomfortable silence. "Were you beset by Indians?"

I shook my head. "Not Indians. Antriders."

"Ant...riders," he repeated slowly. A thoughtful look passed over the secretary's face. "Tell me what's happened."

As briefly as I could, I outlined the events of the past week. The trip along the river, the days of rain, and then the rapid string of events that had occurred along Caney Creek. The loss of the men. The burning of the bridge. The desperate flight to the river. All through this narrative, the secretary watched me closely, but he did not stop me, or ask any questions. Finally, I told how I had returned to St. George like flotsam along the stream.

The old man gave a sharp nod at the end of my talk. "I see." He left the room for a moment, and I thought he was going to fetch the director. Instead, he returned in the company of the portly soldier from the door.

"Sergeant Norris," said the secretary, "I have an important task."

"Sir?"

I wondered if the secretary was going to launch an immediate military expedition in hopes of aiding Captain Valamont's party. However, he took rather unexpected action. The secretary directed a finger my way. "Sergeant, take this man to the Ebo, and see that he's held in irons."

"What?" I stood bolt upright and backed toward the door. "Why would you..."

The secretary spun on his heels and glared at me. "You expect me to believe that trained soldiers were eaten by your fairy tale monsters, Brown?" He shook his head. "I find it far more likely that you ran from your party."

"Why?" I backed away toward the door. "Why would I run away?"

"You said yourself how awful the conditions were. Men often are unhinged by things of the jungle."

"It was a little rain. I'd not run from rain."

"Ah, but what about the Indians?"

"What Indians?" My head began to pound to that I thought my skull might literally crack. "You're the only one who's mentioned Indians."

"We'll know more after you're thoroughly questioned. Sergeant!"

Norris leveled his rifle at my chest. In all likelihood, the gun was not loaded, but that did not make the bayonet that glinted from the muzzle any less threatening. "Come on," said the sergeant. "You know where we're going."

I punched a hand against the wood paneled wall in frustration. "This is a mistake. People are dying."

"And you'll answer for every one that you've killed or abandoned to the savages," said the secretary. "Take him away."

The blade moved toward me. With the bayonet at my back, I left Company House and started back across town.

# 5

*St. George*
*9 August 1832*

Hunger seasons any meal and exhaustion cushions the hardest bed. Or at least, that's what I'd been told. On the question of hunger, I can offer no opinion since I was given no food. When it comes to beds, I can say that any comfort generated through weariness is definitely of limited scope when countered by hard, damp rock.

Anger kept me upright for the length of my forced march back across St. George. For the first blocks of the walk, I attempted to argue with the soldier, and insisted that I be taken to see the director, but Sergeant Norris did not bother to reply. He only aimed me down the street with terse directions, steering my path away from the soft bed that waited for me at the yellow house and toward much harsher quarters.

As in other civilized areas of the British enterprise, the slave trade was no longer legal, but slavery itself continued in Selvanos. Demise of an active market was only recent and most blacks, who made up perhaps a third of the colony's population, were still slaves. Even the rare freed black man was not allowed to own land, and certainly not allowed to hold stake in the company. Most free blacks lived in small shacks of their own making and even these were quite illegal, since they could not officially own the ground to build a home. For the few that lived around St. George, there was Ebo Town.

A decade before, Ebo Town was where slaves were held before being shipped to settlements or works further inland. Auctions were held there, and punishments were meted out to recalcitrant or rebellious workers in the small square. Now that the trading blocks were closed, the Ebo was still one of the few places the free blacks of St. George were allowed to live.

It was a sprawling place of unfinished boards and half-fallen buildings. Only one structure in Ebo Town remained in use by the company. The pens where slaves fresh off the long sea voyage had been sorted for health, temperament, and price, were now used for another sort of human storage. They had become the company's jail.

The jailor was asleep when I was brought to the establishment and it took vigorous shouting and pounding on the part of my escort before a face appeared at the door. "I seen this one around before," said the jailor. He was an older man called Plunket. Whether that was first name, last name, or nickname I did not know. Plunket was nearly as thin as the company secretary, with a horseshoe of grey stubble around his head and deeply sunken eyes. He raised a candle so the light spilled on my face. "This 'ere is the doctor. I've seen 'im 'ere many times, tending to those blacks."

"That's right," I said. "And tending to you. Remember only two months ago, I—"

"Quiet," said the soldier. Norris was one of those that had come to the colony only a few weeks before in the company of Lord Haverset, and for this reason was less well known to me than Captain Valamont or the men who had been on the expedition to Applewash. I knew that he was reputed to be a man of very dark humor and sharp temper, though thankfully I had so far avoided being on the receiving end of these gifts. He held one hand on my shoulder while the jailor pushed open the prison door then gave me a shove into the grey hallway beyond. I caught my muddy boot on the stone lintel and fell to my knees.

"Wait," I said. "This isn't right. I didn't—"

For a reward, I got a boot to the back. "This smelly fellow's to be put in irons."

"In irons?" The jailor bent to study me again. "Cor, what's 'e done, then?"

"Killed three soldiers, including Captain Valamont."

"I did not!" I struggled to my feet before I could collect another boot. "You know me, Plunket, trusted me to doctor your fever. You know I wouldn't do such a thing."

Plunket rubbed at his unshaven chin. "I know you're 'andy with knowing 'ow to keep people a livin'. Maybe you're just so handy when h'it comes time to kill them as well, eh?" He turned and raised his candle. "Come along this way. We've got plenty of room at this 'ere inn."

I opened my mouth to protest, but this time it was not a hand at my shoulder, but the tip of the bayonet at my back. Reluctantly, I followed the jailor into the maze of hallways beyond. The place was made up of dozens of small rooms with stone backs and slat wood fronts. Each of the rooms was small, not six foot across and about the same in depth. When slaves had been traded here, these rooms had sometimes held one man, sometimes a dozen or more. Plunket turned down one hallway then another. Most of the rooms were closed, but I could not say how many of them already held prisoners.

Finally, he pushed open the front of one of the cells. There was no door to speak of. The whole front of the small room opened on rusty hinges. "There's irons hin this one," said Plunket. He stepped in and raised a length of chain from the floor. "This h'is where we put the big bucks when they got to a feisty sort o' mood, see."

The soldier was forced to put down his weapon while he and Plunket fit the legging around my ankle. The thought of putting up some resistance crossed my mind at that point, but though I was angry at this treatment, I still expected my stay as Plunket's charge to be quite brief. That hope, along with fatigue, held me still until the men had locked the clamp around my leg and backed away to the door.

I wished that I could find some sort of threat to make against these men. I told myself that they would soon come to regret what they had done. They would most certainly be in trouble when truth of the situation came out. Then they would be the ones in irons. But I knew well that I had few allies in this affair. The secretary was a well-respected man with decades at the company. Though I was to be a landowner one day, currently I was nothing but a debtor and a bound man.

"I did not hurt those men," I said. "It wasn't me."

Plunket nodded. "Oh, I know, sir. That's what's generally said by men what are about to 'ang." From the look in the soldier's eyes, I could see that this was an outcome that did not greatly interest him, one way or the other. The wooden wall swung shut and I was left in darkness.

My cell was without windows or the luxury of any sort of furniture. I sat on the rough stone floor with my back against the wall and closed my eyes to sleep. Water dripped somewhere, a beat as regular as the company clock. Tired as I was, the hard floor would not let me get comfortable. I lay down. I sat up. I shifted from side to side. Every movement was accompanied by the dull clanking of the rusty chain at my ankle. Each time exhaustion threatened to overcome discomfort, my insomnia was aided by the last words of the jailor. Hanging. I could not believe that this would be my fate, but my subconscious mind was less certain. Men were hanged in Selvanos two or three times a year. Slowly, a line of grey light appeared under the movable wall to show the arrival of dawn.

I was in a fitful half-doze, filled with images of gallows, when the wall at the front opened. The sudden increase in light forced me to squint, but against the glare I could made out the gaunt form of Plunket and the even more skeletal shape of the secretary. "Is the director here?" I asked. "I need to tell him what happened."

"You'll have your chance." The secretary turned to Plunket. "Leave us. I need to speak with Mr. Brown as a friend."

The jailor nodded and left. To all appearances, he accepted the secretary's statement. I did not.

"Pardon me, sir, but you've never shown yourself to be a friend to me." I pulled myself up to my feet and stepped as far from the wall as the chain allowed.

The secretary shook his head. This morning his wig was well set and freshly powdered. He wore a long coat and breeches all of dark brown and a knotted red cloth at his throat. He looked every bit the respectable company man, while I in my soiled, travel-worn, and smelly clothing played the part of beggar. "Mr. Brown, I've been nothing but a friend to you from the moment you took residence with the company," he said.

"How is that, sir? By constantly ridiculing me? By reminding people that I am no true doctor whenever they forget, and reminding me that I am not yet a true landowner?"

"By keeping you from embarrassing yourself or the company. By seeing that you behaved properly." The secretary raised his narrow chin. "Like a gentleman, Mr. Brown."

It was my turn to shake my head. "I'd never look to you to see how a gentleman behaves."

He sucked in his lips so hard that it appeared his head might implode. "Because you have eventual claim to some godforsaken pocket of wilderness, don't think that makes you better than me." He walked a tight circle in front of my cell, casting narrow-eyed glances my way. "Obviously, my efforts on your behalf were wasted, sir. You're not only an embarrassment to the company, you're revealed as both coward and murderer."

"Make all the accusations you want. I did nothing wrong and you have no evidence against me."

"What evidence do I need?" asked the secretary. "You were sent off in the company of Captain Valamont and able soldiers. Now you have returned without them."

"That doesn't make me a killer." I took a step toward him, but was brought up short by the chain. "I've told you what happened."

He gave a dry laugh. "Oh, yes, and quite a story it was. Soldiers killed by fairy tales." He paused in front of me, standing just out of reach like a man taunting a leashed dog. "You repeat that story as often as you like. I'm sure the hangman will be equally amused."

If I could have reached him, I might have wrapped my hands about his thin neck and so justified his condemnation. "Is this why you came here? To laugh at me?"

"As always, I came here to redeem you from your own foolishness, Mr. Brown." He rubbed his hands together and his dry skin made a soft hiss. It was not unlike the rustling noise the antriders had made when they gathered across the stream.

"And how would you do that?"

"You've already made yourself a fool by talking of these fairy tale monsters. If you'll end this farce now, and simply tell the truth—"

"I already have." I walked to the back of the cell and eased back to the stone floor.

"Don't you even want to hear the offer? It may be one you'd find more than acceptable."

I shook my head. "You'd ask me to lie. I don't know why you want this lie, but I can't give it to you."

To his credit, the secretary made no further threat. Which was just as well. Once a man had been threatened with hanging, there was not much point. The secretary slammed shut the hinged wall with surprising force. Moments later, I could hear him stomping off along the hallway.

Strangely, after this encounter, I fell more easily into sleep. I was so completely unconscious, that when the door opened next, it took me several seconds just to remember where I was. I pushed back my lank, unwashed hair and stared up, looking to see if the secretary had come to bait me again.

"Well," said a woman's voice. "You do look quite the criminal."

I stared at the figure in the opening for several seconds before I could place a name to the person. "Miss Marlowe?" I scrambled to my feet.

Though the setting was anything but formal, Genevieve Marlowe was wearing much more proper clothing than when I had last seen her. A dress of solid emerald added to the color of her extraordinary eyes, while a short-brimmed bonnet harnessed, but did not completely tame, her voluminous black curls.

My own unsightly condition seemed much more embarrassing at that moment, even without the heavy chain that bound me in the cell. "Please, madam," I said. "You shouldn't be in a place like this."

"Oh, but I had to come."

"You did?"

She nodded. "I had to see the monster first hand."

"What monster?" I half turned my head, thinking for a moment that the antriders might somehow have accompanied me to my cell.

"You, of course. Everyone in St. George is talking about how you killed three men—her majesty's soldiers, at that—and Captain Valamont from a landed family." Miss Marlowe tilted her bonnet back from her face. "How could you?"

"I couldn't. I didn't." I paced from one side of my tiny cell to the other, the chain dragging at my heel. "How could anyone believe I would do that? Captain Valamont, the others, they were trained soldiers. I could never have outfought those men."

"Of course not. No one believes that."

I sagged against a stone wall in relief. "Thank God for that much."

"They think you poisoned them," said Miss Marlowe.

"What!"

"Oh, the stories are quite clear on that point, doctor. You couldn't kill them in a fair fight." She mimicked the motion of someone pouring liquid from a bottle. "You used your medical knowledge to dispatch the soldiers in the sleep, and then you left their poor bodies in the jungle to be eaten by jaguars."

I stared at her, dumbfounded. "Is that actually what people are saying?"

She nodded. "Some of them. Others say you used witchcraft."

"Witchcraft!"

"Or vodun. Learned from the Africans you treat. Or they say you had a secret arrangement with the Indians." Miss Marlowe smiled slightly. "That last conjecture is very popular."

The thought was so odd, I could not help but laugh. I had been back in St. George only a handful of hours, and it seemed as if every one of those hours had spawned some new tale of my perfidy and villainy. "If that's all anyone can think to say, I should be out of here very soon. It's all too fantastic to be believed."

"I wouldn't be so sure." There was a noise from somewhere in the distance and she paused to look down the hall. Miss Marlowe lowered her voice. "Remember this, Calvin Brown, if a man claims to have caught a large fish, he's doubted from the start. But if he says he hooked a mermaid, well, the sailors will be talking about it for a month."

I was trying to puzzle out a reply when footsteps echoed from the hall. I thought at first that Plunket might be coming to see Miss Marlowe out, but I soon realized there was quite a crowd approaching. A moment later, the narrow hallway was nearly choked by the approaching delegation. At its center was Lord Haverset; close behind followed the secretary, jailer Plunket, and Father Samms, Vicar of the St. George church. At either side of the column stood two soldiers complete with bright red coats and rifles at their shoulders.

Lord Haverset glanced at me as he drew close, but it was Miss Marlowe that he spoke to first. "Goodness, Genevieve, I'm quite surprised to see you here. I wouldn't think your parents glad to hear of their daughter in such a place." He glanced my way. "Or in such company."

Miss Marlowe executed a quick curtsy, the loose hem of her dress brushing the dirty cobblestone floor. "I heard that you were coming, my lord, and thought that I might provide some assistance."

"Really?" Lord Haverset raised a single plucked eyebrow. "You have some information on this matter?"

"Only on the character of Doctor Brown, my lord. He—"

"This boy is not a proper doctor," interjected the secretary. He wagged a finger in my direction. "He's not even a good doorman."

Vicar Samms held up a hand. "Please," he said. "It's not his vocation that's in question here. The issues are a good deal more serious than that."

The clergyman stepped past the others and came closer to my open cell. Samms was a small man, so short that even Miss Marlowe surpassed his height by a good number of inches. He had a ring of snow white hair around a bald pate which he did not bother to hide beneath a wig, and a black coat with slightly frayed cuffs which he wore on all occasions. In the past, the vicar had shown considerable interest in my studies of the natural world. It was common for him to present me with a stone, or leaf, or bird's egg, seeking my identification of his find. I had always found him of cheerful disposition. But that was not the case on this morning.

Samms studied me for a long moment, all the while with his gaze fixed on my face. His eyes were so light in color that they nearly matched his thin hair. At length, he turned to favor Miss Marlowe with a quick smile. "Though your friendship certainly does him credit, madam, I fear the charges against this man are most grave."

The pronouncement was enough to make my stomach jump. If the clergyman thought the charges to be taken seriously, there was little chance that the director would order me free without trial.

In fact, Lord Haverset tuned to me at that moment. He was not smiling. "Tell me what you've done with my men, Brown."

My throat tightened as I tried to reply. Lord Haverset's face was impassive, but behind him the secretary scowled while the soldiers glared at me as if I had not only killed their compatriots, but also eaten them. "Sir, I didn't do anything to them."

"Then where are they?"

"I...I'm not sure."

The secretary made a grunt. "That's not what you told me." He pushed his way up next to the director and shook a bony finger in my face. "When Brown told his tale to me, he said the Captain was dead."

"Really?" said the vicar. He stared hard at me. "Which is it then?"

He said the phrase quite mildly, but I did not mistake the seriousness of his intent. I took a breath. "In truth, I can't say that the captain is dead with certainty, but I find it difficult to see how he could have survived."

"Survived the poison you gave him?" said the secretary.

"No!" I looked to Father Samms and shook my head. "I didn't poison anyone."

The clergyman's pale stare switched to the secretary for a moment then settled again on me. "Is that so? Then tell us, please, what put the life of Her Majesty's soldiers in such peril?"

I drew a deep breath. "Antriders."

At the word, the secretary scoffed and the guards scowled harder. Lord Haverset let out a sharp chortle and the vicar smiled. I wondered at how Miss Marlowe took this statement and turned my head to see her. Even in her handsome features, I could see there was much consternation.

The secretary started to speak again and the two soldiers began to mutter curses. Lord Haverset silenced them all quickly.

"I fear it is as the secretary has warned us," said the director. He leaned over, as if speaking to the vicar alone, but kept his voice at a level that could be clearly heard by all. "This man is guilty, else he would not try to spread such nonsense."

Samms once again focused his uncomfortable gaze. "This is a rather extraordinary claim, Mr. Brown. Surely you recognize that."

I nodded in complete agreement. "Believe me, reverend, I'd have never thought that these creatures existed without seeing them for myself."

The vicar pressed the bridge of his long nose and squeezed his eyes shut. "All right," he said. "Let us hear your tale."

Again, I repeated the story of the trip to Applewash. This time I abbreviated all but that part of the journey concerning the insects and the loss of the soldiers. At several points in my narration, the secretary punctuated my words by scoffs, grunts, and coughs of disbelief, but I maintained my composure well enough to complete the tale.

When I was through, the assembled party only stared at me. While none of them immediately expressed belief, I was relieved to see that none, save the secretary, seemed inclined to dismiss my words out of hand.

"What of this man Richardson?" asked Vicar Samms. "If he made the voyage down river, where is he now?"

"He went to the docks to find a ship."

Lord Haverset turned to one of the soldiers. "Go to the inn and see if this Richardson fellow is there. If not, see if anyone knows where he might be found." The soldier gave a sharp salute and hurried away.

"My lord, this tale of his is a farce," said the secretary. He folded his thin arms across his hollow chest. "You could not possibly considering—"

"No," said Father Samms. "Most likely you are right. Young Brown is guilty."

My heart sank. Already it seemed as if I could feel a rough sisal rope scratching at my throat.

"However," continued the clergyman. "He seems quite adequately confined in this place. I believe we can, through our own efforts and the aid of the Almighty, determine the veracity of his claims without fear that he will escape justice."

"I did not hurt those men," I said.

"No?" replied Samms. "Then where are they?"

Before I could think of a reply, the front of the cell swung shut. Through the slats of the boards, I could hear the people moving away, and caught one glimpse of Miss Marlowe's emerald dress. Then I was left in silence.

The silence stretched out through the day, broken only by increasingly anxious noises which held their origin in my stomach. I tried to think of the last time I had eaten. There had been something, a sodden bit of bread and dried meat extracted from my rucksack while drifting down the river. That had been two days before. Perhaps three. The ache in my stomach no longer felt like hunger. It was something altogether sharper and meaner.

An hour before sunset someone, I assume it was Plunket, opened the cell door and shoved a pail of water accompanied by a shallow tin dish. Before my eyes could adjust to the sudden increase in light, the door was shut again. I sipped at the water and discovered that the plate contained a small portion of brown bread and thin stew. I devoured this inadequate, but much needed, meal in the space of seconds. With the food dispatched, there was little to do but sit in the dark and fret about what the morning might bring.

As it turned out, the following morning brought nothing but another brief visit from Plunket. There were no other visitors that day, or the next. I lay on the cold floor through these days and slept fitfully. Despite my limited movement, the manacle chaffed at my ankle. More painful still were the thoughts that chaffed at my mind—the vision of the gallows never far from my consideration.

It was the evening of the second day, when I was using the last scrap of bread to sop any lingering trace of gravy from the plate, that I again heard the steps of several people approaching. Rather than being hopeful, this sound stirred considerable fear. Since no one had promptly returned to confirm my statements, I could only assume that Richardson had escaped before he could be questioned, and that the approaching footsteps brought with them rope rather than freedom. I stood up and did my best to arrange my dirty, ill-smelling clothes.

The front of the cell opened and again I was forced to squint against the bright light. When my eyes were adjusted, I found that the figures in the opening were those of Father Samms, Plunket, and Miss Marlowe. Immediately, I felt reassured. Had I been bound for a noose, it was sure that the secretary would have been there to gloat.

"What's happened?" I asked. "Did you find Mr. Richardson?"

"I'm afraid not," replied Samms. "He secured a berth on an outbound ship the very night you arrived and made for Kingston before anyone could speak with him."

I shaded my eyes and examined their faces. My initial pleasure melted at their tense expressions. "What?" I said. "Am I to be hanged then?"

"No!" said Miss Marlowe. She stepped toward me and smiled, but the expression was strained. "You're not to be tried. They're letting you go."

"That's good then, but...What's happened?"

"It's Captain Valamont," said Samms. "He's returned."

News of the Second Coming would not have given me more surprise. "That's wonderful!" I clapped my hands together in my enthusiasm and tried to step forward, only to be halted by the chain.

"'ere now," said Plunket. "Let me be taking care o' that, Doctor Brown." The jailor had barely spoken to me over the past two days, but now he seemed suddenly embarrassed at the manacle. He knelt on the rough floor, and with a quick turn of the key, the metal cuff fell from around my ankle. I wasted no time stepping clear of the tiny cell. Without the restraint of the chain, I felt immensely better.

"Has Captain Valamont talked to the director?" I asked. "Did he tell him about the antriders?"

Miss Marlowe looked around at the clergyman and her smile dropped away. "The captain is...injured."

"Then take me to him," I said. "I might be able to help."

Samms shook his head. "We will take you to him," he said. "In fact, we were told to do just that."

"Good. Very good." I turned and started up the hallway. "I'll need to stop at the house to get the medical bag."

The barrister put a hand on my arm. "I'm afraid this isn't the variety of injury that can be attended to with scalpel, Mr. Brown." He lowered his voice. "I'm afraid the poor captain is quite mad."

# 6

*St. George*
*12 August 1832*

The commotion on the streets of St. George was extreme. Men and women fled from the center of town, some on horseback others hurrying on foot, while at the same time still more men pressed toward the square. There were rifles and old muskets in several hands, and few of hands belonged to men wearing red coats. My first thought was that the place looked much like an ant hill that had been stirred by a stick, but then, ants were much in my thoughts.

"What's wrong?" I asked as I emerged squinting into the afternoon sun. "Where is everyone going?"

Miss Marlowe and Vicar Samms came around me and stood at the edge of the muddy street. "It's Captain Valamont," said Miss Marlowe. "People are afraid."

We all stepped back as a buggy raced by, throwing up a sheet of brown water from a puddle. "Why should they be so concerned by the captain?"

"I'm afraid he's already shot two people," said Samms. "Perhaps more."

The idea seemed so odd that I could only stare at the clergyman in disbelief. "He's taken a place inside the fort," continued Father Samms, "and threatens anyone who attempts entry. I expect the company is organizing to roust him from this post. The secretary was hopeful that you might be able to lure him out without violence."

Miss Marlowe rolled her eyes at that statement. "More likely the secretary hopes that if you get close enough, Valamont might choose you for his next victim."

The idea that Captain Valamont was to be hunted down in the middle of St. George was as odd as anything I had seen along the banks of Caney Creek. "I should go to him."

"And get a bullet for your efforts?" Miss Marlowe placed a hand on my arm. "The best thing you can do is stay away."

Father Samms nodded in agreement. "Despite the secretary's summons, it seems clear enough that Valamont has lost all reason. You can tend him after the soldiers have removed him from the fort."

"I was with him out there, and I left him." Guilt narrowed my throat so that I had trouble talking. "I left him for dead, Reverend."

Miss Marlowe's grip tightened on my arm and Father Samms looked down at the ground. "Still," he said. "The danger—"

"I should go to him," I repeated. Before either of them could reply, I pulled away and stepped into the crowded street. I had to step quickly to avoid being run down by a dogcart just as swiftly then reverse myself to miss a horse and rider. In moments, the push of men heading toward Company House had borne me away from the jail, from Ebo Town, and on across the bridge. Several times I looked back, fearing that Father Samms and Miss Marlowe might try to follow me and so be brought into danger for my sake, but the crowd had separated us and I saw no sign of them along the street.

In the square, the number of men easily exceeded two hundred. There were scatterings of soldiers in the group, but they were outnumbered five to one by the landowners and shopkeepers. There were men in good long coats and hatless men with nothing but stained shirts and breeches. Several were boys of a quite young age. I even saw a rifle in the hand of a black African, something that would not have been much tolerated during normal affairs.

Beyond them all loomed up the grey stones of the old Spanish fort. Company House was sprawling, and more handsome by far, but the fort was the largest building in St. George by any measure. The stone walls had been raised by the first Spaniards who landed near the Sarstoon as a defense against what were assumed to be overwhelming forces of native Mayans, and it boasted a curtain wall some twenty feet high with ports along the top and a door formed from foot-thick beams of bulletwood. But the Spaniards had never suffered the expected attacks. Indeed, the

Spaniards lived in their fort off and on for more than a century with barely any sign of natives at all. When the company purchased the area from the Spanish, the fort had come along in the bargain, but the English forces had never used the stronghold for more than storage. Now it seemed there was to be an attack on the fort after all, only it was to be the men of Selvanos assaulting a citadel held by one deranged soldier.

The soldiers in the square were doing their best to organize the makeshift militia, and I caught a glimpse of Lord Haverset as the director barked orders. Rather than join this growing army, I slipped around the outskirts of the square and moved on toward the fort. The density of men on this side of the square was considerably reduced. Only a few dared close to within a hundred yards or so of the old walls.

The idea of drawing closer did not come to me without fear. I stood at the edge of the square and looked at the fort, unsure how or if I should proceed. After two centuries under the tropical rains, the dolomitic stones of the walls were liver-spotted by lichens and opportunistic trees had split the foundations in several places. Still, the place was formidable.

I took a few steps closer to the old walls, cupped my hands to my mouth and shouted. "Captain Valamont!"

There was no response from ahead. I crossed another twenty feet of worn brick and hard packed earth and tried again. "Captain, are you there?"

This time, I thought I heard some muffled reply from behind the Spanish stones, but the exact nature of that reply was drowned out from the noise in the square at my back. It might have been an invitation to come forward. It might have been assurance that one further step would bring me death. My heart beating at my throat, I moved closer.

Only twenty feet from the wall, I came to one of the victims of Captain Valamont's madness. A man in a brown jacket was lying at the side of a hard-tramped trail that led to the doors of the fort. His face and shoulders were half hidden by a luxuriant growth of ferns at the side of the path. Still quite conscious of the looming walls and with the row of gun ports over my head, I crouched down next to the fallen man.

In my experience as a doctor, I had seen many injuries among men struck down while logging or in other occupations. Death was not completely strange to me. But I had not, until that moment, ever seen a man who had suffered the results of a gunshot. It was not a sight I was likely to forget in the future. A large caliber ball had cut through the fallen man's neck and punched upwards toward the base of his skull, wrecking everything in between. Flesh and bone were spread around him and blood dried black on the curling lengths of the ferns. Only his staring, glassy eyes were intact.

"What were you doing here?" I whispered to the dead man. With two fingers, I attempted to close his eyes, but found the eyelids less complaint than they were in books. "What would cause Captain Valamont to shoot you?"

There was a rustling above me. My heart seized, sure that the crazed captain was at that moment bringing his revolver to bear. I looked upward, and was so relieved to see that the source of the noise was only a large red-lored parrot, that I let out a cry of relief loud enough to startle the bird into flight. Even though I had yet to confront the captain, I already felt a trembling weakness in my limbs and the sweat of fear spotted my forehead. If it had not been for the shame I felt over my actions along Caney Creek, I would have gladly slunk away from the stone walls and allowed the crowd growing in the square to dislodge Captain Valamont.

Instead, I turned my attention to the small sapodilla tree that had served as the parrot's perch. The tree had sprouted among the stones at the base of the fort's wall. Large cracks had spread between the heavy blocks as the tree had increased in girth, though the disturbance caused by its growth had not come close to completely breaching the heavy battlements. However, the close proximity of the trunk to the wall did make the sapodilla into a potential means of access.

Wedging myself between the wall and the smooth bole, I made a quick, if clumsy ascent of the wall. In only a few minutes, I cautiously cleared the crenulations along the fort's top and fell onto the wooden platform beyond. The planks were old, perhaps as old as the fort itself, and they groaned threateningly beneath my weight. Again I waited in expectation of a pistol shot, but none came.

"Captain?" I called, though my choked voice could not have been louder than a whisper.

"Quickly," said a voice from beneath me. "Quickly, before they get in."

I crawled to the edge of the rotting platform and looked down into the small courtyard of the fort. Captain Valamont was working just below me, stacking flat stones against the door in a structure that was somewhere between a wall and a disorganized heap. Looking further, I could see the gaps in the courtyard floor where the captain had liberated flagstones and used them to build his barricade.

"Captain Valamont?"

He paused in his labors and looked up at me. Had I not been told that this was the same man who led our expedition out of St. George the week before, I doubt I would have recognized him. His face was gaunt, overgrown with stubble, and marked by half-healed cuts along with splatters of both blood and earth. He wore no topcoat. His shirt was torn open to the elbow. There were other rents along the chest and shoulder, as if the man had ridden break-neck through a patch of thorns. Whatever colors his clothing might once have held, they were now reduced to the red-brown of soil. The only clean patch on him was the pistol shoved through his belt.

"Brown," said Captain Valamont, his voice surprisingly unchanged by whatever ordeal had put him in such a state. "Get down here and help before it's too late."

I hesitated for a moment, watching to see that the captain did not take his pistol in hand, then I walked carefully across the sagging boards and made my way down the equally decrepit stairs to the courtyard. Captain Valamont rushed past me to grab another stone from the yard. As he passed, I caught a rank order that mixed blood, mud...and lemons.

"Hurry," he said. To my astonishment, he prized the next stone from the hard ground with no instrument but his fingers. As he came back, staggering under the weight of his burden, I saw that his fingers were torn and bloody. Blood spotted the stone he carried and was scattered across his barricade like a pox.

"Captain," I said. "Why don't you let them in?"

"What?" Immediately, he whirled toward me, his eyes wide and wild as any creature in the forest. "You mean to let them in!"

"I think it would be best," I said. I tried to keep my voice slow and calm. "I'm only trying to help you, sir."

Valamont blinked and his expression flashed back and forth between exhaustion and anger. "You...you weren't there. You don't know."

"I know," I said. "I saw what happened."

"You don't. You can't." The captain let the stone fall from his grasp. It crashed to the ground and broke into fist-sized cobbles and dust. Valamont barely seemed to notice. "You weren't there."

I took a step toward him. "I was there, sir. At Caney Creek. I saw Sergeant Harness fall."

"Harness," he repeated slowly, as if it were a word from some foreign tongue. "Caney Creek." He shook his head. "You weren't there. You didn't see the fires. You didn't see the works."

"The works?" A chill went through me that overcame the heat of the afternoon. "You can't mean Grey's Works?" The Works were another settlement, off the side of the road we had taken on our march. However, the distance from Caney Creek to Grey's Works was several miles, more than twice the distance from Applewash to the bridge that Richardson and I had burned to halt the antriders' advance. If something had happened at the works—if the antriders had reached that point—then not only had sacrificing the bridge failed to stop them, they had more than doubled their previous pace. The settlements near Weir and along the Qualm could already be threatened. This was news that demanded immediate action.

While I was working out the implications of this development, there was a shout from outside the door. Rising noise indicated that the crowd in the square was on the move.

Valamont spun toward the door. "I hear them," he said. "They're close. So close."

I risked another step toward him. "It's only the soldiers," I said. "They want to help you."

He grimaced and shook his head violently. "No. No, no one can help."

"They're soldiers," I said. "Your own men. Surely you know that they—"

His reaction was so swift that I did not have time to move a muscle. In the space of a heartbeat, Valamont drew his pistol, turned, and leveled the open bore toward my face. "You're working with them," he said. "That's why you weren't there. Maybe it was you who set those fires."

I backed away, hands raised. "What fires? I burned the bridge, yes, but—"

Captain Valamont gave a small grunt. The hammer on the pistol rose and fell. But there was no explosion, no pain of impact. There was only the hard, dry noise of metal on metal. Whether it was a misfire, or the pistol was empty, I did not wait to find out. I rushed toward the captain, my hands tightening into fists as I advanced.

It would be more pleasing to report that my own martial skills overcame the captain, but in truth I never struck a blow. As Captain Valamont stepped forward to meet my rush, his heel came down on one of the broken bits of flagstone. He staggered, swung his arms, lost the pistol, and fell back against the stack blocking the door. By the time I reached Captain Valamont, his eyes were already glazed and he was quite insensible.

There was a thin trickle of fresh blood emerging from his scalp, but the damage did not seem severe. I positioned him as comfortably as I could in the shade of the platform then set to removing the stones in front of the door. It took a few minutes to drag the flagstones clear and a few moments more to slide free the large iron bar that braced the door. When the bulletwood panel opened, I found myself facing fifty men and as many weapons. They seemed as surprised as I.

"Surrender," shouted one soldier.

"Gladly." I raised my hands. "Gentlemen, Captain Valamont is not well. Could you help me get him home?"

The soldiers in the front ranks only stared at me at first, but after a moment first one and then the next lowered their weapons. Six red coats took Captain Valamont from the old fort and carried him across the courtyard into Company House.

# 7

*St. George*
*14 August 1832*

Cleanliness may not truly deliver sanctity, but after a week covered in filth, a warm tub did deliver a fair measure of heaven. Mrs. Dillworth, the keeper of the yellow house where I kept my rooms, was kind enough to prepare a bath as soon as I arrived. She went so far as to heat additional water while I was enjoying my first soak and little Alice laid a fresh pot at the door so I could replace the mud soup of my initial rinse. Whether Mrs. Dillworth was motivated by kindness, or merely sought to diminish the stench coming from my person, her actions were much appreciated.

The large indoor iron tub at the yellow house was a luxury installed by an earlier occupant, made only marginally less useful from the lack of piped in water. Still, the opportunity to bathe in relative seclusion was one not enjoyed by most of St. George's residents and was counted a great luxury among those of us lucky enough have rooms in the house. More than once, I dozed off in the tepid water. I might have enjoyed a longer sleep there had it not been for fear that, having survived jail, the river, and the antriders; I would die by drowning in my bath. Reluctantly, I pulled myself from the cooling water and prepared to face the world again. Brought to a state proximate with acceptable cleanliness, I then completely rejoined the ranks of the civilized through the agency of dry clothing— including the item most overlooked in fair circumstances and most desired when absent, dry socks.

The circumstances I faced on leaving the bath were bound to be considerably less friendly and comfortable than the confines of the tub. Even my freedom had been a subject of some considerable debate inside Company House. Stopping Captain Valamont earned me praise from some quarters, especially among some of the soldiers that had served under his command. However, the captain had killed two men in making his entry to the fort and the town had been organizing to take him by force. My interruption of their plans was viewed as disappointing, if not pure interference in the delivery of justice. Whether I was to be considered a hero or a scoundrel was still to be determined. For the moment, I could only rejoice that I was allowed to go home—though even home was not completely comfortable.

My period as an occupant of the yellow house had been very brief, and I had barely settled in before I had been secunded to the ill-fated expedition to Applewash. Stepping from my bath that afternoon, I found myself brought up short by the changes in my absence. My rooms, formerly well-scattered with books and folios, pages of notes, boards festooned with pinned beetles, stacked envelopes of butterflies, jars, interesting stones, puzzling bones, and piles of pressed leaves had, under the care of Mrs. Dillworth, been turned into a model of organization. Books were on shelves. Specimens arranged in cabinets. It certainly brought an impression of order, though the taxonomic associations so generated might well have driven Linnaeus into paroxysms.

While I was still contemplating these changes in my surroundings, I found myself pressed back into the role of physician. Mrs. Dillworth appeared to direct me into the sitting room, where a fisherman was waiting. The man presented a hard, calloused hand that had received a mean gash from a swordfish and was now swollen so badly that the fingernails were half-buried in the flesh and the skin taut as a sausage. Before I finished tending to this problem, the woman who owned the waterfront inn appeared, bringing with her a young daughter peaked with a fever. From there I was encouraged to pay a call on a neighbor coughing his way through the final hopeless stages of consumption and a sailor at the inn who was shivering under a bout of malaria agues. I left the house, bag in hand, and dispensed what comfort I could in these situations, which chiefly consisted of tincture of opium and a few words of reassurance. Each visit seemed to lead to new requests, and I soon found myself with enough patients to carry me through the afternoon.

It was gratifying to ply my trade and serve the people of St. George— though it seemed that some had called on me not from any pressing illness, but to wheedle from me the story of my journey and imprisonment. On this aspect, there was more interest in the affair with Captain Valamont than in the events at Applewash and I said little about my encounters with the antriders.

I started my rounds with renewed energy, but the week's events soon caught up with me. Late in the afternoon, with the sun barely above the trees to the west and great flocks of brown pelicans settling around the docks, I dragged myself back to the yellow house, prepared to examine the patients that had remained in hospital at my rooms even in my absence, and then prescribe to myself a full night of sleep. Like most of my plans of late, this one was very short-lived.

Approaching the house, I saw that an officer of the guard was stationed at the front step. As I drew closer, I saw that it was the disagreeable Sergeant Norris. He carried with him a long rifle with fixed bayonet, but held the weapon causally. His dress was a formal day coat, with blue sleeves and red facing above a cream-colored waistcoat. Together with his white breeches and high dark gaiters, it made quite a splendid costume, but on seeing it, my heart sank. This scowling soldier at my door, no matter how well dressed, could only mean I was to be sent back for another evening in Plunket's cell—if not to somewhere even less pleasant.

The man straightened as I approached. "You're that Doctor Brown, now aren't you? I didn't know who you were the last time."

I nodded my head. "Yes, sergeant. What am I charged with this time?"

Norris looked at me in surprise. "Charged? Why, sir, not with nothing, so far as I know."

"Then why are you here?"

"I'm here because I go where Lord Haverset goes." He gestured at the door with the sharp end of his bayonet. "And the director is here."

It took my tired mind a moment to sort this bit of information. "Lord Haverset is in this house?"

"Less he climbed out a window," replied the soldier. He smiled, revealing a jagged dentition that suggested a proclivity for fisticuffs. "Seeing the dolly who opened the door, I doubt he's in a hurry to leave."

I could scarcely credit what the soldier had said—titled directors of chartered companies were not prone to visiting houses only a block removed from the Ebo Town, and for all Mrs. Dillworth's admirable qualities, there were few men who would consider her a particularly handsome woman. I stepped past the man and passed quickly into the house. There I saw that he had spoken truly: the small front parlor of the yellow house was fairly packed with the leadership of the British Central Lumber Company.

At one side of the room, the secretary stood in front of a glass-fronted case filled mostly with a collection of metallic beetles. From the depth of the frown on the secretary's face, I suspected his expression had been fixed hard since the last time we met. Vicar Samms was beside him. The clergyman seemed much more relaxed, with the top button of his vest released and a book of bird paintings in his hands.

"Good evening, Brown," he called as I entered. "You've quite a library here."

"My predecessor gets the credit for that, sir," I replied. "He left me well supplied."

At the far end of the room, Lord Haverset held the lounge to himself. He sat with his long legs straight out in front of him and his arms stretched along the arched back of the lounge. He would have appeared for all the world like a man at ease in his own home, were it not for the disparity between his richly brocaded jacket and the worn velvet of his seat.

"Brown!" he called with such force that I rocked back on my heels. "I understand you've been out tending to the needs of the community. Very commendable. Sit down, sir, you look to be exhausted."

This appearance of the director in my home—even if it was a borrowed home—and his familiar greeting, struck me as the most surreal of all the events that had happened in the last tightly packed week. Before I could recover my wits and manage a suitable reply, young Alice emerged from the kitchen. Her dress, which had been mud-stained and rain soaked on our first meeting, was now scrubbed cloud white and her hair bound back from her face by a strip of red ribbon. She appeared quite the little lady, as she approached with a porcelain teapot in one hand and a cup in the other. She promptly placed the cup in my surprised grip and commenced pouring so quickly that it was all I could do to get the cup in position. "You better sit down," she said, "you're spilling it all over the floor."

I had some quibble over the cause for this spillage, but since my sitting was the one action on which everyone seemed in agreement, I crossed to a high-backed chair and sat.

Miss Marlowe entered just as Alice departed. On this evening, she wore a pale yellow dress trimmed at collar and sleeve with cream-colored lace. Her dark curls were caught up in a net that glittered with small cabochons of chrysoprase and jasper and there were pearls at her neck. She looked every bit a daughter of the most respected family in Selvanos, and far too regal for the shabby sitting room. She smiled at me agreeably as she crossed the room. "I see you've returned from making your visits, Doctor Brown. Did you find anything serious?" she asked.

"Nothing that warrants alarm, miss," I replied. Though, in truth, I was quite alarmed by the scene I found waiting at the house. I was more frightened at that point than I had been when I first saw the soldier at my door.

"That's good to hear," said Miss Marlowe. "We certainly have enough to worry about without facing another run of fevers." She sat down a chair quite close to the director.

I looked around the crowded parlor and addressed the director. "I'm sorry, your lordship, but can I ask what this is about?"

Lord Haverset cleared his throat and leaned forward from his place on the lounge. "I came for a brief visit."

"I would have been happy to come to you, my lord."

"It wasn't you I came to visit," said the director. "It was Genevieve." He stretched out a long arm and placed a hand on Miss Marlowe's shoulder. "She suggested that this location would be advantageous considering the nature of our discussion."

My face warmed with my embarrassment, and I risked further tea stains on the rug by climbing back to my feet. From across the room, I heard the dry sound of the secretary's laughter. "I'm sorry, sir. I thought..."

Lord Haverset favored me with a smile. "I've heard of the work you've done, sir. Quite decent work, in lieu of an actual, properly educated physician."

"Thank you, my lord. I had best go see if someone else needs my care." I made a quick bow, which delivered a fresh spot of tea to the floor and drew another laugh from the secretary. Before I could generate additional merriment at my own expense, I straightened and made my way past the amused secretary to the bedroom. With great relief, I escaped into the bedroom and closed the door on all of Selvanos's finest.

Through the paneled door, muffled voices drifted. I could identify the baritone bark of Lord Haverset and the sharper tongue of the secretary, but I could not make out the words. Miss Marlowe's contralto joined the faint conversation and there was a general chorus of laughter. They might have been discussing the poor prices recently paid for logwood or setting a time for my trip to the gallows, though why they would chose to come to this place to talk, rather than meet within the confines of Company House, I could not fathom. Whatever the subject, I had little desire to join the conversation.

Irrationally, I found myself angrier at that moment than I had been through the course of my imprisonment. This house might be the property of Mrs. Dillworth, but it was still my home. Surely my rent should secure me some measure of privacy. The presence of the director and the others was an uncomfortable intrusion. The secretary had been calling for my neck only hours before. Now he was in the parlor, fingering my books. Lord Haverset had been equally ready to believe in some sort of foul play on my part. Now he sprawled on the couch.

And I did not like the familiar way he behaved with Miss Marlowe.

Contemplating these affronts, I sat down in a wicker chair beside the bed to stew upon the unfairness. Within the space of a heartbeat, I was sound asleep,

I woke to a touch at my shoulder. When I opened my eyes, I found Alice standing by my side. The little girl's face was extremely serious. "She sent me to get you."

I felt a bit dizzy and had to rub at my eyes to clear them. "Who is it that wants me?"

"My mum," said Alice. "She says you're to come straight away."

My limbs felt logy and numb as I stood and I had to lean on the back of the chair for support. "What about Lord Haverset, is he still here?"

The little girl shook her head. "Not since last night. Come on now. Mum's waiting for you."

Until that moment, I had not noticed the light slanting through the bedroom windows. Evidently, I had passed the whole night in the wicker chair. I felt quite cheated by this discovery. Even after leaving the jail, I still could not manage to find my way to a soft bed.

Alice took my hand and pulled me forward insistently. I stumbled behind, still yawning as I walked. Mrs. Dillworth was rolling bread on the kitchen counter, her arms white with flour up to the elbow. From the scowl on her face and the unpleasant lumpish look of the forming bread, I had my doubts about its impending edibility. Meals were not Mrs. Dillworth's forte.

"You shouldn't go," she said.

"Go?" I extracted my fingers from Alice's grasp and rubbed sleep away from my eyes.

"I would have let you sleep," said Mrs. Dillworth. "Lord knows you need it." She pulled up the ill-formed loaf from the counter, looked at it critically, and pounded it against the boards again. "Since you agreed to go with them, I thought you'd want at least a few minutes to get ready."

"Go?"

Mrs. Dillworth shook her head. "You do nothing but repeat yourself this morning. Are you part parrot, Mr. Brown?"

"No, it's just that, well, I have no idea what you're talking about."

Mrs. Dillworth cocked her head to one side and for a moment her brown hair masked the wounds that puckered her left cheek so that her face seemed miraculously restored. "The company is sending another troop of soldiers back to Applewash, and you're going with them. I heard Miss Genevieve say you'd be happy to go."

The idea of making a second trip to the interior was so startling that I felt my legs go weak at the thought. "Why would anyone think of going back to Applewash after what happened last time?"

"It's because of that soldier," volunteered Alice. "On account of how the Indians attacked you."

"Indians?" Rather than understanding, I was growing more confused by the moment. I looked back and forth between Mrs. Dillworth and her daughter. "What have Indians to do with anything, and what soldier are you talking about?"

The glance that Mrs. Dillworth gave me made it clear she thought me either dim or daft. "The soldier that you took from the fort," she said. "That one as shot people."

I felt relieved to understand that she was talking about Captain Valamont, though why she was talking about the captain was still beyond my reach. "Am I going to be tried?"

"What?"

"For helping Captain Valamont, the soldier from the fort. Am I to be tried?"

Mrs. Dillworth shook her head. "I don't know anything about a trial." She let out a breath clearly tinged by exasperation. "All I know is that Miss Genevieve told them you'd go along to Applewash to see how the Indians attacked your people."

Now that I understood the whole of the thing, it made less sense than the pieces. I could not pretend to understand why would anyone believe such a thing, or why Marlowe should volunteer me for this fool's errand. "No Indians attacked us. It was those insects, the antriders."

"That's not what Lord Haverset says," she replied. "He said it was Indians all along." She looked thoughtful for a moment and pushed loose hair back from her face, leaving a streak of flour across her forehead. "Could be they're right, I suppose."

I stared at her in amazement. "But you know what happened. I told you."

"Folks get confused," said Mrs. Dillworth. "Especially when there's people hurt and all."

"I didn't get confused, madam." I kicked at the floor in frustration. "And unless these Indians have six legs and stand the size of a hazelnut, the director has taken leave of his senses."

"Sure now, I'll be quick to tell him you said so," called a voice from the door. I looked around to see the stout form of Sergeant Norris lounging in the doorway. "We're waiting on you, doctor. The sooner you get yourself outside, the sooner we can get this circus on the road."

"You shouldn't go to Applewash." I took a step toward the soldier. "No one should. The danger is too great."

Norris pushed himself away from the door frame. "Oh, I'm going to Applewash, and so are you. Be ready in ten minutes, or we'll drag your down the road." The sergeant gave a quick nod to Mrs. Dillworth, then pushed himself away from the door frame and left.

A headache began to force itself toward the front of my skull. I pressed my temples and squeezed my eyes shut. "Where is Miss Marlowe?"

"Gone," said Alice. "She left before the sun was even up."

For a long moment, I stood there in the kitchen and contemplated mutiny. If I refused to go with the soldiers, it was altogether likely that I would again find myself a resident of Plunket's less-than-reputable establishment. However, sleeping in a cell seemed imminently preferable to what was waiting down the road to the west. Finally, I opened my eyes and, without another word of complaint, began to gather my things.

Much as the idea of traveling toward the insect horde might frighten me, I felt I owed it to the other men who would be compelled into making this journey. If they were actually convinced that the cause of all the troubles was Indians, then it was likely that they would ride straight into the real menace and meet the fate of most of those on the first expedition. They did not trust my judgment or my story of what had happened near the Caney Creek Bridge, and that was exactly why I had no choice but to go.

# 8

*St. George*
*15 August 1832*

The scene that greeted me along the south bank of the Sarstoon was the most extravagant display of martial force I had seen in my years in Selvanos. Fully twenty men were gathered along the western road, with a like number of horses and a well-loaded wagon. The soldiers wore full red waistcoats with gold turnbacks and deep blue piping. Both muskets and side arms were in evidence. It appeared we were not going so much to visit Applewash as to invade. Seeing the size of this expedition gave me a momentary feeling of confidence—surely a force of this magnitude could come to no harm. On the heels of that feeling came another. Confidence was not what was needed. A group of men this large would fully expect to overcome any opposition in their path. And that expectation might only lead to disaster.

I had assumed that Sergeant Norris would be leading this sortie, but that task fell to another officer, a young lieutenant who was a distant relation of Lord Haverset. This officer was a well-formed man, with a firm chin and broad shoulders, but he held the unfortunate name of Lawrence Bland. I had seen him only a few times since his arrival in Selvanos, as he had been in charge of escorting various parties to Honduras or accompanying ships to Jamaica. His experience in these outings was clear as he directed the forming troops with vigor and seemed to be ready to overcome the flavor of his name by decisive action. Within a few minutes of my arrival, all the men were loaded, mounted, and ready to proceed.

The brief notice had given me little time to consider what I might require for this trip, but I held two hastily packed bags in my hand and the rucksack which had somehow survived the from the previous trip, slung over my shoulder. I brought with me more equipment that I hoped would be useful in the capture and study of the antriders. I was also careful to bring along some of the medical equipment left to me by the departed Dr. Wilmater. Considering the number of men and the direction we were going, it seemed all too likely that this equipment would be needed.

Little attention was given to me as the men prepared. I stood by, reluctant to interrupt the arrangements and still hopeful that I might be told to stay in St. George. As the front rank trotted off to form an advance guard, I walked alongside the road, looking for an empty mount. It quickly became evident that no such animal was present.

"Excuse me," I called to the lieutenant. "Where is my horse?"

Bland turned to look at me as if quite surprised to find me in his company. "Why would we give you a horse?" he asked.

The confusion that had plagued me all morning was on me again. "I thought...That is, Sergeant Norris told me I was to come with you."

"You'll come," said the lieutenant, "but you've already lost one horse belonging to king and company. This time, you'll ride in the wagon." He walked off without further comment.

The rest of the soldiers began to pass as the troop moved forward. I was forced to rush to reach the wagon and secure a seat beside the driver before the conveyance was put in motion. My placement among the baggage was certainly intended as a slight, and Sergeant Norris did not miss the chance to sneer as he rode past. Why these soldiers should be so angry at me, and not glad for my rescue of Captain Valamont, was something I didn't understand, but for the most part, I did not mind this demotion to the wagon. While the lack of my own mount limited my ability to wander afield from the course of the expedition, it also left my hands free and made it possible to take more notes while I traveled — though I cannot vouch for the legibility of any notes made in a flat board wagon traveling a heavily rutted road.

With an early start and cooperative weather, we made good progress that first day. The countryside that had seemed so rain-soaked and dreary on the first trip showed a happier face under clear skies. I observed coati mundi unexpectedly active in the middle of the day as they scurried into trees at our approach. Near noon, I watched as an enormous harpy eagle, *Harpia harpyja*, swooped down to snatch a woolly monkey that had been happily raiding fruit trees near the road. The burden of the prey was so great that the bird came down to earth with a crash. After a moment's pause, the eagle managed to get airborne once again and few off north, clearing the fields by no more than a hand's breadth as the luckless monkey dangled into its grip. Shortly after the bird left my sight, we came close to the river again. The lack of rain over the last few days had brought with it a drop in the river levels when compared with my previous excursion, leaving behind wide splays of grey mud and revealing steeply cut banks along the outer edge of meanders in the stream.

These observations, and the notes they generated, were enough to keep me distracted through much of the morning. The driver of the wagon, who held the odd sobriquet of "Muley," and was not a soldier, but a wayward American, displayed some interest in my notes and began to question me about the geology of the area. At first, I took him for a man with an interest in the sciences. However, it soon became clear that he had drifted down to Selvanos on the basis of unlikely rumors of gold.

I explained to him that many people had thought the western area of Selvanos suitable for either gold or silver, and perhaps the source of some of the fabulous wealth of Mayans further north, but after extensive study, it was now thought neither were present in any quantity.

At this, Muley's questions faded into disappointed silence. It appeared that his interest in the surrounding stratigraphy extended only so far as it offered the possibility of wealth. Still, he was amiable enough, and with the soldiers holding some unstated grudge against me, it was good to have someone to share a conversation.

Progress that first day was much more rapid that it had been with the stormy conditions that had reigned during the first foray. We crossed the Glaize Creek Bridge well before noon, stopping only for a brief meal along its banks. As night approached, we drew within sight of the small village of Harbridge, just short of the Sarstoon Ferry. It was one of several settlements that Captain Valamont had passed without pause on that initial expedition, however given the size of our force on this second foray, I expected that we would camp there and wait for the morning to move to the north bank. There was an inn at Harbridge, and at least a few of the men could be guaranteed a good bed. But Lieutenant Bland proved as impatient as his predecessor. He was not about to lessen his pace for the sake of comfort. He rode ahead of the party and arranged with the boatmen to start moving the troops across the river as soon as we arrived. By the time the wagon rolled in at the end of the column, the first group of men had already crossed and the boat was returning for more. The size of our expedition required four trips, with myself, Muley, and the wagon taking an entire ferryboat for ourselves.

Full dark had fallen by the time we saw the north bank and the river men were navigating their craft by lantern light. The exhaustion of making so many trips was clear on their faces, but they took their payment and headed back to their homes on the south side in short order.

There were few landholders along this stretch of the river, and none that could handle twenty men and horses on short notice. The lieutenant continued on for perhaps a mile, and then ordered that camp be made right there at roadside so that the company might move again at first light. While the men unloaded tents and sleeping rolls from the wagon, Lieutenant Bland selected two soldiers and rode off to dine at one of the smaller farms some distance yet away. He did not invite me for this trip.

Muley served double duty as the cook, proving himself capable of preparing a meal for twenty men with no more than some pots and an open fire to serve as a kitchen. The food was not elegant, and was perhaps spiced a bit more strongly than the average in St. George, but it was warm and made more than palatable by a day's hard travel. After watching Muley work for some minutes, I elected myself assistant cook and went about gathering the supplies he needed to make the meal. Muley spoke freely while he cooked, detailing adventures in his search for gold, which had taken him through Mexico, Selvanos, and much of the territory in between. His adventures were made humorous in the retelling, but I suspect they had been quite harrowing in the living.

When the meal was ready, I moved to aid in handing out the food. I was surprised with first one then another of the soldiers deliberately refused to take stew from my ladle, but waited until they could get their food from Muley. I tried to question these men, but they seemed in no more mood to exchange words with me than they were to share a meal. It was not until Sergeant Norris came up to get his portion that I was able to press my question.

"Why are your men so angry with me?" I asked.

"Oh, that's not something special for you," he replied as he took a ladle of stew onto his plate. "They treat all cowards the same."

I felt as if I had been struck across the face. "Coward?" My voice was loud enough that several of the men around the fire turned to look my way. Warm with embarrassment, I lowered my voice and continued. "Do they think I'm afraid just because I'm not in the army?"

Sergeant Norris shook his head. "It's on account of the way you were with Captain Valamont."

"Captain Valamont thought I was a coward?"

"After you run off and left him to the Indians, I guess he did."

Before I could manage a reply to this, the sergeant walked off to the fire and sat down on a stone near the men. Shortly afterward, there were several glances in my direction and general laughter. I had no doubt about the subject.

For several moments, it was all I could do to stand. My hands were balled into fists and my chest heaved with the effort of my breathing. After all that had happened, to be labeled a coward seemed monstrously unfair. And again there was this madness about Indians. If Muley had not laid a hand on my shoulder, I think I would have flown at Sergeant Norris right then and there.

"Let it go," said the cook.

"How can I?" I pushed his hand away. "A man can't allow himself to be labeled a coward, and for no reason. A stigma like that could ruin me. Even if I gain my father's lands, I'll have none of the respect that should come with it."

"Maybe so," said Muley. "But I see better than a dozen men over there, all of them trained to fight, and some of them still wearing pistols. I doubt you'd get the pleasure of laying your knuckles long side his chin."

It took a few more breaths before my anger began to subside, but I could see the sense in what the American was saying. Attacking Sergeant Norris was unlikely to clear my name and was sure to generate more troubles. I would have to bide my time until I was in a position to attack the lies at the root of this accusation.

After the meal, some of the men produced a dog-eared deck and played cards by the firelight while others spread their bedrolls out in ranks. I was relieved to see that they posted not one, but three guards for each shift of the night, two at fixed positions along the road and another a roving picket. With this insistence on blaming all events on actions of the natives, I had feared that this troop would evince no caution until we neared Applewash. It was good to know that they were taking care even though our journey was barely started.

As the men started to bed down, we were treated to a show by one of Selvanos's most extraordinary coleopterans. Giant lightning beetles of the genus Pyrophorus emerged from the woods like a cloud of stars and moved right across our camp as the beetles went to dance above the open fields on our left. More and more of them joined the party, swinging through the trees and coming low over the camp. These insects are near as long as a man's finger, and thick-bodied. The two luminescent spots on their thorax tend to be whiter than those of other light-producing insects and are so bright that you can read by holding one near a page—a fact I attempted to demonstrate that night. When several flashed together, the flare cast a distinct shadow from the surrounding trees. But Muley showed little inclination to discuss these insects, and the soldiers wanted nothing to do with me, so my pronouncements on their extraordinary nature attracted little notice. At last, I lay back on my bedding and contented myself with admiring the passing insect comets until at last I fell asleep.

Sometime later, there was a loud call from deep in the woods, and then a crashing among the tree limbs. I sat upright on my bedroll and fought to control my breathing. My first thought was that these sounds marked another exodus of creatures like that we had witnessed on the first trip, but soon enough the chorus of frogs, geckos, and insects resumed its usual level. It took me a good while longer to recover and I lay awake for an hour or more before my nerves calmed enough to permit rest.

When I rose, the sky was just becoming bruised by dawn, but the soldiers were already up and Muley was busy at the breakfast pots. Lieutenant Bland had returned to us sometime in the night and was deeply engaged in his rapid barking of commands. The men managed to wolf down bacon and coffee, and then it was time to grab our things and move on.

I had just taken my seat on the wagon bench and the soldiers were still engaged in saddling their mounts, when there was the sound of a horse pounding up the road at our rear. The soldiers bristled and Sergeant Norris sent two men who had completed their preparations back to guard against attack, though I don't know how anyone thought the natives would be attacking us from horseback. A single rider soon appeared, driving hard up the road. As the horse drew closer, I was surprised to see that it was Miss Marlowe, and even more surprised to see her dressed in mannish shirt and breeches, a skimmer pressed down on her dark curls.

She drew up her mount as she came up to us and looked down at Lieutenant Bland. "I need the doctor."

"The doctor's to come with us," said Bland. "I have that order from Lord Haverset directly." The rest of us were rumpled from our overnight on the road, but the lieutenant appeared fresh, the horsehair collar of his coat stiff and his breeches were unspattered by travel. I wondered if he had brought along more than one uniform, or if his diner with local planters had including disrobing so that his clothes could be laundered.

"One of my men is injured," said Miss Marlowe. "I need the doctor's services right away."

I moved to get down from the wagon, but Bland stuck up his hand. "This man has been accused of crimes against company, crown, and soldiers of this army," he said.

The anger that I had felt the night before came back instantly. "What crimes?" I said. "I have a right to know of any accusations."

Neither the lieutenant nor Miss Marlowe bothered to answer my demand. "It's little to me what he's done," she said. "I only know what I need. I'll bring him back when he's through."

"We're departing in moments," said Bland. "And he's to come with us."

I looked back and forth between to two of them, feeling much like a prize in some contest. Though, not a prize of any particular merit.

Miss Marlowe eased her horse forward and made a slow turn around the lieutenant. "You've twenty men and a wagon. You're not likely to move along faster than a single rider. My man can be cared for, and I'll have the doctor back to you before you've traveled ten miles."

If Miss Marlowe had not been of the most prominent family in Selvanos, I have no doubt she would have been refused, but after a few seconds, Lieutenant Bland gave a grudging nod. "If you must. But see that you hold him no more than two hours. This company moves quickly, and

I expect to reach the Qualm before dark and bivouac this evening by Grey's Works. Be sure that Brown is with us."

"He will be." Miss Marlowe looked my way. "Well, get mounted. My man won't last without attention."

"I don't have a horse," I said.

Miss Marlowe looked back at the lieutenant. In the space of a minute, an unhappy private had surrendered his horse and I was mounted with my instrument bag in hand. We started off back toward Harbridge with Miss Marlowe leading at a hard trot.

It took only seconds before the winding road and the thick forest took us out of sight of the soldiers. We continued on at brisk trot for what could have been only another hundred yards before Miss Marlowe abruptly reined in her horse and turned to look back over her shoulder. "I think we've gone far enough," she said.

"Far enough?" I pulled my own unfamiliar mount to a ragged halt a few lengths further on and looked around. The forest surrounding the road at this point was unbroken, with no sign of trail or habitation. "Is your injured man nearby?"

Miss Marlowe pushed her wide hat to the back of her head. "No," she said. "Mr. Brown, Calvin, I'm sorry I didn't get a chance to talk to you before you left, but there was no time."

"Your man was hurt two days ago?"

"No! No." She shook her head sharply. "There is no one injured, I'm afraid that was just a story I made that up so they'd let you come with me."

"I don't understand." I believe that was the truest statement I had yet made. Considering everything that had happened since I departed St. George on the first trip, I wasn't sure there was any feature of my life I could list as a solid fact and not open to speculation. "You told the director I'd accompany this mad expedition, and now you drag me away from them on false pretenses. Are you seeking to get me shot?"

"Hardly." Miss Marlowe took another glance over her shoulder. "There's not time to discuss this, but I believe Lord Haverset really does want you dead."

"Dead!" I said it so loudly that several birds took wing in the forest. "Dead? Why would the director want to kill me?"

"Because he thinks you helped the Indians."

A frustration that was near to insanity pounded in my head. "What Indians? Why is everyone always talking about Indians?"

Miss Marlowe drew in a deep breath and spoke quickly. "Lord Haverset thinks that Indians attacked Applewash and your group. He thinks that because he thinks Indians are behind everything wrong with the colony. I suspect he thinks they dance to cause the rain."

"But that still doesn't explain why he..."

She held up a hand to stop me. "You came back carrying on about these insects—which is a story the settlers learned from the Indians—and then Captain Valamont appears, saying that it really was Indians behind it all."

"But Valamont is insane! The director must realize that much."

"Insanity, like beauty, is found in the eye of the beholder." Miss Marlowe slipped down from her mount, walked around, and gave the horse a stroke along the side of the neck. "Valamont's resting in a bed at Company House, telling the director exactly what he wants to hear. The captain is a military man. He's also a landowner, so naturally, his opinion is respected. He says Indians attacked your group and you ran away."

"I ran, that's true enough, or I'd not be here now, but—"

"And you were found over Valamont with a gun in hand."

"Valmont's gun! I saved Valamont!"

"Or attacked him to keep him from telling what you had done."

I wiped the sweat from my forehead. "Captain Valamont killed two people. Half the men in St. George were preparing to attack him."

"They were," she agreed. "But you got there first. In Lord Haverset's mind, that's proof you were out to silence Valamont before he could share the truth about what happened in the west."

The situation, now explained, seemed more incredible than any fantasy I might have fabricated. "The director is prepared to believe a murderous madman over me?"

For the first time, Miss Marlowe appeared somewhat flustered. "For God's sake, Calvin, you've told the director his company is under attack by some kind of imaginary creature." She walked around her horse and stared up at me. "A whole town's been abandoned and soldiers lost and you blame it all on fairy story ants. Are you surprised he doesn't believe you?"

"I..." I stopped, and for a long time there was nothing but the sounds of birds and the distant noise of foraging monkeys. Slowly, I eased myself down from the horse and stood close to Miss Marlowe. "Is it only Lord Haverset who doubts me, or do you share his opinions?"

To my surprise, she actually smiled. "If I didn't believe in you, you wouldn't be here."

Though my anger and bafflement had not completely faded, her smile was contagious. I thought back to the events of the last days, from the moment of my return to St. George, through my abrupt departure. "The secretary," I said.

"What?"

"It's the secretary." I looked at her and nodded. "He's hated me for years and he was the one that sent me off to jail. It has to be the secretary that put Lord Haverset against me."

"He may hate you, but don't think this starts or ends in his office. The secretary didn't want you killed."

"He didn't?"

Miss Marlowe shook her head, sending the hat swinging against her curls. "I heard him tell the director that you weren't a soldier, and shouldn't be treated like a deserter. He only wanted you exiled from Selvanos, or kept in jail."

A ship to Jamaica or time in Plunket's cell was certainly better than mounting the steps to the gallows, but I didn't find this news particularly comforting. Still angry, I shook my head. "This can't be right. If the secretary wanted me jailed, and the director wanted me killed, why am I out?"

"Because I wanted it." Miss Marlowe reached out and laid her fingers against my arm. Her touch was light, but I felt each fingertip as though it were charged with an unnatural heat. "Because my father controls the largest tracts and shares in the company. Because I told Lord Haverset that you would prove your worth on this expedition. Because I wanted it."

What I felt then was a surprise so great it nearly buckled my knees. Because she was a landowner, I had never considered that Miss Marlowe might regard me as more than a tradesman. Because she was female, I had not thought her to have great influence within the company. On both counts, I had misjudged her.

As I struggled for a proper reply, she seemed to realize my distress. She reached out and stroked the nose of my horse. "You need to get back or the soldiers are likely to send someone after you."

"I suppose you're right." Though her hand was no longer on my arm, a sensation lingered where her fingertips had touched. I was acutely aware of her nearness, as if her warmth were detectable above the heat of the day. "I...I want to thank you for your help."

"You needn't thank me," she said. "Only go prove that I didn't lie when I told the director you'd acquit yourself well on this journey."

With that, we both climbed onto our mounts. I started back along the road toward Applewash, she toward Harbridge. I looked back only once, but Miss Marlowe was already out of sight behind the screens of trees.

# 9

*Central Selvanos*
*16 August 1832*

The soldiers had moved along quite briskly during the first day, but I caught them that morning no more than two or three miles from where we had spent the night. Progress had been somewhat delayed by the commotion caused in my departure, and further interrupted by the discovery of a tamandua, *Tamandua tetradactyla,* among the supplies. This smaller form of anteater is more rarely seen than the giant I had run into with the first expedition, as unlike other anteaters, they tend to an arboreal existence and come to the ground only when necessary. However, something in the wagon must have attracted the attention of the animal.

Discovery of the tamandua had ended badly on both ends. Stumbling into a camp of twenty armed men had been the last action for the relatively peaceable creature. When I caught up to the expedition, the yellow and black body of the tamandua was draped over one side of the wagon with the animal's long narrow head bouncing at every jolt of the wheels. The man who had first encountered the creature was also a casualty, though his injury was decidedly less fatal. He had cornered the anteater within the wagon and earned a slash from the tamandua's powerful fore claws which had torn through the meat of his hand. No sooner had I arrived, than forward progress was halted while I sutured the soldier's wounds.

When that was completed, I was quickly removed from my horse and returned to a place on the wagon a few feet from the sad remains of the tamandua. Muley gave me a summary of the tumult resulting from the anteaters's presence in the camp and the anger displayed by Lieutenant Bland at this interruption of orderly progress. Within a few minutes, the expedition resumed its pace through the rolling hills.

The weather, which had been cooperative to this point, showed signs of resuming a more contentious nature. Heavy cumulus piled along the horizon and the trees to our right began to sway with gusts of wind. Lieutenant Bland ordered an increase in pace. He was still hopeful of reaching Grey's Works before nightfall. No matter what the officer ordered, some of the horses were in no mood to agree. The pace of the previous day had tired the animals, and they had to be walked more frequently and ridden more slowly. This did not help Lieutenant Bland's disposition.

Shortly after noon, we reached the field of mixed grass and lavender that I remembered well from the first trip. The field looked beautiful, but seeing it brought tightness to my stomach as I recalled how close we were to the Caney Creek Bridge and the scene of my last encounter with the antriders.

By this point, the expedition was no longer so neatly grouped as it had been on the first day. The Lieutenant's desire to keep moving had taken the lead soldiers on off down the road and gradually spread the group over more than a mile. Within a few hours, the force had become so dissipated that I could not see the men in front of us. Sergeant Norris and a private named Hadley, the same man who had suffered from his encounter with the tamandua, remained behind the wagon, bringing up the rear of the train. Otherwise, we were alone.

"I hope your Indians don't come after us now," said Muley as he eased the wagon over a stretch of particularly rough road. "The others are so far off, the Indians would have us scalped before anyone could get to us."

"There are no Indians here," I told him. "None that would attack us. Anyway, Indians in Selvanos do not take scalps." From his expression, it was obvious that the American did not believe me.

The rising storm continued to build in the west. Where the tall forest allowed views in that direction, the sky was bruised purple and mustard yellow. The fields along our left had been planted with African sorghum grass, which was widely used as a source of sugar in Selvanos as cane seemed to dislike either the weather or soil. The tall, bicolored blades of sorghum shivered under the tempest wind and leaves and small bits of branches blew out from the woods on the right with stinging force. From the nearness of the clouds, it was clear that the rains would be on us in no more than minutes. Those men who had hurried along at the start of the line might still make it to shelter at Grey's Works with no more than a damp hat. Those of us at the rear of the line were in for a soaking.

Thunder rumbled out from the clouds. The first drops, fat as hen's eggs, stuck the road ahead of us and sent up puffs of dust. There was another crack, and a sharp rattle in its wake.

"What was that?" Sergeant Norris jerked sharply at his reins and brought his mount up alongside the wagon. "Did you hear that?"

"The thunder?"

The sergeant shook his head. "More than thunder."

Lightning forked down from the clouds. A few seconds later the ground shook and my ears were popped by the passing wave of air. "What did you hear?" I asked.

Norris held up his hand and turned his head side-on to the road ahead, listening. We waited there for what must have been a minute. The horses were nervous about the storm and Private Hadley experienced quite a bit of difficulty in keeping his mount still. Even the placid, heavy-bodied pair that pulled the wagon began to flick their ears forward and mutter as the storm moved toward us.

Finally, Sergeant Norris shook his head. "It must have been nothing but thunder after all," he said, though he did not seem convinced. "Come on, let's go get wet."

The rain arrived then as if he had summoned it. Great buckets of water fell in the fields and on the road. Limbs crashed down in the forest and the gusty winds threw water, mud, and broken branches into our faces. Sergeant Norris moved around in front and led the way. I could hear him cursing as the storm went on, though the exact words were often drowned by the thunder. Considering the nature of that portion of his speech that reached my ears, I was not sorry to lose the majority.

It grew swiftly darker. What had been full daylight only minutes before was reduced to a blue-grey submarine glow. The sergeant was little more than a silhouette along the road in front of us, the forest a black wall rising on the right, the fields flashes of gold and green lit by the frequent lightning. Cold rain swept over us in waves, and I was soon colder and, I believe, wetter, than I had been when floating along the Sarstoon. The storm seemed determined to extract revenge for every moment of good weather we had enjoyed on this trip. The road was swiftly overrun first by puddles, then by flowing streams. The wagon team had increasing difficulty in dragging the metal-rimmed wheels through the soupy mud.

"We should be near," I said.

"What?" asked Muley.

"Grey's Works!" I raised my voice to be heard above the storm. "We should be within a mile or two, I recognize the stream we just passed."

The wagon driver nodded in reply and gave the leads a good shake. The horses moved on with no more vigor than before, stolidly planting one big foot after another in the mud.

Private Hadley's horse was not withstanding the storm so easily. Whenever I glanced back, the gelding was as likely to be on two legs as four. Considering the injury to the private's hand, it was a wonder of horsemanship that he was able to stay in the saddle as his horse jumped, twisted, and bucked along the road. Coming down from one jump, the horse's front hooves slipped on the muddy course and the animal's legs splayed out to the side. I feared that the horse would go down, but it managed to recover, mostly due to good guidance from the private.

"You're a fine rider!" I shouted across to Hadley.

He returned a weak smile. "I've never been on a horse before yesterday," he said. "Not sure I want to be on one again."

"If this is your first time, then you must have a talent," I replied. "You're a born cavalry man."

The horse twisted around, and Private Hadley held on tight. "I think I'd sooner learn to drive a wagon," he shouted back. In these conditions, the soldiers seemed to have momentarily forgotten that they were supposed to show me nothing but disdain.

Sergeant Norris reappeared from the screens of water ahead. "Hurry on!" he said. "I can see buildings at the next turn. We're almost there."

I was thankful to know what we were close to shelter, though at that point I was as wet as I was going to get. Private Hadley allowed his nervous horse to move around the wagon and together he and Sergeant Norris led the way to Grey's Works. A few moments later, I could make out the faint form of a barn through the sheets of rain, and then a small wooden slave house, some sheds, more slave quarters, and then the tall tank used for boiled molasses. Another hundred yards, and we came to the front of the large main house.

The previous expedition had been greeted by such excitement that it surprised me to find no one at the front step. Even if the Greys were staying in from the storm, I would have thought they might send out a slave to see us to the barn. Since we had been left to our own devices, I was about to call out to Sergeant Norris to let him know the route around to the large horse barn. Before the words could leave my mouth, I noticed something odd.

The storm had made the area quite dark, and night was almost on us, but there was no light through any of the windows. The front door hung open, bouncing back and forth in the wind. It had to be allowing rain into the front hall, but no move was made to stop it. I leaned out from the wagon and drew in a deep breath. Over the smell of ozone and wet vegetation stirred by the storm, I could just make out the faint smell of lemons.

"Sergeant!"

Norris looked around. "What is it, Brown?"

"They're here! They've already been here!"

"The lieutenant? I should say. He's probably inside drinking warm wine and..."

"Not Lieutenant Bland!" I shouted. "Not any of the men. The antriders."

The sergeant looked as if he might laugh. "Your little fairy story knights?"

I shook my head. "They're not knights, and they're no fairy story." I leaned out from my seat on the wagon and looked down. There was nothing to be seen on the ground but water and mud. "We need to get away from this place."

"Now?" Lightning split the air behind us, and for a moment the conversation paused while we waited for the thunder to die and Private Hadley to calm his frightened horse. "I'm not moving from this place," said Norris. "Not until this storm is over, and not until I have orders."

"If we stay here," I said, "it's likely we'll all die."

I feared that the sergeant would only laugh, but he looked at me seriously for a moment and then nodded. "We'll take a look," he said. "You and me. These two can stay out front while we see what's what."

"I'd like to get down off this horse," said Hadley.

"You'll be down soon enough," replied Norris. He climbed down from his own mount and looped the reins across a fence row at the side of the road. "Come on, Brown. Let's see if it's any drier on the inside."

"And if the antriders are there?"

"If we see your beasties, then you'll find out just how fast I can get back to St. George. I didn't join up with the army to get eaten by any buggering bugs."

Norris waited by the end of the walk. Reluctantly, I climbed down from my seat on the wagon and together we headed for the open door. Mentally, I was measuring the distance at each step. Five paces back to the wagon. How fast could Muley turn the wagon if I came running back? Would the wagon move fast enough to outrun the insects on the muddy roads? Would the antriders themselves be slowed by the rain? I made a hundred guesses as we made the last steps onto the porch. I remembered how the Grey's had arrayed themselves across this same porch when Captain Valamont approached, but no one came out now.

The sergeant hesitated by the door. "It seems deserted, I'll give you that much." He looked back toward the road, squinting against the rain. "I wonder where the lieutenant has gone off to?"

I feared that I had an answer to that question, but was not ready to pronounce the soldier's doom. Even with what I had seen along Caney Creek, it seemed impossible that twenty men could vanish so quickly without leaving a trace. Sergeant Norris went to the door, hesitated a moment, then stepped inside. I followed at his back.

The front hall of the Grey's home was cool and dark. Where children and slaves had poured forth in their fine clothes on the previous call, there was only silence. Though we had seen nothing, the silence itself clearly showed that something was badly wrong. It took a few minutes to locate dry matches and then to fumble along the tables to find a lamp. The yellow light added warmth to the hall, but no life.

"Halloo!" shouted Sergeant Norris. "Lieutenant? Anyone?"

There was no reply but the rumble of more thunder from outside. Norris handed the lamp to me, then tugged his pistol free of its holster and held it ahead of him as we passed down the hall and into a parlor. Some of the furniture here had been overturned, and there were dark stains on the rugs. The smell of peppered lemons was mingled with a harder, metallic scent.

"You smell that?" I said. "That's their smell."

"Your bugs?"

"Yes."

It wasn't clear if the sergeant was ready to believe me, but he nodded and moved on. We explored a smoking room and a large dining room, again with some items overturned, but no signs of the inhabitants. As we passed through each of these rooms, I felt a growing guilt over the fate of the Grey family and their others that had shared their works. I had floated by this place nearly a week before on my way back to St. George from the encounter at Caney Creek. I had been fully aware of the antriders and the threat they posed, but I had made to effort to reach the banks. If I had left Richardson on the river and come to shore at this place, I might have warned these people in time. Instead, I had clung to the timber and spent several days making the journey in St. George. The Greys had paid for that decision.

Sergeant Norris left the kitchen and I followed him into the pantry. Here, too, there was a general disturbance, with tins and jars lying open and boxes of salt spread across the floor.

"Your bugs are poor housekeepers," said the sergeant. He kicked at an overturned barrel of pickled maize. "You think your little knights could throw down a barrel?"

"Not one, or ten, or even a thousand," I replied. "But there are a lot more than a thousand."

Norris gave a noncommittal grunt. "I'll believe it when I see it."

"Then I sincerely hope you never get a chance to believe." I walked through the back of the pantry and stepped onto the rear portico. There was a baking kitchen ten steps out along a hard-packed path, barely visible in the light of the lamp, a large brick building that had two chimneys. It was a kitchen such as could bake three dozen loaves in a morning. Only there was no smoke there now. I might have gone out to check the kitchen, but the thought of the dead woman I had encountered near Caney Creek was with me strongly. Besides, it was still raining very hard.

The sergeant had moved on to another room and I could hear him shuffling through the dark. "Brown." he said. "Bring me that lamp."

I made my way across the hall into a bedroom. Sergeant Norris was standing by the foot of the bed. Curtains streamed back from open windows and I could see that the whole room had been soaked by blowing rain.

"What is it?" I asked.

"Over here."

Lightning flashed and I caught a glimpse of something tan and red on the puddled floor. I rounded the bed and the lamp revealed the body of a soldier lying face down on the floor.

"Be careful," I said. "They could still be here."

Sergeant Norris crouched down next to the body. "Your bugs might shift a barrel, but I don't think they could swing a knife." He pulled a long blade from the back of the bloody coat and held it up to the light. "What we have here is a murder."

# IO

*Grey's Works*
*16 August 1832*

The soldier was an older private by the name of Reynolds and he was most definitely dead. He'd been one of Lieutenant Bland's favorites, one of the men who rode near the head of the column, and I'd had little chance to speak to him during the journey. It was clear I'd not be speaking to him now.

I knelt on the carpet beside the body and held the lamp close to the torn coat. In the yellow light, it was obvious that Reynolds's uniform was much darker than it should have been, the wool stained deep crimson by spilled blood. The gash made by the knife had cut through the thick red coat and the light linen shirt beneath. The blood on the garments obscured the details of the wound, but from what I could see, the blade had skirted the spine and entered at an oblique angle between the dorsal curve of the thoracic ribs. Carefully, I laid two fingers across the back of the soldier's neck. "This happened recently."

"Of course it did," said Sergeant Norris. "I saw this man not two hours ago."

"No, I mean very recently." I took hold of the dead man's arm and pushed the body onto its side. The limb moved with a slight degree of stiffness, but did not display the first signs of full rigor. "If he had been dead more than a few minutes, his body would be much stiffer."

Sergeant Norris raised his head and looked off into the gloom. "The savages could still be here."

"Savages?" I studied the wound in the dead man's back. "You think this was the work of Indians?"

"Who else?" said Norris. He walked to the edge of the circle of light cast by the lamp. "There's eighteen soldiers missing, along with all the folks that lived in this place. That's not the work of one killer." He turned back to me. "Come on, let's get the others out of the rain before we're pulling knives from their backs."

I dropped poor Reynold's arm to the floor and followed the sergeant back through the house. There was still the smell of lemons in the parlor and this distinct scent was very strong in the front hall. I was sure that the antriders had been there and might account for the absence of both the inhabitants and Lieutenant Bland. However, the manner of Reynold's death certainly bolstered the hypothesis of a human agent behind the killing and made me look even more the fool.

The rain had slackened while we searched the house. A few fat drops fell against my face and shoulders as we followed the path back to the road, but already I could see tattered openings in the clouds and a few bright stars peeking through. Muley and Private Hadley were still waiting at the gate. The American had climbed down from his bench on the wagon and the private had dismounted his nervous horse. The two men were standing so close together it would not have been possible to slot a sheet of paper between them.

"What did you find?" Hadley called as we approached. "Is the Lieutenant here?"

Sergeant Norris held silent until he was close enough to speak in a quiet tone. "There's no one here," he said. "No one alive anyway." He raised up on his toes and peered across the road at the dark screen of trees. "Could be there's savages close by."

"Savages?" said Muley. He twisted his head around to look at the woods on the far side of the pike, then back at the sergeant. "Somebody's been here, I tell that much."

"Why do you say that?" I asked.

"Look here at the road." Muley took a few paces away from the wagon to where a trail branched off toward the complex of barns and sheds behind the house. "See here? Our boys all turned left here."

Sergeant Norris stepped over beside the man and bent for a good look at the muddy track. From what I could see, any story the road had to tell had been nearly erased by the brief deluge, but Sergeant Norris appeared to believe Muley's tracking. "We should find the mounts in the barn, then."

Muley shook his head. "No you won't. Because then they came out again, riding hard." He took another step forward. "See here? This horse was moving quick, sir, damn quick."

From the expression on the sergeant's face, he was as perplexed as I had been over the last week. "Why in god's name would they ride in then ride back out again? Especially when they had just made shelter and a storm was coming?"

None of us had a ready answer to that question. For a few minutes, we stood there in the road, dividing our attention between the rain-blurred hoof prints in the mud and the threatening darkness of the forest. Finally, Sergeant Norris made a decision. "Let's get inside," he said. "If the Lieutenant headed out after savages, he'll be coming back for us. He'll expect us to stop here, and we've no way to find him."

"If he's still alive," said Private Hadley.

On that rather glum note, we moved to put the horse team into the barn, along with the mounts belonging to the two soldiers. The supplies in the wagon were covered, then I held up the light and Muley unhitched the team where they stood. I then assisted him in leading the tired pair along the track toward the barn. The two of us walked in front, while the soldiers walked their own horses behind. Sergeant Norris had not yet mentioned the unfortunate fate of Private Reynolds, and I followed his example. I could appreciate that he wanted to keep order and get us into a position to defend ourselves while waiting on the Lieutenant, I only hoped that he would mention the dead man before either Muley or the private stumbled across the body.

Near the barn, I began to catch the scent of lemons again, mixed with odors of hay, horses, and mud. When the lamp showed something white gleaming at the entrance of the barn, I was not completely unprepared.

"The antriders have been here," I said.

"What's an antrider?" said Private Hadley.

"Be quiet," said Sergeant Norris.

The big grey gelding tugged at the line in my hand. I tried another step forward, but the horse balked and took a step back. Beside me, Muley seemed to be having no better luck. He cursed, and slapped at the flank of the horse with his wide-brimmed hat, but the animal would not enter the barn.

"Something in there they don't care for," said Muley. He reached down and picked up one of the small white bones from the ground. "There's bones here."

"Horse bones?" asked Private Hadley.

I looked at the small bone in the American's hand. It was slender, with rounded processes at either end. "Not horse," I said. "Man."

"Man bones!" Hadley dropped the reins of his horse and went to pull free his rifle.

Sergeant Norris spat on the ground. "You don't know that."

"I do. That's a tibia, one of the two bones making up the lower part of the leg. From the size of it, it's from an adult. Most likely a male."

"You don't know," the sergeant repeated. He stepped past us, dragging his own horse forward. The sergeant's chestnut mount seemed less disturbed by what it sensed around the barn. It followed docilely enough as the sergeant reached the doorway and paused at the edge of the darkness.

There was a sound of movement from inside the barn.

"Brown, get that light up here," said the sergeant.

I looped the lead for the reluctant grey horse around a nearby fence rail then hurried to join Norris at the door. There was another sound. I raised the lantern with great trepidation, sure that it would reveal a mass of antriders sheltering in the barn. Instead, I saw several stalls, many of them closed, and piles of dried hay near the door. There were more bones here, and the sharp smell of the antriders hung heavy in the air, but there was no sign of a red and black horde.

Down the row, something shifted in a stall. For a moment, I thought it was the oft-mentioned savages come to finish us, but a moment later the lamp shown on the fear-whitened eyes of a horse. "It's all right," said Norris. "Get your bloody horses and get them inside."

The wagon team was still reluctant to cooperate, but we took them one at a time, pulling at one end and slapping at the other, and soon enough brought them into the barn. Private Hadley entered last, leading his black horse with one hand and still clutching his rifle in the other. He started at the number of bones that littered the hay. "These all come from people?"

I shook my head. "Most are from horses, See how large the vertebrae are? And over there is a skull." The skeletons were disarticulated and some portions appeared to be missing. As best I could tell, there appeared to be remains from perhaps four or five horses in the barn, not nearly enough to account for all the mounts of Lieutenant Bland and his men. And even accounting for what I had seen along Caney Creek, I was not prepared to believe that the antriders could reduce horses to clean bone in the time that had passed since we had seen the rest of the expedition.

Muley came up beside me. "I've seen bones like this from cattle," he said, "when they die out in the fields and varmints and weather get after them. How long has this place been abandoned?"

"It's not abandoned," I replied. "I was here little more than a week ago and the whole farm and log works held at least forty people. Maybe twice that."

The American obviously had a hard time associating such a short passage of time and the dry bones on the ground. "Well," he said. "These folks didn't take very good care of their horses."

Private Hadley finished removing the tack from his mount and went to see about the only living inhabitant of the barn. "I know this horse," he said. "This is one of ours." The frightened animal stuck its head over the railing and Hadley stroked it along the nose. "This is Bill Reynolds' mount, sure enough."

I glanced at Sergeant Norris and saw that he was looking back at me. He gave a grudging nod and turned to the others. "Reynolds is inside."

"Bill's here?" said Private Hadley.

"He's here, but he's dead." Before any questions could be voiced, Norris went on to explain our discovery of the unfortunate soldier and his condition. "The savages as killed Reynolds are probably still close by. I'd wager the Lieutenant is putting an end to the brutes right this moment."

"We should go help!" said Hadley. He began to finger his rifle again.

"No," said Sergeant Norris. "If the lieutenant had wanted us with him, he would have waited till we caught up. It's dark out there and the road is poor. If we go farther, we'd have to leave the wagon behind, which means leaving our supplies." He shook his head. "We're staying here until morning. It's likely the lieutenant will be back by then. If not, we'll move on at first light."

It took several minutes to see the horses relieved of their saddles and get them settled in stalls. Private Hadley kicked the fallen bones clear of the stalls before he would put his mount in one of the places. Even then, he seemed more skittish than the horse.

As we walked back to the house, I caught up to Sergeant Norris and spoke with him quietly. "You can't think that the Indians killed those horses."

"And why not?" asked Norris. "I didn't see any of your little knights around."

"You saw those bones." I moved around in front to block his path. "Those horses, and those people, they were taken apart. Not a scrap of flesh left behind. Why would the Indians do that?"

Norris scowled at me. "Savages don't have to have a reason. That's what makes them savages." He shoved hard against my shoulder, sending me staggering across the wet grass. Before I could recover, he had reached the door of the house.

Inside, we found more lamps and braced the rear door with cabinets dragged from the pantry. The sergeant seemed satisfied with these precautions, but though the door was effectively blocked for any person that might enter that way, I knew that it was not tight enough to shut out smaller intruders. For the antriders, there were a hundred ways into the house.

Reynolds cooling body was left in the room where it lay. Private Hadley stuck his head in for a moment and saw the figure on the ground, but seemed to have no desire for a close inspection. Under the sergeant's direction, all four of us moved to the parlor just off the front hall, a position from which we could easily monitor the remaining entrance. More lamps were gathered and lit from my own, which was nearing the end of its oil, and soon enough the place was blazing like noon. It was comforting to be bathed in such light, but it ruined our vision for seeing outside and made the glass panes of the windows little more than mirrors.

The furniture of the parlor was quite fine, as fit the Greys' position as wealthy and influential land owners. Stuffed chairs were run over in pale silk and thick green cord-du-roi. A chaise bore fluted legs in the French style and the rug on the floor was embroidered with scarlet and deep blue. The four of us took positions around the room, and I accompanied Muley on a return trip to the wagon so that we might retrieve the bedrolls. It seemed a waste to sleep on thin blankets thrown on the floor when the house contained several bedrooms with tall, well-cushioned beds, but Sergeant Norris would not hear of us dispersing through the house and insisted that everyone stay in the parlor until the others returned.

No formal periods of watch were set, with only the four of us to share the night. Instead, we all moved restlessly around the room, occasionally lying on our beds, then pacing around again, staring at our reflections in the dark windows. Along around midnight, lightning began to once again flash off to the west. The deep rumble of thunder vibrated the walls and rattled the windows in their frames. This storm was more persistent than the first, and we were all thankful that at least we were spared the rain. Private Hadley hung near the window, holding his injured hand against the cool glass as he watched the new storm drag past. Sergeant Norris sat in one of the imported chairs, gnawing at a succession of biscuits, while Muley reclined on the floor, half-asleep.

My mind was in as much tumult as the weather and eventually I surrendered any idea of rest. I walked the limits of the room, wondering if all the people that had once inhabited this house were now dead. I wondered if the antriders had found them all at home, if they had died in their beds, if they had run or fought, or perhaps if they had miraculously escaped. The antriders had been there, I was sure of that much, but that bare fact left open the question of where the insects had gone. If they had moved on toward the east, then we should have encountered them along the road from St. George. Of course, the creatures had proved themselves capable of crossing a moving stream at Caney Creek. They might have used the same skills to cross the Sarstoon itself. At this moment, they could be harassing the works along the Qualm.

Shuffling back and forth across the room in my agitation, my attention was captured by the dark stains along the edge of the rug. I had assumed that these stains were blood, and this was verified when I bent down for a closer examination. From what I could see, only a small amount of blood had been spilled in this place. There were streaks, perhaps reflecting the direction that a body had been dragged across the room, but the total blood on the floor might have been measured in teaspoons. However, there was an unexpected quality to this stain. The blood was hard and black, matting together the threads of the rug into stuff tufts.

"This is old blood," I said.

Sergeant Norris glanced round from his seat in the silk chair. "What of it?"

"Reynolds was killed today," I said. "Only a few minutes before we arrived, but this blood has been here much longer."

"You're sure of that?"

"Yes, absolutely."

The sergeant thought for a moment, then shrugged. "Then savages must have been in this place for days. That explains why the horses are all down to bones. They probably went into the stew pot." Norris finished with a satisfied grin.

His theory did not appease me. The house showed signs of fights here and there, but it had not been ransacked for its valuables and it showed none of the signs I would have expected if an army of natives had taken to squatting inside a home. I got back to my hands and knees and studied the stains on the carpet, thinking I might deduced in which direction the body had been taken, but no sooner had I put my eye near the floor, than something new caught my attention.

I reached between the matted fibers of the rug and drew out something red, and shiny, about the size of a toothpick. It was quite a familiar object—I had taken one just like it from my own ankle. It was the weapon of an antrider. "Look at this," I took the tiny bit of chitin over to the sergeant. As I did, the others moved in for a closer look.

Norris squinted at the small object between my fingers. "What am I looking at?"

"You called the antriders little knights," I said, "well, this is part of a lance. The weapon of an antrider. It shows that they were here, as I said."

Both Muley and Private Hadley leaned in so close that they shadowed the item in my grip, but it was clear that Sergeant Norris was not interested in any better view. "That could be anything."

"It's from an antrider," I said. "I know it. The antriders were here. I have little doubt that they are the cause of the deaths at this house, not your savages."

"You're that sure of yourself?" said the sergeant. He slapped at my hand, sending the miniature weapon flying into the shadowed distance. "Are you forgetting how Reynolds died? That little scrap of twig didn't look anything like the knife we pulled from Bill's back."

I opened my mouth to reply, when my attention was caught by a noise from outside. A moment later, we had all heard it and together we rushed to the window to peer through the glass. The storm was nearly played out and the first light of dawn was purpling the sky to the east. The trees across the way were visible as dim shadows and I could make out the faint forms of barns and sheds around us.

Sergeant Norris grasped the window and pushed it open. Cool air flowed in, bringing the scents of rain and jungle. The sounds that we had all detected was much cleared how. Horses. Horses were approaching, moving fast by the sound of them.

Private Hadley ran to collect his rifle, came back to the window, and worked to fix a cap in place. Sergeant Norris shoved down on the barrel of the weapon. "Indians don't ride horses."

"They do in the states," said Muley.

"Then thank the good lord we're not in your states," replied the sergeant. He leaned against the window frame. "That has to be the lieutenant returning."

"If it is," I said. "He's in a hurry."

A moment later the horsemen came into view. There were six of them, packed in such a knot that they might have passed for riders nearing the finish of a race. Mud flew from the hooves of their horses. They were crouched low over the necks of the mounts and even in the faint morning light I could see that the coats of both horses and riders were heavily spotted by mud. Not one of the men retained their hats.

I feared for a moment that they actually were natives. Indians that had taken to riding as did those Sioux of the North American plains. But as they crossed the space in front of the turn off to the barns, I began to make out faces. They were, in fact, our men, members of the expedition, and right in the center of them was Lieutenant Bland.

"Lieutenant!" Private Hadley shouted. "We're here, sir!" He pushed to the window and waved at the men.

The riders did not slow. They crossed in front of the Grey house and kept on moving to the east. The light was good enough as they passed to make out the foam on the horses. The animals were all heavily lathered, clearly ridden out, and close to exhaustion. But the soldiers had no mercy. They drove their heels hard against the horse's ribs as they rode, urging them on. In the space of ten seconds, they were past the house and kicking up mud on the road toward Harbridge and St. George. In thirty seconds, they were out of sight.

The passage of the lieutenant left us all shaken and Private Hadley near in shock. "He didn't stop," said the soldier. "Why didn't he stop?"

"They might not know we're here," said Sergeant Norris. "If Bill Reynolds was dead before they left, then they might think there was no reason to stop."

"Where are the rest of them?" asked Muley. "There should have been three times as many."

Sergeant Norris offered an idea that the others might yet be farther down the road. The reason that the lieutenant was riding so hard might be that he needed the supplies from the wagon. The rest of the men could be arrayed along the road in a major engagement with the Indians.

"Which way should we go?" asked Hadley. "Should we go join in the fight, or try to catch the lieutenant?"

Norris had some reply to this, but I did not hear his suggestion. Another sound from outside had caught my attention.

It seemed at first like a rising wind, and I thought we might be facing still another round of storms, but as the sound increased it became more distinctive. A hissing, dry sound, like a man rubbing callused palms together.

"Oh, God," I said. "Run."

# I I

*Grey's Works*
*17 August 1832*

The rising sun cast long, distorted shadows as I leaped down from the porch and hurried toward the barn. The wind blew in from the west, bringing with it the smell of vegetation and damp earth. For the moment the hissing noise had faded, and I could detect neither sound nor scent that signaled the approach of antriders. But my own heart was beating in such alarm that I could barely hear anything else and I had no doubt about what was approaching.

The door banged open behind me and Sergeant Norris shouted across the lawn. "Where do you think you're going, Brown?"

"To get the horses." I turned, but continued walking backwards across the grass. "The antriders are close. They'll be here any moment."

"Antriders?" Norris stepped down from the porch. "You think bugs sent the whole troop to running? It had to be Indians."

I tripped over a branch blown down by the storm and barely kept from falling on the soggy ground. "Insects or Indians, if they sent the lieutenant into flight, do you really want to meet them with only the four of us?"

Norris opened his mouth, shut it, nodded and dived back into the house. Through the open door, I could hear him shouting at Muley and Private Hadley to gather their things.

The barn seemed nearly as dark as it had in the middle of the night and this time I had no lamp. I blinked and shuffled toward the sound of the horses moving in their stalls, unsure as I raised the bar at the front of the stall if I was releasing one of our mounts or only opening the gate on the dry bones of horses left by the Greys. A big form moved past me in the shadow, and a moment later I saw one of the horses from the wagon team step into the light. I feared that the animal might bolt and be off before any of us could move to hold it, but Muley arrived while the horse was still standing at the door and took it quickly in hand.

"Get Old Mary," he said. "I'll take Trip on around."

"Right." My eyes began to adjust and I picked the other wagon horse between the stalls holding the darker cavalry mounts. My actions were made clumsy by fear, and it took me several tries to fumble open the gate. Still, I managed to secure the horse and lead it from the barn just as Sergeant Norris and Private Hadley charged into to retrieve their mounts. Muley had already positioned the first horse by the time I got the second around.

"You think they're coming, your bugs?" he asked.

I nodded. I looked down the road, stained orange by the rising sun. There was still no sign of danger. "We need to get moving if we're going to be out of here before they arrive."

"Five minutes," said Muley. "That's what I need." He relieved me of the second horse and began to tie it into the hitch.

The time requested was short enough, but I feared it was more than we had. Sergeant Norris emerged from the barn leading his horse. On his heels was Hadley, struggling under the weight of a saddle and tack. While Norris held the animal steady, Hadley wrestled the saddle into place. I stood by them, feeling rather useless. My years in St. George had required little knowledge of horses and on the previous expedition it had been Donnel who cared for my mount. I could be of little assistance as the men worked so hard to prepare our departure.

I stepped back out to the road and looked again. The light was rising, and though there was a fine fog around the trees on the far side of the pike, I could see some hundred yards or more without problem. The antriders had not yet appeared, but once again there was that noise. A hissing, dry noise, like a hundred sheets of paper rustling at once, like dry sand shifting over stones. Like antriders on the march.

I stepped raised my eyes and looked along the road. The thin fog was roiling, as if disturbed by the passage of some breeze. Along the ground, a sea of black and crimson was rolling forward.

Shivers went through my skin. I turned and sprinted toward the wagon.

"They're coming!" I cried. "They're coming!"

Muley was still working at the harness and neither the sergeant or Hadley was in sight. It was clear that neither of them was prepared to go, which only increased my terror. "Hurry! We've got to hurry!"

Norris stepped out of the barn, shading his eyes against the rising sun. "What are you screaming about?"

I staggered to a halt beside the wagon and pointed back down the road. "The antriders, they're coming!" When I followed my own pointing finger, I saw that my warning was incorrect. The antriders were not coming. They were already on us. In the time I had covered the dozen or so yards to the wagon, the antriders had covered an equal distance. The black line spread left and right as far as I could see. There was little doubt that the mass of insects was even larger than the force I had encountered at Caney Creek, and they were surging toward us like a rising tide.

Muley's response was succinct. "Well damn," he said. "Get on." He dropped the lines he had been working at and jumped up to the wagon bench.

I followed, one eye on the barn. Sergeant Norris mounted the one horse that had been led outside, only to discover that it was still tied to the rail. Cursing steadily, he dropped from the saddle and pulled the reins loose, then put his foot to the stirrup and vaulted back up. "Hadley!" he said. "Come on man!"

The private came out of the barn leading the second horse. Its girdle had not been fastened and the leather straps lay on the ground. The antriders were ten yards shy of the barn.

The wagon lurched into motion as Muley whipped at the team. The horses were squealing, frightened as the humans that drove them. Sergeant Norris was struggling to hold his mount in check, the chestnut rising on its rear legs and kicking out of the air. He called again and again for Hadley, but the private seemed frozen, staring at the wave of insects as they drew to within twenty feet. Ten.

At the last possible moment, Private Hadley scrambled to mount his horse. The saddle, which had not been secured, swung hard to the side and threatened to fall free, but Hadley found his place and pulled himself erect. The lead elements of the antrider wave were around the horse's hooves and the animal hopped and pranced. It was too far for me to see, but I can well imagine the stinging lances that were jabbing the poor gelding.

With Hadley on his mount, however precariously, Sergeant Norris at last turned his own horse and galloped hard for the road. In a moment, the private followed, one hand tangled in the mane of his horse, his head low over the animal's neck.

The wagon team was moving forward at a rate that, when combined with the less than perfect character of the road, jarred my spine like hammer blows. I did not complain. My only concern was that the hitch, which was still incomplete, might part, leaving us behind while the horses galloped to freedom.

The pace of both wagon and cavalry was enough to pull away from the insects. The antriders were extraordinarily swift for their size, but I could see now that their pace was more a match for a walking man, than for a running horse. In a few seconds, we had opened a gap of a dozen yards, and this was quickly doubled. It seemed to me that the antriders were actually slowing, perhaps realizing that we had made good our escape. I began to feel a sense of relief. This had been a very close thing, but we had avoided the fate of the first expedition.

Sergeant Norris rode up alongside the wagon, still driving his horse at a fast trot. "Good God," he said. He shook his head and then repeated these words several times more. "What are those things?" he said at last.

"Insects," I said. "Antriders. Surely hymenoptera of some sort, like ants and wasps. There are army ants in the jungle that—"

"I've seen army ants. Even had them run though my tent. They're nothing like that great bloody flood back there."

I nodded. "Very different, but they are a related form, I think. These antriders travel in larger groups, and are certainly more dangerous."

The sergeant considered this for a few steps. "I'll never believe that those things are nothing but ants." He looked at me with an expression I had not seen before and had little means to decipher. "But it's sure they're not Indians. Any man can see that much."

Once again, my sense of relief was buoyed. Sergeant Norris had never been my friend, but he saw the truth of what I had been saying. His words would exonerate me from the charges made in St. George.

Before I could reply, there was a hoarse shout on my right. I looked over, thinking that Private Hadley had finally lost his hold on his mount, but the man was still on horseback. He was looking ahead of us, his eyes, and the eyes of his horse, were wide and white.

"A trap," he said, in a voice that barely carried above the sound of wagon and riders. "They've set a trap."

I looked around and saw that the road was covered in boiling blackness. The antriders were ahead of us.

In another second, we would have been among them, but Muley gave an enormous pull on the lines and the wagon slewed sharply right. The jolt as the wheels went through the ditch along the side of the pike was enough to bring notes of splintering wood from the wagon floor and groans of protests from all points along the frame. We were still alongside the sprawling barns, sheds and houses that together made up Grey's Works. After we bounced and flew over cut cane for a few yards, the wagon was forced down a narrow alley between two out buildings. The space was so tight that the wheel hubs tore gashes in the boards on both sides and I had to lean toward the center of the wagon to keep from brushing against the passing walls.

We emerged from the end of the gap. "Which way?" said Muley.

"I don't—"

"Which way!"

"Left. Turn left."

He did so. One side of the hitch came completely loose, and the wagon teetered for a moment on two wheels, but it completed the turn. The horses were still running side by side, though one of them was now carrying most of the burden of the wagon. There was another cluster of buildings ahead. Barns and storage bins, a cleared circle where mules had paced around a molasses press. The gap between the buildings ahead was small, and I began to suggest that we go around rather than attempt to pass between, and then the need for any such suggestion was gone.

There was a sharp crack, a lurch, and the wagon was torn apart. It might have been a broken axle, or only a fractured wheel. In any case, the vehicle halted so suddenly that I was thrown clean through the air like a stone launched from a sling. At one point in my flight, I put a hand down and found myself touching the back of a horse. There was even a fleeting thought that I might land on the animal, bareback, and continue my escape. Instead, the horse passed below me, I completed my brief trajectory, and fell breathless to the ground.

Standing up was a slow, painful effort. The air that had been pounded from my lungs was in no apparent hurry to return, and I stood there, working my mouth uselessly like a fish hurled to the bank. I saw Muley on the ground a dozen feet away. One of the wagon horses was there, and from the blood that flowed freely down its flank, it was going no further. Some portion of the shattered wagon had speared the poor beast. The other horse was missing, as were Sergeant Norris and Private Hadley.

I had the sense of some terrible circular moment, left again with a single companion, all the other men of our expedition scattered or dead. Antriders pouring through the distant buildings like a spill of night along the ground.

Finally, a breath squeezed down my aching throat. I coughed, and broke my momentary trance. I crossed to Muley and grabbed at his shoulders. "Get up!" I shouted, the words tearing at my throat. "They're still coming!"

Under my urging, the wagon driver was on his feet in a few seconds. He cast one anguished look at the bleeding horse, but followed as I started across the field. I made the nearest pace I could manage to a run, though in the muddy field and with my own condition, that was not very close. At every step, the soil, which had a high content of red clay, clung to my boots. Each time my heel struck ground, it seemed to leave burdened by another pound of soil. I ran on, making no conversation but the grunts and hisses of my exertion.

There were four structures directly ahead of me. One was the small box of the molasses press, with a long arm and wood collar at one end to accommodate a mule or oxen. There was a good mound of cut sweet sorghum piled beside the press, but I could see no way that this instrument could lend us shelter. Further back, there were two small barns adjacent to the round tank in which the thickened molasses was stored. And past that were was only mile on mile of field and wood stretching back to the ferry at Harbridge.

In my first encounter, I had managed to stay ahead of the antriders with no more cleverness than my own two feet. But on that occasion there had been a stream within half a mile—a clear goal in my effort to elude the insects. There were several streams along the road west of Grey's Works, but none of them were a third as big as Caney Creek and the first of them was some miles distant. I feared that even if we reached it, it would prove scant obstacle to the antriders. And I did not believe we could reach it.

The only chance seemed to lie with the two barns. All the inhabitants of Grey's Works had been killed, but they had not known what was coming. It was possible, though unlikely, that we could find some place in the barns that could be hardened against the antriders. We might ride out the attack as those who enter a cellar against a storm.

The closer we drew to the barns, the less I believed this plan. The structures were roughly built, as with most such buildings, with poorly thatched roofs and gaps between the boards wide enough to accommodate my forearm. Unsure that either building would prolong our lives for even a second, I decided that the barn on the left was slightly more substantial and turned my lumbering steps that way.

Muley came in just behind me, his face flushed and running with sweat. The two of us stood there panting for what might have been half a minute while the antriders closed the distance across the field.

"You have any idea what we ought to do now?" asked the American.

I shook my head. "Not really, no."

Together, we pushed closed the doors and began kicking earth around the base of the boards. The barn was still porous enough to allow more wind to pass through than what went around, but it was a start.

Satisfied that the doors were as secure as they were going to get, I turned my attention to the barn's contents. There was a rick of split wood against one wall and a good cord of logs remaining to be split against another. In the center of the structure was a great mound of white ash that marked the place of a large fire. I looked up and saw that the center of the roof was open. Chains dangled down from the beams on either side of the opening. This would be the boiling room, where the thin syrup of the sorghum was reduced to the considerably thicker molasses through a slow process of heating and evaporation. There was a mound of enormous iron pots stacked in the corner that climbed nearly to the ceiling and were undoubtedly used for this purpose. The pots were certainly sturdy, but they were not large enough to hold a man and I could see no way we might use them in making ourselves secure against the antriders.

An ax with a well-used appearance was half-buried in the end of one of the logs. Muley quickly wrenched the tool free and weighed it in his hand. "This should do."

A shook my head. "I can't see how it would help against the antriders."

"I wasn't thinking of them," he said. "I was thinking that when they get in here, I could finish myself before those little bastards set to biting."

This morbid suggestion was barely out of his mouth before I heard a scrambling at the boards. The first of the antriders had arrived.

I stepped into the ash circle and stared upward. If we were to climb to the top of the pile of pots, we could likely make it through the opening, though I wasn't sure what that would gain us. My first episode with the antriders had demonstrated their ability to scale buildings quite readily and if we were forced down from the barn, we would only be back to facing a hopeless run across the fields.

"There's matches," said Muley.

"What?" I asked.

The wagon driver held out a handful of sulphur matches. "These were over by the wall," he said. "You think it would help to start a fire?"

Fire had saved me from the antriders at Caney Creek, but there was no bridge between us here. Still, it seemed as good an idea as anything. "Start up the wood," I said. "Maybe we can arrange something."

The scrambling on the outside of the building grew in volume. One of the antrider pairs slipped through a crack at the level of my shoulder and began traveling along the inner surface of the wall. In seconds, it had been joined by a dozen of its fellows. Shadows fell inside the barn as the antriders moved over the gaps on the outer walls in larger and larger numbers. I could well imagine that the outside of the building was growing dark with the covering of insects.

"Here," I called to Muley. "Stand here." I directed him to a spot in the center of the cold ash while I scattered a armload of wood around us. Muley caught the idea instantly and joined me in carrying wood into a ring. While I went for a third load, he fumbled at the matches and bent to light a fire.

A sharp sting struck at my thigh. I slapped down, feeling the bodies of insect mount and rider smashed beneath my hand. Another lance jabbed into my shoulder. At the back of my neck. At my shin.

I dropped the load of wood and swatted madly at the insects. The creatures were streaming in through an opening behind the woodpile almost as if being forced through under pressure. I tripped over a piece of wood and sat down hard in the ash pile. A white cloud rose up around me. I coughed and waved the soot away from my face. Behind me, I heard the sharp pop of a lighting match and smelled the acrid scent of sulphur and phosphorus mixing with the sharp tang of the antriders.

My eyes watered. Another antrider jabbed at my ankle. I pulled my feet toward me and, when my vision cleared, saw that we were surrounded by antriders that coated the floor in a shimmering, hissing blanket. All but for the circle of ash.

The insects stepped into the white powder again and again, and just as quickly drew back. I saw thumb-sized bodies, turned pale by the ash, staggering away. Tiny riders tipped from their mounts and were lost in the swarm.

Quickly, I stood and shuffled to the center of the circle. An antrider sprinted toward me, tore a small gully through the ash, and stopped dead an inch short of my toes.

"They don't like wood ash," said Muley.

I nodded. "I see that. But don't expect it to stop them for long."

Muley's match had managed to start a small blaze among some small slivers of dry bulletwood. He bent and pressed a larger chunk of wood against the fire. It was clear the flames were spreading quickly, but it was less clear how this could be of any aid. Even if he should manage to strengthen the flames, we had only a small amount of fuel within reach.

The antriders backed away from the limits of the ash, leaving a small barrier of bare dirt between themselves and the white circle. It was very dark in the barn now, the whole place weighted with a burden of insects. The restless, susurration of their movement grew softer.

"What are they doing?" asked Muley. "Why don't they move?"

I looked at the still bodies coating the floor. "They're waiting."

"For what?"

"Maybe they're waiting for us to make a mistake, but I expect they're planning something." Ten thousand insect eyes glittered in the dim light, and I thought of those little yellow antriders that had appeared at Caney Creek with spiders in their grip. The same trick might not work here, but that didn't mean the antriders didn't have another means of crossing this obstacle. "They're clever. Very clever."

The fire moved from one bit of wood to another. Muley pushed the quartered wood carefully, arranging a woefully thin wall between us and the antriders. Even when it was all ablaze, it was little more than a scattered campfire.

"Let me have a bit of that." I took up one of the burning logs, pulled it back, and made an underhand toss toward the woodpile. Muley moved to stop me, but the log sailed in among the heap of split wood.

"Why did you do that?" asked Muley.

"These things don't like ash, and they don't like fire," I said. "If we can drive them off, maybe they'll leave us along long enough that we can get out of here."

"Maybe you'll just burn this shed down and us with it."

I shrugged. "In that case, you'd best keep your ax handy."

My attempt to spread the fire began to take hold. Small yellow flames licked at the stacked wood and along the back wall of the shed. At the same time, the antriders made their first attempt to breech the ash.

Something large moved at the door, and for a second I thought Sergeant Norris had come to join us, but the object moving was a branch, a branch still well stocked with green leaves that marked it as having come from a kapok tree. The antriders on the floor of the barn cleared a path while a hundred others dragged the branch forward. There was no mistaking their goal. In seconds, they were forcing the branch out into the ash the way a man might balance a log across a chasm.

Muley kicked at the cluster of twigs and leaves as it came near his feet. "Get away from me," he shouted at the bugs. "You stay back now."

The antriders did not listen. Despite his kicks, and despite the fire that smoked through the branch, the insects swarmed across their makeshift turnpike by pairs then by dozens. Muley cried out and tried to brush away the creatures that were already climbing up his legs. He staggered, and would have fallen clear of the ash, had I not grabbed him by the arm and pulled him back in. Still, I saw him wince again and again at the stings the riders delivered. He crushed one that was crossing his face and flung down his hat to get at one in his hair.

We might have been overrun in that first effort, but the branch the creatures were using itself caught fire and burned up the antriders faster than they could cross. While they wriggled in the fire, I took hold of one unburned end of the branch and flung the whole thing away. The antriders hissed their disappointment.

Muley jumped up and down to crush the last of the riders under his boots. "God's blood, that was close," he said. "What do you think they'll try next?"

Another branch appeared at the door of the barn, and another beside it. The antriders were pulling a forest of green wood toward us.

"You little bastards," said Muley.

We had only moments before our defenses would be breached in a dozen points at once. I looked desperately around the room and saw that the fire I had started in the woodpile was burning fiercely. Smoke rolled up the wall and escaped through the opening made for the molasses fires. A large area on the back wall of the barn had been reduced to black charcoal that glowed cherry at the edges. The antriders had pulled back from the flames, leaving a clear lane on that side.

I pulled the ax away from Muley. "This way," I said.

"What? Into the fire?"

"Not in. Through."

I took one step, raised the ax above my head, and jumped. One of my boots found a precarious purchase at the edge of the flaming woodpile. Heat washed over me and I drew in a breath that scorched my throat and lungs. I brought the ax down on the wall as I plunged helplessly onward.

The wall broke open in a shower of ash and embers. I fell into hard sunshine on the edge of a trimmed field. All around me the coals from the burning wall smoked as they hit the damp ground. I drew in a chest full of clean air, coughed, then breathed again.

I turned, and was stunned by the blanket of antriders that covered the barn. The swarm of creatures hugged most every surface, as if the building had been painted a shiny black veined through with red. The only exception was the wall that I had broken through. The insects had abandoned that hot and smoking surface, and with it this whole side of the barn. For the moment, the antriders did not seem to be moving in my direction.

Muley emerged from the opening with smoke rising from his boots and embers burning holes in his jacket. "Where now?" he asked before he had even cleared the barn.

There seemed to be few choices. There were two dozen other buildings in the complex that made up Grey's Works. Some of them might have offered better shelter against the antriders; only all those buildings were on the wrong side of the barn. Between us and anything that might have offered safety was an acre covered in antriders.

The only object between us and the open fields was the molasses vat. It was tall, a good twenty feet in height, and with an equal width. "This way," I suggested. I hurried toward the vat, still clutching the ax in one hand.

I had some hopes that we might scale the vat, and perhaps even shelter inside. With a tank this tall, there was surely some kind of ladder to allow workers to empty their pots into the top. But if there was a ladder, it was missing now. There was only the tight wooden sides, bound in by three broad hoops of iron, and a tap at the bottom for letting out molasses. I looked up at the smooth wood and shook my head. "I'm sorry. I don't know what to do. I suppose we've got to run." Just saying it made my aching muscles give a twinge.

The antriders had finally noticed the route of our escape and were now coming toward us. The shed was burning quite well, and it made a hole in their advancing ranks, but the reprieve was strictly temporary.

"Here," said Muley. "We'll run, but not just yet." He took back his ax and pulled it back for a swing. In two quick blows, he parted the bottom ring around the cask. The metal snapped away with a sound like a ringing bell. Muley extended the ax above his head and swung again. The second ring was a good eight feet above the ground, and Muley could barely reach it. He struck it three times. Four. The ring would not part.

The antriders were ten seconds away.

"Muley..."

He swung again. The upper ring broke in pieces, one of which went through my right sleeve and brought a warm flow of blood down my arm.

Muley dropped the ax. "Now," he said. "Run. Run like hell."

We turned ourselves to the east and began to sprint. We had taken no more than three steps before a deep, bass groaning sounded from behind us. There was a snap as sharp as a rifle shot, then a long series of booms. I looked over my shoulder just in time to see the sides of the tank tear open like damp paper, releasing ten thousand gallons of golden molasses.

The liquid spread in all directions, carrying bits of the shattered tank, clods of earth, and clusters of antriders. The wave was still knee high when it caught up to us and the force of the molasses was strong enough that I was sent sprawling. For twenty feet or more I was bounced along the ground, caught up in the sticky, thick flood.

I finally managed to arrest my movement, raised my face free of the liquid, and dragged down a much-needed breath along with a mouthful of sweet syrup and gritty dirt. I was forced to wipe the mess away from my eyes before I could force them open, and even then the syrup dripped down to obscure my vision.

The molasses had cleared a circle in the field at least two hundred feet in diameter. The burning shed had been collapsed by the flood and lay in a steaming heap. Drifts of mired antriders had been left in rings, like flotsam along the banks of a falling stream.

"You alive?" said Muley. He looked ridiculous. Head to toe he was coated like a goose basted in the oven. Dirt and grass and dead antriders were stuck to him everywhere. The whole horrid mess dripped from his chin, slid along his shoulders, and flowed in dirty streams down his legs. I could only assume that I looked no better.

"I'm alive," I said. "Though I can't say I'm well."

"Alive is something," said Muley. "If you want to keep that much, you better get on your feet."

I looked back again. A million antriders might have been halted in the flood, but the supply was all but infinite. And they were still coming.

# I2

*The Western Road*
*17 August 1832*

After an hour in the sun, we smelled remarkably like a pair of baked yams.

The molasses had dried to a sugary coat at my knees and elbows. It cracked at each step or motion, but not before providing enough resistance that every effort was doubled. My clothing had collected such a coating of mud and twigs that I might have been a man of daub and wattle, a scarecrow shambling across the fields.

There were infrequent puddles left by the previous night's rain in depressions along the field. These we used to wash some of the drying molasses from our faces. Which was a good thing as we soon gained the attention of another insect that seemed nearly as numerous as the antriders: biting flies.

These flies, or more properly midges of the Ceratopogonidae, are familiar to anyone from any quarter in Selvanos. They are tiny, sometimes no more than a mote in the air, yet capable of such a potent bite that the suspicion exists that, should one be placed under a magnifying lens, it would be revealed as little more than a pair of fangs supported by wings.

Though these mites make their meal on blood, something in our sweet coating was attractive to them. They gathered about us in great clouds as we struggled to the end of the field and bit repeatedly at those parts of our anatomy still well covered in molasses. They left our somewhat cleaner faces mostly alone, which was the only blessing. After no more than a few minutes of their attention, I felt sure that I was fairly drained of blood. Swatting at these tiny insects was a hopeless action. The only measure of revenge we could extract was in observing how many of them became caught in the molasses and ended as part of our bizarre coats.

The cane fields gave out a half mile southeast of Grey's Works and our surroundings changed over to native grasses and occasional shrubs. Another few miles, and the vegetation changed again. Across a stream too small to be counted as a trickle, we found ourselves facing a screen of tall grasses. A family of brocket deer that had been nibbling along the edge was sent into flight at our approach. They darted into grass and bounded away, their course visible by the shaking grass heads. I could not blame them for running. Considering our appearance, I would not have been surprised to see jaguars fleeing in terror.

I paused at the edge of the high grass and eyed it warily. "Wait," I said, putting out a hand.

"What is it?" asked Muley. "You see something?"

"Nothing," I said with a shake of my head. "And the deer seemed to make it through. Only..."

"Only what?"

"The antriders got around us once and set a trap. What if they're trying the same thing again?"

Muley scowled at the grass then twisted around and looked back over his shoulder. "They're still back there."

"Yes, but they're not moving as fast as they were. That's what worries me."

The antriders had chased us away from the works at a speed that kept us running for the first few minutes, but by the time we left the cane the antriders had reduced their pace. It was a blessing, in that both Muley and I were near to exhaustion, but I didn't know what it meant. Perhaps the antriders were distracted by other prey, perhaps we had moved beyond the range of their senses and they were forced to cast for our trail. Perhaps they were simply not so indefatigable as they had, at first, appeared. Whatever the cause, the insects had dropped to the velocity of a slow walk, and were now several hundred yards in our rear. If we could keep our feet, we might yet keep alive—though that was by no means guaranteed.

Muley kicked at the edge of the grass. "If there's bugs in there, we're dead anyway. Might as well go on."

It was a good point. Together, we waded into the grass.

Because the antriders were pressing us ever onward, we had been unable to make a return to the road. Instead we had held to a course that was close to due east. The gap between us and the best path back to Harbridge had opened from a few hundred feet to a span of at least half a mile. Now that we were in the high grass, we began to angle our course to the south, hoping to intercept the pike. We made little attempt at conversation while we walked. Many times I thought of the long silent float down the river in company of the settler, Richardson. I wondered if Muley would also seek passage as soon as we reached St. George and thought it likely. After all, his wagon and team were lost, he had realized none of his dreams of gold, and there was no good reason to stay in Selvanos.

I was quite lost in thought when I noticed a rising sound, like a wind blowing over the grass. The idea of a breeze was welcome, as it was by then close to noon and the heat and humidity in the field was stifling. But the welcome breeze never arrived. When the sound grew louder still, I looked around. At first, I saw nothing. Then I noticed a phenomenon. No more than twenty feet away, the grass heads were trembling, shaking as if they were being cut by an army of tiny lumberjacks.

"Run!" I shouted. "They're on us."

Muley took off without so much as a glance to his rear. Grass heads slapped against my face as we sprinted blind and tall stalks cut at my arms. Even over the broken grass smell and the sickening sweet odor that rose from my molasses covered frame, I could smell the sharp lemon-spice of the antriders.

Each time I looked back, I could see the movement of the antriders. The motion of their passage spread though the grass like the ripples from a stone in water. The distance between ourselves and the antriders was never more than thirty feet and sometimes less than ten. I felt sure that were either of us to fall for so long as a second, we would be lost. That run through the grass had no fires, no collapsing tanks, no streams or structures to hide behind. It was simply the endless effort of two exhausted men, stumbling on and on, pursued by an unseen army that spread out over a vast front. I think it was a closer, more desperate thing than either the events at Caney Creek or at Grey's Works.

After an impossible time, we stumbled from the grass, side by side, onto the main pike. The change of scenery was so abrupt that I almost stopped, but Muley grabbed me by the arm, urging me on. We pounded east along the rutted clay, with the grass on our right and the jungle on the left. For some time, the antriders did not appear on the road, but paralleled our course through the grass. Then I could no longer see the grass moving. It was tempting to slow, but we did not dare. The antriders might have fallen back, but they might just as well be plotting to catch us unawares. By this point, I was ready to attribute a great tactical genius to these animals the size of my thumb.

We were close to the field of mingled lavender and wildflowers when I heard the sound of horses approaching from the east. Both Muley and I raised our voices and waved our hands—though there was no one yet to see or hear us. A moment later, five riders came into view.

They were not, as I had expected, Lieutenant Bland and the remnants of his command. Instead, the figure on the first horse was that of Miss Marlowe. With her were two hands from her family's plantation, both of them Mestizo. The other two riders turned out to be, to my considerable surprise and pleasure, Sergeant Norris and Private Hadley.

Miss Marlowe brought her mount to an abrupt halt in front of us and looked at us with an expression that could not seem to settle between horror and amusement. "What in the world happened to you?"

I gestured at the coat debris that clung to my body. "It's molasses."

"I can see that," Miss Marlowe replied. "And half the bugs north of the Sarstoon stuck to it."

Sergeant Norris came up at her side. "We thought you were dead." He surveyed us a moment longer. "Looks like maybe you are."

"We thought the same of you," I said.

"How did you get away?" asked Hadley. "We saw those things chase you out across the fields, and saw the wagon go down."

"We went to this shed," said Muley. "Then we had a fire, and well, it's a hell of a long story. You got anything to drink?"

Sergeant Norris handed down a canteen, and Muley drank deeply before passing the water to me.

"You're lucky those things gave up on you," said Private Hadley. "They chased after us for nearly a mile, and we were mounted."

"They chased us," I said. "In fact, they're chasing us still."

"Here?" Norris shook his head. "We must be five miles from Grey's."

"More like ten," said Miss Marlowe. "You mean to say these ants of yours chased you for—"

Before she could finish her sentence, I saw her eyes go wide. The lumber hands behind her cursed and Private Hadley's excitable horse reared to paw the sky. Already fearing what I would see, I looked back along the road and confirmed that the antriders were emerging from the field. At first they were a stream, then a torrent. Black and red they poured onto the road behind us. The dry hiss of their motion filled the air.

"Come along," said Sergeant Norris. "Let's move while we still can." He reached down a hand, and Muley quickly took it. In a second, the American was mounted on the horse behind the sergeant and the two of them were off.

I moved toward Private Hadley, expecting to share his mount, but Miss Marlowe moved between us and put down her hand first. "Hurry," she said.

"But..."

"Get on now, or we're both dead."

I climbed on. She turned the horse, giving me one last look at the antriders. Then we were moving east, following behind the other horses.

"You better hold tight," said Miss Marlowe. "If you don't want to fall."

I moved my hands toward her waist, but hesitated. Not only was there a problem of propriety, but I was also filthy, sticky, and odorous. "Maybe we could—"

"Hold on!" she said. "If you fall, I'm not coming back for you."

With my hands around her waist and my face close to the back of her neck, we pounded down the road. "Where are we?" I asked, shouting to be heard over the noise of the horses.

She tilted her head back to reply, putting her curls against my face. "Five miles short of Harbridge. I hope to all the saints that the ferry is waiting when we get there."

I nodded in agreement. "Do you have any other workers on this side of the river?"

Her shoulders slumped and after a moment she nodded. "There's a crew cutting logwood. They're two miles this side of the landing. If we can get them in motion, we should all be well enough."

We came to the track leading to the Marlowe crew only a few minutes later. By this point, the antriders had been outdistanced and were no longer in view. Still, the time it took to warn the men and get them in motion toward the ferry was nerve-wracking. There were not enough mounts for everyone, and several men were forced to run the remaining miles on foot. I suggested to Miss Marlowe that I climb down to join them, but she would not hear of it. So I continued sharing her horse, acutely aware of the looks I got from her men, as well as from Sergeant Norris.

The ferry was in midstream when we arrived, bound for the north bank to cart a single rider up from the far south. Sergeant Norris fired his pistol into the air to gain their attention. By shout and by hand signal, the ferrymen were convinced to return for us all. When they arrived, eight horses and twice that number of men attempted to crowd onto the boat in one load. The ferry settled low in the water, and the owner of this small vessel was loath to let us proceed. Pellion, the man who styled himself captain of this collection of boards and logs, objected most strenuously, speaking of the risk to both boat and passengers, and finally issued a flat refusal to push the boat away from the bank until at least two of the horses and five men agreed to wait another turn. At this point, Sergeant Norris drew his pistol again, this time to point it at the ferryman.

"We're not waiting," said the sergeant. "Not one of us. You'll make for the north bank, or by God you'll stay here and I'll find someone else who can man a pole."

This statement motivated the captain. The ferrymen leaned to their poles. A serious exertion was required, but we were soon in motion. It was clear that the overloaded boat posed a challenge to the ferrymen, but they made no further objection. The craft moved downstream as before, straining so hard against the rope that I thought the system of wheels might let go. When possible, every man not at a pole crowded in the center of the boat as best we could, being careful not to tip the vessel to any quarter. Though our journey was somewhat precarious, with every yard of brown water that was put between the ferry and the land, I felt myself relax a bit more.

When we were just shy of the river's midpoint, a black smudge appeared on the southern road. The hands shouted and pointed it out. The ferrymen stopped and let the boat sag against the cable as they strained to see.

The dark stain spread along the pike until the landing was covered over in black and crimson. The blackness covered the landing and spread both ways along the water's edge. The south bank of the Sarstoon River, and the whole southern half of Selvanos, was now given over to the antriders.

# I3

*Harbridge*
*17 August 1832*

There were few amenities among the small houses of Harbridge, but there was a flowing stream, a scrub brush, and a good supply of soap. I gathered the latter two items, and set out to find the first, intent on cleaning myself of the results of my second escape from the antriders. I was decorated crown to boot in an unpleasant encrustation composed of equal parts molasses, plant matter, snared insects, and horsehair. After a day in the sun, the mixture smelled much like a pie left far too long in the oven.

To scrub myself, I settled on a site near where the fast-running Glaize Creek emptied into the Sarstoon River. The water dropped into a pool that was deep enough to reach halfway to my knees and the bottom was a firm ledge of limestone. I first checked to be sure that no one was in view—and, more importantly, that I was in view of no one else—then sat down on a rock and began to strip off my ruined clothing.

It felt impossible that only that morning I had been at Grey's Works. After passing a night without sleep and the exhaustion of the long chase, that silent plantation house seemed more a dream than a memory. Surely if I were to go across to the north bank and go down the road, I would find the Grey family ready to show off their children and their servants, and everything I remembered of the day would actually be a singularly unpleasant nightmare. I shook away this illusion and returned my attention to my molasses covered buttons.

As I undressed, I noted a uniform buckle and the torn sleeve of a red jacket near the pool. Evidently, I was not the first to bath here on this day. Lieutenant Bland, the leader of our failed expedition, and his surviving men had reached Harbridge some hours before. It was their arrival that prompted Miss Marlowe to search for any other survivors and fortunately locate me. One of Bland's soldiers must have chosen this same pool before me. If so, he was gone now. The lieutenant had urged his men back toward St. George with the same haste he had shown on the outbound leg of our journey.

My molasses-soaked shirt came off without much trouble, though the process did remove a good amount of the hair from my chest and arms. I likewise removed my socks and spats without much incident. It was only while removing my pants that I learned the molasses had trapped more than midges and weeds. Adhering to the cuff of my left leg was an antrider pair, both rider and mount, still locked together in death. Evidently, the insects had been in the process of climbing my leg when they became candied in the sugary flood.

I loosed the laces and slid the pants down my legs carefully, so as not to dislodge the antrider. Then I dipped the pant leg momentarily in the water to thin the molasses. Holding the insects up to the light gave me a better chance to see the details of the animals than ever before. My initial impressions had not been too far from the mark. The mount looked not unlike a harvester ant, though of considerably larger size than an average member of Pogonomyrmex, which gave me some notion of the creature's affinities. I could see a distinct alteration of the thorax, with a quantity of ridges along the dorsal surface and a lengthening along the central axis to provide a better saddle, but no one would mistake this insect for other than a large ant.

The rider was another thing altogether. I could still see that it was an ant, but it was an ant far transformed from the traditional design, and I doubted anyone not well-versed in the pliable forms of insects would have named it so. The angle between the abdomen and the thorax was severe, even more so than that seen in the ant's close relatives among the hymenoptera, the wasps. It was this angle, approaching eighty degrees, which allowed the rider to sit its mount, laying its abdomen parallel to the body of its mount while keeping its thorax approximately upright. Similarly, the head dipped hard toward the ventral surface. In all, the rider's body was figured in a flattened Z-shape, giving it something of a mantis-like appearance.

Then there was the matter of the limbs. Both pairs of rear limbs were reduced, with the central pair being no more than a set of jointed hooks. Looking carefully, I could see how these hooks were designed to keep the rider attached to matching grooves on the thorax of the mount. The right forelimb was similarly reduced, with several processes at the end that might have been used for gripping, almost like a minuscule hand. It was the left limb that was most transformed. It extended into the impressive lance, half again the length of the creature's body. Held up to the light, I could see that the little weapon was well shaped for penetration, with serrations along the edges and an incised groove along the side.

I measured the insect's lance against my little finger and tried to remember the first pair I had seen. Had that one kept its lance on the right? I held the insects as carefully as I could and transferred them to a rock were they would be safe while I took my bath. I wished I still had the satchel that had been with me when I left St. George. Among the medical supplies had been vials and denatured spirits that might have been used to preserve the specimens. I would have to see if substitutes might be found.

"Rum," I said to myself, taking a few steps toward the center of the pool. "A little rum will—"

"I think we might all do with a bit of rum at the moment."

I looked up to see Miss Marlowe observing me from the opposite bank. I started to reply before I realized that except for a few remaining patches of my melting molasses veneer, I was completely naked. My clothing was out of reach, and putting it on would take time, so instead I dropped into the pool and sat down in the water. The flow from the stream evidently came from the distant mountains as the water was quite cold, but I hugged the bottom until I was submerged to my chin. I began to regret the water's clarity. "I'm not decent."

"I can see that," she said. "I'm not offended." She sat down at the water's edge as casually as she had joined Lord Haverset for tea. She had removed her wide-brimmed hat, and loosed her hair so that it surrounded her face in an aurora of dark curls. Her boots had been removed and her feet were bare. Once again I was struck by the sharp difference between the elegant young lady I had seen on visits to Company House, and this completely different creature revealed away from the capitol. She let her toes dip into the stream as she leaned down for a closer look at the two insects I had left on the rock. "These are the things that were chasing us?"

"Yes," I said. "The same creatures that attacked Applewash and the first group sent to investigate." I began to describe what I knew of the antriders, and though I was never completely comfortable with speaking to her while in such a state, I did become enthusiastic about the subject and went on at some length. It was a relief that for once I was not being doubted. After all the nonsense with Captain Valamont and his story of Indians, this time I could at least be sure that I would not be plunged into jail on my return to St. George. No one could think I was the cause of the losses to Lieutenant Bland's party. Every survivor would surely testify to the threat posed by the antriders. My word would be no longer in doubt; my reputation and my life no longer in peril. As I spoke, I felt a burden lifted from me that I had not even realized I bore. Despite the events of the day, I was very close to ecstatic.

Miss Marlowe lowered her face until her nose was only a few inches from the antriders and her green eyes focused on the insects. "They're so different from each other."

"But of the same species, I'd wager," I said. "Ants and other colonial insects often have many different castes, each with its own task. There are workers and warriors, even gardeners in some colonies."

She turned her face toward me, holding back her hair with one hand. "How many of them are there, do you think? Your antriders?"

"I don't know that I would want to claim them as mine," I said. I paused to consider her question. "A colony of army ants, the more common army ants, is said to have a million individuals. The antriders are larger, but also more numerous. Certainly tens of millions, more likely hundreds of millions."

Unexpectedly, she smiled. "A hundred million horses and riders. Think of it. Even Napoleon never mounted anything like such a force. This is a cavalry that dwarfs every other on earth, a force as large as there are citizens of the empire."

It was a staggering idea, and I was pleased to see that Miss Marlowe was giving real thought to the antriders. "There are other kinds as well," I said, "besides the knights and horses."

"There are?"

"I've seen at least one other," I said with a nod. "There's a pale yellow sort that appears to hold the role of engineers. They build bridges. They forded the stream at Caney Creek and I suspect that there are...are..." I paused. The smile had abruptly faded from Miss Marlowe's face. "What's wrong?"

She sat up straight and stared at me with a wide-eyed expression that was a close cousin to fear. "They can build bridges?"

"Yes. Somehow they can fix bits of wood and leaves together, using silk coaxed from spiders. Then they arrange rafts together in a way that allows them to bridge a stream."

"A stream," Miss Marlowe repeated. "But not a river." She looked toward the wide brown expanse of the Sarstoon at our side. "Not a river like this."

I looked at the swirling waters. The Sarstoon was an enormous river. The south bank so far away at Harbridge that it could barely be seen, with islands, eddies, and a thousand floating logs in between. It seemed ridiculous to think that something so small as an antrider could span this obstacle. But as I thought, I remembered the deliberate actions of the antriders in crossing Caney Creek. They had demonstrated an astounding flexibility again when at Grey's Works I had hidden from them within a circle of smoldering ash. These creatures were adaptable and industrious. And their numbers were huge.

"Yes," I said at last. "I think they can cross. I expect they will cross."

Miss Marlowe stood up abruptly. "Is there anything we can do?"

"I'm not sure," I said. "We could certainly watch them. The antriders might not try and bridge the river here. They might move downstream, or upstream. If we know where they are crossing, we might be able to act against them."

"I'll see that the ferry goes out." She stepped back from the stream, water dripping from the soaked cuffs of her trousers and running along her bare feet. "Then we'll need to go to my family's works. If those things are coming, I need to get everyone away."

"If you could get word to your father," I said. "Surely he could arrange the removal."

"My father has been dead for two months," said Miss Marlowe. "Fairhill is mine, and my responsibility alone."

Astonished, I stood up to follow her, quickly realized that I was in no condition to do so, and sat back down with a splash. "Tell the ferry to wait for me," I called to her retreating back.

It was a shock to think that a woman, and one as young as Miss Marlowe, might pass into control of the largest works in Selvanos. It was within the company laws to have a woman as a property owner, but it was rarely done. Of course, women who wore trousers and rode out with their workers were also a scarce commodity.

As quickly as I could, I washed the worst of the dried molasses from my hair and scraped both bugs and weeds from my skin. Warm water would have done a better job at dissolving the rind of sugar, and I could not remove all of the grime that coated me, but the stream was far better than nothing. In a few minutes, I was returned to a state slightly more proximate to humanity and felt myself ready to dress. The clothes I had been lent were a good fit, though I was obliged to wear the same shoes, still dirty and now damp from the stream. Energized by my bath, I made my way back to the houses of Harbridge.

A crowd had been gathered near the dock. Miss Marlowe was in loud and urgent discussion with Sergeant Norris and the ferry captain, while others looked on. There seemed to be great disagreement concerning the urgency of the threat on the north bank, with Miss Marlowe voicing alarm, and several others supporting her position. However the ferry owner, Pellion, was arguing that the water offered safety.

"Will you not just take out the ferry?" I asked. "We can see what they are doing. If there's no threat, that's well and good. If there's danger, it's better to know."

"That's what I suggested," said Miss Marlowe, "but he won't budge."

The ferryman waved his hands. "Now, now, Missy Genevieve, you know I want to help. My boat is already cracked from all the weight and all that thumping we took on that last passage, bringing you all over so quick like. We take another trip without some repairs first, we'll be swimming back."

"We'll load it lightly," said Miss Marlowe. "Only a few men. No horses."

"Maybe." Pellion rubbed at his sunburned chin. "You'll excuse me, Missy, but I'd need to be paid special, so as to fix my boat."

The demand was ridiculous on its face, the boat being nothing but poorly trimmed logs and split lumber, which was the one thing Selvanos had in plenty. But the ferryman was in a good bargaining position and was clearly ready to exploit this opportunity. Having no coin to offer, I left Pellion and Miss Marlowe to haggle over the price and went down to the river to see if I could observe any change in the antriders.

Standing near the water, I spotted Muley. Like me, the American had changed his clothing and taken some effort to clean himself of the sticky coating. However, I could still smell the molasses on him as I approached and wondered how long it would be before either of us stopped smelling like a pan of oat cakes. Muley was standing at the edge of the water, shading his eyes as he squinted at the far bank.

"What do you see?" I asked. "Are the antriders still there?" I could make out little myself, though I imagined that the distant bank was darker than normal.

The wagon driver nodded. "Best I can tell, though they don't look so populous as at first. Could be they're wandering off. Any case, I was more interested in the fire."

"What fire?"

"Over there." He raised a finger and pointed across the river. "See that smoke on the other side of the trees?"

Now that he had pointed it out, the rising plume of grey was obvious. It did not appear to be a great fire, something more akin to what was produced when a farmer burned off the fields for fall. The wonder was that there was any fire at all. "There was no fire when we left."

"No," said Muley. "We'd have seen it for sure. But it was burning when I came back down from my scrub, burning a bit fiercer then, to judge by the smoke. Now it's about died out."

The smoke was on the decline. In a few minutes, the column had faded to an off white smudge against the sky, quickly tattered to invisibility by the winds. "Who could have set that, I wonder?"

"Whoever it was, I hope they weren't counting on that fire to stop your bugs, because it's out now." Muley picked up a stone from the bank and skipped it toward the water.

I continued to look across the river for some time, hoping to spot some other activity. There were other settlements across there, several large ones along the north road that ran down toward the mountains. Someone coming up that way might have been besieged by the antriders and set a fire in defense—as I had done now on two occasions. But the location of this fire seemed more westerly, along the same road we had followed in our retreat from Grey's Works, and I did not want to contemplate the fate of anyone trapped along that route.

Miss Marlowe came down to the river's edge, the negotiations over the ferry apparently ended. "We'll be leaving shortly," she said. "As soon as he can gather his crew."

"You're coming?" I said. "Wouldn't you be better if you stayed here on shore?"

The look she gave me left no doubt about her opinion on this suggestion. "I paid for the trip, Mr. Brown. I get to see the show."

"I only meant that you could be better employed in warning the people away from your family works," I said. "And to persuade the other landowners in the area."

She was somewhat mollified by this statement, but her position on going along on the ferry was unchanged. Within the hour, I had clambered back onto the flat deck in the company of Miss Marlowe, Pellion, and a tall, lanky ferryman whose name I did not know. The two military men who had been with us on the retreat along the south bank, Sergeant Norris and Private Hadley, also decided to join in. However, Muley, along with every man in Harbridge, elected to remain on the south bank.

Lightly loaded, the ferry rode high in the water and moved away from the bank easily even though only Pellion and his one crewman were manning the poles. The rope slid between the rims of the wheels as we moved out into the water and I heard the now familiar groan as the slack was removed from the line and the raft slipped slightly downstream. With so few people on board, we felt more confident in lining the edge of the rails without fear of upsetting the craft. We stood in silence through the first leg of the voyage, staring across the shrinking distance to the north bank. As Muley had said, the dark stain representing of the antriders was still obvious along the landing, but they did appear somewhat sparser than before. They might have been moving on east along the north bank, or even returning the way they came. However, as we closed the distance, the sun dropped down among the western hills, making it more difficult to make out activities on shore. To further complicate our efforts, mist began to rise off the water.

"We'll have to be stepping on those things before we know they're there," said Sergeant Norris.

Fortunately, Pellion had made some preparations for the coming darkness. He mounted lanterns at each corner of the ferry and filled them with oil. "As long as you're content to wade the last twenty feet, you can step on all the bugs you want," he told Sergeant Norris, "but I'm not taking my boat to that shore. You just be sure you wipe your boots before you step back on my ferry."

The ferry moved easily toward the first island. There were fewer logs drifting in the water now, fewer even than there had been when we crossed before, and I wondered if it signaled the extinction of all the works upstream from Harbridge. Had the antriders also swept through the homes and settlements along the Qualm? Had they captured every far-ranging crew? The pitiful few logs in the water argued that the insects had performed a remarkable job of scouring the interior free of humans.

Just beyond the first island, at a place where rushes showed the river to be no more than knee deep, Pellion called a halt. His crewman held us in position with a tight grip on the rope while the ferryman visited each corner of the raft in turn, lighting the oil lanterns. Rather than being much improved by these lights, I found my own view of the surroundings rather diminished as it limited my vision to a small circle around our craft, but Pellion seemed pleased enough and ordered his man to proceed.

We passed a small island to our right that was another anchor point for the rope system, then another on the left. On the second of these, bright eyes reflected the lantern light, marking a group of spider monkeys that had made their way to the island. Past this point, there was a long stretch of open water, where the only excitement was a log that turned out to be a crocodile floating downstream.

The density of logs increased as we neared the north bank and I was happy to improve my gloomy estimates of conditions upstream. But the increased traffic of lumber forced the ferry to slow. The logs were difficult to see in the thickening mist and the water in this part of the course moved at a good pace. We proceeded with caution, the ferry moving backwards almost as many times as it went forward to avoid collisions. Finally the fog-shrouded south bank came in sight.

"Where are they?" said Sergeant Norris.

I squinted against the rolling mist and shook my head. "I don't...wait, there they are!"

All of the others, Pellion included, gathered near me. Even lightly loaded as it was, the boat was unbalanced enough by our concentration that water washed around my feet. No one seemed to notice as they strained to see what was happening on shore.

The antriders were still there. They had moved back from the very edge of the water and now waited some yards short of the stream. Occasionally some individual would dart down to the river's edge on a mysterious errand, then hurry back to rejoin its companions. But the bulk of the colony stood farther back. They were visible through the fog only as a thousand pinpricks of light where the lanterns caught their unblinking eyes and glossy carapaces.

"What do you think they're doing?" asked Private Hadley. "Are they sleeping?"

"I'm not sure," I admitted. "Army ants huddle together to sleep at night, but from what we've been told these insects attacked Applewash in the darkness, so I wouldn't be certain that they're asleep."

The raft stayed in that position some ten minutes or more, a brief stone's throw from the shore. Logs drifted toward us, but these were deflected for the most part by a push from Pellion's pole, and those that did strike the raft did so quite slowly. Finally, it was Miss Marlowe that called an end to our viewing. "Gentlemen," she said. "I think we've learned all we can here. Let's go back and get some rest. At daylight, if the creatures are still to be seen, we can—"

Her statement was interrupted by a splash from somewhere just upstream. Another followed on its heels.

"What was that?" asked Sergeant Norris.

"I could have been an animal trying to escape the antriders," I said. Briefly, I recounted the experience of the first expedition in the woods short of Caney Creek and how we had been overrun by every sort of beast fleeing before the insect flood.

"There's something up there," said Miss Marlowe.

All eyes turned to the upstream side of the boat. The something in the water was a dark oval, nearly the size of a man. I thought at first that it was some animal, paddling toward us, but as it swam into the lights, its true nature was revealed. "It's them," I said. "It's the antriders."

It was a raft, similar in structure to the ones the creatures had built at Caney Creek, though this one seemed more boat than bridge. It was perhaps a yard in width, and nearly twice that in length, and loaded from front to back with the glistening bodies of antriders. No sooner had this first craft entered the circle of light around the ferry, than a second one came into view.

"Go!" shouted Sergeant Norris. "God's sakes man, get us away from here."

Pellion barked a command to his assistant and the two men hurried to press their poles into the mud. From almost the first moment, it was clear that they would not be fast enough. The boat moved along well enough once started, but it was in no hurry to begin its motion. The antriders would strike our side before we could get away.

"Stand ready," I called. I braced myself at the rail, ready to fend off the insects as they attempted their boarding party.

I need not have bothered. Miss Marlowe stretched and took down the lantern from the top of one of the corner posts. When the antrider raft was no more than a two yards shy of the ferry, she tossed the lantern right into the center of them.

The lantern passed straight on through the intruder's creation, punching a hole that let in the river, but not without setting dry leaves and antriders alike on fire. Before it had moved another pace through the water, the antrider raft was disintegrating, falling apart in a flurry of sparks. The water around the collapsing structure boiled with drowning insects.

Private Hadley cheered, and the rest of us soon joined him. "Good thinking, Missy," said Pellion, but when Sergeant Norris went to grab a lantern to throw at the second raft, the ferryman stopped him. "We can dodge that one easy as sink it," Pellion said, "and save me a lantern." He bent to his pole and his prediction proved correct. The second antrider raft went past along the northern nose of the ferry, missing us by no more than a yard. The insect craft, and the thousand or more passengers it carried, soon vanished in the fog.

"Where do you think they'll fetch up?" asked Sergeant Norris.

There was no good answer to his question, and we all looked at each other uncomfortably. The antriders might be swept into an eddy, or snared against a bank, but every day a hundred of more logs completed the trip down to St. George. The antriders might be in the capital before we could even reach them with word of warning.

"Another coming!" called Pellion's assistant.

We hurried back to the upstream side of the raft and saw several more dark forms in the fog. Some of these shapes were clearly bound to strike us, and I started for another of the lanterns, but Pellion warned me off again. "Logs," he said. "They're just logs."

There was great relief, but we still had to deal with the dangers of collision. Pellion and his hand moved around and raised their poles toward the first log, so they might slow its force and keep us from being struck a damaging blow.

"Careful now," Pellion said. "Move it off southwise." His pole landed solidly on the front of the log and the ferryman grunted as he absorbed the impact. "Ease it off," he called to his helper. "Ease it off."

The second man put his pole in place and began to push. A moment later, he began to scream.

Antriders. Antriders by the hundreds were swarming up the side of the log and scurrying up the poles toward the men. Pellion hurled his pole away at once, and it splashed in the water beside us, but his helper held his pole as the riders came closer, screaming as they moved toward his fingers.

The antriders passed over the man's arms and across his shoulders. They jumped from his body down to the raft. One went right into his open mouth and his scream ending with a fit of coughing as he finally dropped the pole and stepped back from the side.

All of us were jumping and shouting, kicking at the antriders. The raft bucked and plunged, throwing up gouts of water. The sergeant bellowed as he was speared by a knight. The ferry hand fell to the deck and rolled over and over, giving strangled cries. I was run through on both legs, and had the unpleasant experience of feeling an antrider scurry up my leg, under my shirt, and emerge to jab me in the back of the neck. I slapped at it furiously, and said things that would have made me blush in other circumstances. It would have embarrassed me still had not others, Miss Marlowe included, said far worse.

No longer held back by any pole, the log that the insects had been riding collided against the side of the ferry with enough force to send me staggering. Someone was more than staggered, as I heard splashing on the downstream side of the raft. Before I could render assistance, another antrider struck at the back of my leg and I was back to my personal battle.

The ferry was shaken again by another log. "There's more of them," said Sergeant Norris.

A lantern whistled overhead and smashed against one of the logs. The night was pushed away by an explosion of light and even from twenty feet away I felt the rush of heat. The ferryman who had held onto the pole was lying near one corner of the raft. His clothes were soaked through with blood and I could not tell if he was alive or dead. Sergeant Norris was near him, dancing like a mad Scotsman as he brought his boots down on one insect after another, each one dispensed with a curse. Pellion was on his knees at the rail, trying to push away the logs that had jammed against us. I could see him shake as antriders jabbed at him, but he did not stop his work. Miss Marlowe was off to my right. Her shirt was torn open at the shoulder and blood was streaming from the corner of her mouth. I moved to help her, but she waved me away.

"Private Hadley," she said. "See to him."

I spun around, but there was no sign of Hadley on the raft. Then I saw a spot of red in the water and knew that it was the private that had fallen. I rushed to the side and reached out for him. "Here," I said. "To me. Swim to me."

Hadley barely seemed capable of swimming at all. He foundered in the water, flailing at it with his arms and sending splashes in all directions. He drifted toward me as much by luck as by purpose, but after a moment I was able to snag the stiff collar of his coat and haul him back aboard. He collapsed to the planks and began to retch what appeared to be a good portion of the river back into its proper place.

During my struggle to save Private Hadley, the others had seen to the remaining antriders. The flaming log had been pushed away, and Captain Pellion was beside his fallen helper, talking to the man and holding him by the shoulder. I took this as a good sign that the man still lived.

"We have to get away," said Miss Marlowe. "There could be more of those things bearing on us right now."

The ferryman got to his feet. I could see that he had taken several stings to the face, and blood was fairly pouring from an open gash on his forehead. "We have no poles," he said. "We'll have to pull ourselves back along the rope."

This task turned out to be much harder than it appeared. The rope was thick, nearly the diameter of my wrist, and made of coarse cords that abraded the hand like boar's bristle. Private Hadley came to join us when he had recovered himself well enough to stand, and Miss Marlowe also tried for a time to pull the rope, though I winced to see her hands bloodied by the effort. Where pushing the raft along with poles was a fairly slow process, it seemed like a gallop when compared what we managed on the rope. Still, we were moving. Several more logs went past, some on either side of the ferry, but we had only two remaining lanterns and I could not say whether or not the antriders had made these logs into their vessels.

We passed the first of the islands, getting a momentary rest as Captain Pellion worked the wheels over the junction in the ropes, then it was back to grunting and bleeding as we moved on to the south. Thirty feet further on, the effort suddenly grew much greater. It was a teeth-gritting effort to force the ferry on for another five feet, then we could move no further.

"The wheels must have jammed," said Pellion. He lifted one of the remaining lanterns and went to examine the problem. No sooner had he reached the south end of the ferry, than he shouted and drew back. Again there was an explosion of light and heat from a shattered lamp, only this one was on the deck of the ferry itself. In this light, I could see antriders streaming along the rope. They clung to it top and bottom. It was their bodies, ground between rope and wheels that had halted our progress.

"Put out the fire," said Pellion. "Put out the fire or we're all dead." He dropped to his knees and began splashing water onto the flames that already covered half the boards.

"Why did you start the fire?" shouted Sergeant Norris.

Pellion threw another splash into the flames. "I didn't mean to. One of those bastards bit me and I dropped the lamp. Now put it out before we're roasted."

"Cut the rope," I said. ""They're getting aboard."

"We can't," said Pellion. "If we cut the rope, the raft will drift. We'll have no way to get back." He splashed an armload of water across the deck, quenching a good portion of the flames.

Above him, antriders were running along the rope, over the frozen wheel, and jumping past the flames. The rope on the other side of the wheel looked twice as thick, completely encrusted with antriders and more streaming along every second. "Cut the rope," I said again, "or it won't matter where we're bound."

Pellion appeared more striken by this idea than by the stabs from the antriders. "No," he said. "You can't."

Sergeant Norris wore a sword at his waist. I stepped forward and pulled the weapon clear of its scabbard, an action that brought Norris roaring to his feet. The soldier spun toward me, clearly intend on retrieving his sword. At the same time, I brought the blade down on the rope. The cord was thick and tough, but it was under considerable tension and the sword was exceedingly sharp. At the first touch, the rope parted.

The ferry surged forward and spun with the sudden loss of tension on the line. I had enough presence of mind remaining to drop the sergeant's sword and grab the fallen end of the rope as it went past. The pull of the raft was enough to drag me against the rail, and threatened in a moment to take me over. Hands closed around my waist.

"I have you," said Miss Marlowe. "Hold on."

"You fool!" Pellion was on his feet, ignoring both what remained of the fire and the antriders that darted around his feet. "It took me two months to set that cable." He started toward me, but to my surprise, Sergeant Norris blocked his path.

"Those bug's made your rope into a turnpike," he said. "They'd have been past us and on to Harbridge if Brown had not stopped them."

The end of the raft that had pointed north was soon turned to point downstream. My arms ached with the effort of holding on. I swear I could feel my shoulders being dragged from their place and my hands left bloody prints on the big rope. Sergeant Norris and Captain Pellion managed to extinguish the fire as the ferry fell downstream. "Let go," said Miss Marlowe. "We're at the end of the rope."

I could feel the increasing strain my arms and saw the rope growing taut again. We had to be directly downstream from the first island. Miss

Marlowe was right. Holding on now would bring us no closer to shore and in any case there was no chance that I could hold on against all the forces of the river on the ferry. I let go the rope, Miss Marlowe released my waist, and we were drifting free.

Any fears I held about repeating the float to St. George were short-lived as we became wedged on a mud bank within minutes. "We'll have to walk from here," said Pellion. "The good news is, we can." He demonstrated by jumping overboard and showing that the water was only hip deep, though a good half of that was clinging mud. Sergeant Norris and Private Hadley worked to carry the fallen ferryman. The rest of us had nothing to carry but ourselves and even that was a challenge.

Before we left, Pellion took the last remaining lantern and threw if hard against the deck, setting fire again to the vessel he had worked so hard to extinguish.

We made it ashore at a point about a mile east of Harbridge and began the walk back to the settlement. Muley, and a group of Harbridge stalwarts, met us before we reached halfway.

The American shook his head when he saw me. "Whoever lent you those clothes," he said, "ain't going to be much impressed by the care you've shown them."

# 14

*The Road to St. George*
*18 August 1832*

I have read that when the crusaders crossed Europe in their quest to reach the Holy Lands, they took with them servants, wives, children, carts, wagons, horses, cows, goats, and chickens. I had often wondered how such a mixed parade might fare over a long march. The answer, it seems, is not very well.

The people of Harbridge began to gather their things soon after the disastrous end of the ferry. A few held out and refused to budge, but seeing the ferry lost, and hearing our stories, set most of the town to running. By sunup, there was a steady stream of people and wagons moving eastward along the road. I would have liked to go with Miss Marlowe to see to the people at Fairhill, but there were enough places to visit in the stretch between Harbridge and St. George that we were all called on to mount and ride in different directions.

The landowners I visited were not inclined to vacate their claims on the basis of what I had to tell them, and at one location I was seen off at the point of a musket, but as the locals became aware of the others passing down the road, most of them opted to leave. Few would admit to fearing these unseen insects, or that such a thing could even exist, but a holiday in St. George had abruptly become a popular thought along a wide section of eastern Selvanos.

By mid-morning, the road was packed so tightly that progress was all but stopped. Wagons overloaded with trunks, chests, tables, and even birdcages became mired in low points of the road. Horses more suited to pulling a plow than a cart grew restive among the crowds. Cattle balked.

Children cried. And nature responded with that one commodity which was even more plentiful in Selvanos than trees—rain.

Rain started as a drizzle and before long became a downpour. As winds whipped sheets of rain over the long, slow moving column, people began to leave the road. Some took what shelter they could find among the trees on the right of the road. Others took up temporary residence in abandoned houses, whose original occupants could be found somewhere farther along in this strange procession. It was troublesome enough to worry about these few that had fallen aside, but they were no bother compared to those who took up camp in the road itself.

I began the day on horseback, but by the time noon approached, I was afoot, trying to convince one of the stragglers to resume their place in the march. The landowner in this case was a man with thick shoulders and a thicket of dark hair that circled round a bald head and looped down across his upper lip in an extravagant mustache. He looked hearty enough, but after a few hours on the road he appeared already exhausted and was unwilling that he, or his family, should take another step toward St. George.

"Sir," I said. "This is not a good place. You should come along with the rest."

He shook his head, water pouring down the long slope of his freckled forehead. "No, we're going back." He pulled his wife against his side with one arm and looked at me defiantly.

"But sir," I tried again. "Everyone is moving east. You're blocking the course for everyone else."

"Then let them move around us," he said. "We're going back." He took the traces of a cart in one hand, his wife in the other, and began to drag both against the flow of traffic. Already, there was an open space of some hundred yards at his back and a crowd of at least a dozen waiting to pass.

"The antriders are coming," I said. "It's not safe."

"The devil take your bugs. I'm going home."

Thudding hoof beats sounded along the road. Sergeant Norris approached, riding his horse off to the side of the pike and kicking up a grand wake of mud and water in his passage. He brought the horse to a halt beside us. "There you are, Brown," he said. "I've searched half the morning for you."

"I'm trying to get this...this good gentleman to proceed," I said. "Can you talk to him?"

Norris nodded. "I can do better than that." He pulled out his pistol and leveled the barrel toward the recalcitrant landowner. "Move on, you great fool, or I'll see that you remain here as part of the road."

The man blew out a hard breath, sending his mustache into a flutter. "You wouldn't—"

The sergeant pressed back the hammer on his weapon. "Can't say as I didn't warn you." In the space of a heartbeat, the landowner reversed himself and began hurrying along the pike so quickly that twin sprays of water rose from the wheels of his cart.

"You didn't actually intend to shoot that man," I said.

"No," said Sergeant Norris. "I didn't. My powder's so damp I'd never get the shot off. Had I dry powder, I'd have shot him." He took another look at the pistol and returned it to his jacket. "Where is your horse? We need to move along ourselves."

I pointed back along the lane. "There was a man with a gouty leg. I gave him my horse to ride."

"Why in hell would you do that?" asked Norris. I started to explain further, but the sergeant waved my words away. "Doesn't matter now. We need to find you another mount."

He turned and faced the next group of settlers coming down the road. This group was from a larger hold than the last. There was a man on a large grey horse, with a hand driving a two-horse wagon, a young wife, a good number of children, and a pair of slaves who followed on foot.

"You," said Norris. "Give over your horse."

The landowner looked at him with black anger. "I will not. I own two thousand feet along Glaize Creek and I have my rights as a stockholder. This is my property."

"And this is company business," said Norris. He pulled out his pistol again and directed it at the man. This landowner did not move quite with the alacrity of the first, but after a bit he reluctantly handed over the horse and moved to join his family on the wagon.

I took hold of the big grey and mounted, though I had to jump to make its saddle. For all its size, the horse was cooperative enough and I was shortly moving along the muddy track that the sergeant had blazed alongside the pike. "Do intend to make a regular habit of pointing that pistol at landowners?" I asked him.

"I haven't tried it before today," said Sergeant Norris. He looked admiringly at the weapon. "But I have to say, it works bloody well."

We passed several groups of wet, unhappy landowners before Sergeant Norris led the way off to the left toward the river.

"Where are we going?" I asked.

"Hadley came down this way to water his horse," he said. "He found something that I think you ought to see."

The slope was muddy and we had to ease the animals forward before we came under the canopy of kapok trees. Passionflowers clung to the trunks and spread across the ground, their petals open to the rain. The overhead canopy was so thick that the rain did not fall with the steady, even dispersal seen out on the road. Instead, it would gather in leaves and vines until the vegetation was overwhelmed, releasing a pint or more of water at a time to splash on the forest floor. Sergeant Norris did not seem to notice either the beauty or the irregular deluge as he urged his horse on into the wood and right to the edge of the slope above the river. The trees were so dense there that I was almost on Private Hadley before I saw him standing beside his horse not twenty feet ahead.

"Thank goodness you're here, doctor," said Hadley. "I was starting to think I'd be waiting alone all day."

"Have they moved?" asked Norris.

"No, sir, not so much as a whisker."

I pushed my borrowed mount closer. "What are you talking about?" I asked. "Has who moved?"

"Your antriders."

My heart jumped at the word. "They're here?" I raised myself in the saddle but could see nothing. "Why aren't we running?"

"Because they're not chasing," said Norris. He nodded toward where Hadley was waiting. "Go have a look."

I climbed down from my horse and joined Private Hadley on the ground. I still did not see what it was that had captured their attention until I took a walked a bit closer to Private Hadley. There was a bull's-eye pattern decorating the leaf mold; a pattern edged in black, red, and yellow. It was perhaps twenty feet across. It was made from antriders.

"They been like this since I arrived," said Hadley. "Don't even seem to notice we're here."

The outer circle of the antriders was composed of knights and riders, all of them facing outwards. The little knights held their lances extended so that the whole circle bristled like a ring of thorns. Behind this barricade was an empty space a good yard wide, so clear of plants and fallen branches that I was sure it had been groomed by the insects. Then came a second circle, the same as the first but half its size, another void, and finally an inner mass that mixed the black and red of the riders with the pale yellow color of the bridge builders. And something else as well, something large and flecked with spots of blue.

"What are they doing?" asked Hadley. "Why don't they move?"

I shook my head. Slowly, I took one step closer, then another, as I tried to get a better look at this fourth caste of antriders. The insects at first seemed oblivious to my actions, but when my third step landed within ten feet of the outer ring, there was an immediate reaction. The riders along that section of the ring elevated their lances, jutting the weapons toward me. There was a hiss of insect limbs moving like dry sand, and the antriders at the center of the circle boiled with activity.

"Careful now," said Sergeant Norris. "You've riled them."

"I see that." Moving with extreme deliberation, I lowered myself to my hands and knees. The antriders had not forgotten my presence. As I eased to the ground, their weapons gradually lowered with me, keeping the points of the tiny blades directed at the center of my body. It was impossible to see any detail of the creatures at the center of the ring, but I fancied they were watching me as well. I pushed one hand closer. Again the antriders reacted. The ring became slightly distorted as the riders on either side of my arm turned to face this new challenge.

"They're going to charge you," said Norris. "Come away."

"I don't think so." I moved my hand left and right and watched as the insects shifted to follow. "I don't think there's enough of them."

"Not enough? There must be ten thousand of them here. They could pick your bones clean fast as your could spit."

"They could, but I don't believe they will." I backed away from the circle for a few feet before standing. Mud was smeared along my knees, but considering the state of my wardrobe in general, it was not a concern.

"My guess is that these creatures only attack when they're in a large mass. Until others arrive, they're going to wait." I stood on tiptoe and looked through the trees. "I think I see more."

Sergeant Norris and I left our horses in the care of Private Hadley and explored further down the river. In the space of a hundred yards, we found two more groups of antriders, both arrayed in similar circles, and both waiting just as patiently. Near the second mass, I picked up the remains of a crumbled antrider raft and held it up for the sergeant to see.

"It looks as if they washed up here," I said. I studied the damp mass of twigs and leaves. The construction was not quite regular, but neither was it random. It was clear that a floor of leaves had been laid out and then reinforced by an under girding of twigs—not unlike the manner of construction used for the Harbridge ferry. "They must move away from the water when they land and wait for others to arrive."

"Suppose they don't arrive," said the sergeant. "More of them, I mean. Will these wait here forever?"

I let the insect construction fall from my hands. "I don't know." The antriders near me shifted slightly. As I turned to look at them, I caught a edge of odor. Spice. Cinnamon, perhaps. Or perhaps more like allspice. "Sergeant."

"Yes?"

"Let's get back to Private Hadley." The scent grew stronger and sharper. "Quickly."

We hurried through the damp wood, while fresh buckets of rain splashed the leaves around us. By the time we passed the second group of antriders, I could see that their defensive circle was beginning to dissolve, and as we reached Private Hadley, the original ring pulled back sharply into a tight, writhing mass of insects. The points of blue were more generally dispersed through the mass. The smell was quite strong now, lemons and spice. It was fragrance that was becoming all too familiar.

"Ride," I said. "Get back to the road."

The soldiers needed little encouragement. The three of us were soon off. My last glimpse of the antriders was of the three masses merging together to form a horde several yards across.

"We should have killed them," Norris said as we picked our way back to the road.

"And how would you do that?" I asked.

"Fire," Private Hadley suggested. "We could burn them."

I shook my head. "Not unless you have a gallon of lamp oil. It's far too wet to set any of this wood to light."

"We might have rolled a log over them," said Norris. "Crushed them where they stood."

"We might, but I doubt they would have allowed such a thing. Just because they didn't attack us doesn't mean they wouldn't defend themselves."

It was clear enough that neither of the soldiers were satisfied with this answer. They pulled back from me and rode beside each other while we returned to the road. Back out of the jungle, we found that the rain had diminished somewhat, but the flood of people down the road toward St. George was still flowing as strongly as ever. For the moment at least, they were making progress. I watched for a bit, and was relieved to see that few were turning around or leaving the road. The man from whom Sergeant Norris had liberated the horse was no longer in sight, which was just as well. If I had seen the man, I would have felt obligated to return the animal, but since I did not, I felt entitled to continue riding.

Back down the road to the west, I saw what looked like the end of the long procession, with a quartet of riders bringing up the rear. From a distance, I could not tell if any of these were Miss Marlowe, but I was preparing to go and see for myself when Sergeant Norris rode closer.

"Is this it then?" he asked.

"What?"

"Running away," said the sergeant. "Is that all we're to do?"

I shrugged my shoulders. "It's all we can do. We've no way to defend these people out here. If the antriders overtake us, there will be hundreds killed."

"Fair enough." Norris removed his hat for a moment, and let the rain fall through his dark hair. "And should we get them to St. George. What will we do then?"

"We'll..." I paused, my mouth open, but with no words to issue. The threat of the antriders had been enough to set everyone in motion, but the escape had become a goal in itself. "The antriders might stop before they reach St. George."

"And if they don't?" said the soldier. "These bugs have come halfway across Selvanos. Why should they stop now when they've got us all nice and gathered up like sheep brought into the pen?"

This was another fine question, and again I had no fair answer. "There are bound to be ships in the harbor," I said. "We can get some people away."

"Some. That might be. But there'll be more than a thousand people bottled up, maybe half again as many by the time we bring home everyone from the works along the way. You're not like to fit half so many on the lumber ships that happen to be anchored in the bay."

I frowned and twisted around in my seat. Back there in the jungle, the antriders were massing at that moment. Soon enough, they could come pouring from the wood, harassing the slow progress of the escape. Even if we should avoid that small army we had seen on the riverbank, there could be other groups of antriders waiting closer to the town. And if we should avoid any confrontation on the road, we would reach St. George, only to be assaulted there. As Sergeant Norris had indicated, we were animals driving ourselves to the slaughter, and I saw little way to avoid it.

"We can't stop," I said.

"No," he said. "On that we agree."

"Nor can we go back. So the only thing to do is keep people moving. See that they reach St. George."

"And then?" he said again.

I tried to smile, but I was afraid my expression came quite short of the mark. "Lieutenant Bland is a full day ahead of us by now. He's probably in St. George this minute, telling Lord Haverset what he's seen. By the time we reach the capital, they'll have something ready."

Sergeant Norris gave a short bark of laughter. "You trust Haverset and Bland to take care of this mess? And here I was thinking that you had a brain." The sergeant put heels to his horse and rode off along the pike, paralleling the long line of settlers on the march.

I sat and watched him for some time. In truth, I did not trust Haverset. How could I, when the man had been set to have me killed on no better evidence than the ravings of an injured and maddened soldier? Even if Lieutenant Bland and his surviving men had reached St. George, there was no way I could know what story they told. Perhaps the director would finally realize that my assertions about the antriders were true. Perhaps he would choose to cling to his stories of Indians, no matter the evidence before him. The confidence I had felt back in Harbridge had vanished, but there was nothing to do but go forward.

"What has you thinking so hard, Mr. Brown?"

I twisted round and nearly fell from my saddle when I found Miss Marlowe right beside me. "I was thinking of St. George," I said. "And of what we'll do when we get there."

Miss Marlowe took off her hat and wrung it out between her hands. "I'm not up to worrying about that yet," she said as the water poured from the sodden hat. "Getting there is worry enough."

I noticed then that she was mounted on a large bay horse, not the chestnut we had ridden together into Harbridge. From the mud splattered on both her legs and the horse's coat, she had seen some hard riding along the muddy road. "Have you had problems?" I asked.

"I've had antriders," she said.

"They've crossed?"

"Not all of them."

Miss Marlowe described a small group of antriders, something similar to what we had seen in the woods, and told how they had chased the last of those leaving her family works. "We could have come straight here," she said. "But I was afraid we might lead those bugs right onto the trail of all these people. So we went south into the hills, then down the east slopes, then back again. We made them a good chase."

I was amazed to think of Miss Marlowe leading men off through the jungle, the antriders in pursuit, all to keep them away from the rest of us. "You might have been killed," I said. "What if your way had been blocked?"

"We followed the old trails," she said. "The Indians keep them clear."

Not for the first time, I was struck by my own ignorance of events outside the boundaries of St. George. "Your lands are that close to the natives?"

"We see them all the time."

As we talked, the tail of the procession had moved on down the road. We urged our mounts forward and went forward at an easy walk. For hours after that, we followed at the rear of the retreating settlers. Miss

Marlowe talked at some length about her family's lands and the workers that she had put in motion for St. George. At first, I kept up my share of the conversation, telling her something of my duties at Company House and the lands I hoped to inherit once my debt was paid. But as hours went by, I rested against the slowly pacing horse and limited my answers to nods or single words.

A hand touched my arm. "Calvin."

I started and opened my eyes. The scene around me had changed. The rain had stopped, and the sky was midnight black. A few stars winked between torn streaks of swiftly moving cloud and a quarter moon lent a faint light. In front of me, the column of landowners and workers had stopped. Families had spread out to either side, and makeshift tents had been pitched with blankets or oil clothes.

"Where are we?" I asked.

"We're there," replied Miss Marlowe. "We're right on the edge of St. George."

Once she had said this, the scene came into better focus. I could make out familiar landmarks. The capital was a stone's throw away. "Why have we stopped?" I asked. "Why not go on into town?"

"Go and see for yourself."

Still blinking away sleep, I got down from my horse. My limbs ached from hours in the saddle and I was deeply embarrassed that I had fallen asleep in this middle of this ordeal. At least I had not pitched off into the mud.

The settlers barely looked at me as I passed through the middle of this sprawling camp. Now that they were all put together in one place, rather than being spread out along miles of road, the scale of what we were doing was much more apparent. There were as many people standing, sitting, lying on the wet ground, as there were citizens in St. George. Selvanos was not a populous land, but we had emptied the homes of a third, perhaps half, of all the people in the colony and put them out in the weather. Those who did not know my part in this barely glanced at me as I worked my way through the waiting people. Those settlers who I had sent running myself, glared at me in resentment.

I had walked little more than a hundred feet when I saw a line of lights ahead. The houses and shops of St. George were near, but not this near.

After another minute, I saw that the lights were lanterns, and that they were mounted on some new structure. In a state near shock, I stepped closer.

There was a wall around St. George. A wall of tables, chairs, boards, logs, wagon beds, sections of fence, mounds of bricks, and heaps of books. At places it raised up ten foot or more. Nowhere was it less than six. Clearly, Lord Haverset had not ignored the warnings of Lieutenant Bland.

No settler was within a dozen yards of the wall. I stepped past the last of them and advanced up the pike. The wall had been made particularly thick along the road, with no sign of portal or gate.

"Careful there," said a man at the edge of the camp. "You best come back here."

"I'm just going up to—"

The heavy crack of a musket broke off my words and a ball smashed into the road so close to me that sand was thrown in my face.

"I warned you!" shouted a voice from the other side of the wall. "I warned you! No one comes close or they're dead."

# 15

*Outside St. George*
*19 August 1832*

Dawn rose, the rain stopped, the bright sun pulled steam from the damp earth, and still we were still kept from entering St. George. I called to the soldiers on the ramshackle ramparts, as did Sergeant Norris, and Miss Marlowe. None of our arguments showed any sign of reaching those inside. There were several men among those camped on the road who suggested the soldiers inside would not dare fire on a landowner. After all, those with claims to land were also stockholders in the British Central Lumber Company. These soldiers, many of them common boys born in Selvanos, would not dare fire on such august property owners. However, though this claim was repeated several times, we seemed short of men willing to put their theory to the test.

Sergeant Norris grew more restive by the hour. "We are bottled up here," he said. "Tight as a cork in a jug." He pointed to the river that was close on our left. "We've got the main course holding us one way, and a smaller one not far south. We know we can't march back, and now we can't go forward."

"We have to go forward," said Miss Marlowe. "We have to get these people to safety in St. George, or around to the harbor."

"You can march all the folks toward that wall that you want," said the sergeant, "but I promise you the arsenal is well stocked. There's more than enough balls to put one in all of us."

Frustration and exhaustion warred in me. I wanted to rush the tumbled barrier, or to lie down in the grass at roadside and sleep. Neither option seemed immediately available. "I don't understand why they would hold us out. The antriders are not a disease. It's not like we're carrying some forest ague."

"They could be worried that we're not carrying enough supplies," said Norris, "that we'll eat the town into starvation. Or that the antriders will rush through when they open the door to us. But I expect they haven't thought about it that much."

"Then why are—"

"Because they're afraid. Because people do foolish things when they're afraid."

Miss Marlowe fumed and stared at the wall. I could see the way the tension tightened her jaw and pulled at the corner of her lip. "A lot of these people are mine, and I'm not going to let them die out here. Not from the antriders, and not from the idiocy of that syphilitic bastard who calls himself the director."

I stared at her in some shock, though her words brought a great smile to the sergeant's face. "Well, that is, I suppose...No. We'll definitely find a way in," I said with more surety than I felt. "Even Lord Haverset cannot allow his company to die right under his nose."

Private Hadley appeared from the camp, with Muley at his side. "There's some more of them bugs by the fork," he said. "Little groups in a circle, like we saw before."

"How many?"

"We saw three of those circles," said Muley. "First two were quiet as paintings, but the last one was casting around, moving along the bank."

I stared back across the camp at the thin trees that remained along the river. The banks near St. George had long ago been logged out, but there was enough scrub wood and brush to block any view of what was happening. "They'll merge together, I expect, these and the ones that crossed upstream. When there's enough of them, they'll come for us."

Sergeant Norris nodded. "Like I said, we're bottled." He scowled toward the wall. "When time comes, I know I'd sooner take a ball than deal with those bugs. Besides, I taught gunnery to most of those fools on the other side of the wall. The best of them couldn't hit a man if he was pinned onto their bayonet."

The debate over our limited options continued, and I confess that my mind drifted so that I caught only one word in three. There was some discussion of floating the settlers down the river on logs when I saw something that caught my eye. I stepped away from the group and squinted to be sure. In the south part of the town, there was a bright point of light. It vanished, then reappeared. After a moment, I realized that it was a mirror being maneuvered so as to catch the rays of the sun. "We're being signaled," I said.

The others stopped their discussions and followed my pointing finger. The light repeated itself several times, stopped for a few moments then picked up again.

"Who is it, do you think?" said Private Hadley. "Maybe some of the soldiers decided they'd rather have us inside than out."

The rest of us had some doubt about this, but whoever was signaling, it was worth determining the source. However, reaching this light proved somewhat problematic as the flash was coming from that side of town on the north bank of the Sarstoon. We searched along the bank and were fortunate enough to find a tiny coracle, which the lumbermen used in gathering logs that drifted up here. The boat was so small, that to fit two men inside was an act requiring very careful positioning. Still, it was the only option available. Taking care to stay back out of sight of any sentries at the wall, I folded my legs inside the boat and crossed the river in company with Sergeant Norris.

Once on the north bank, we took a circuitous route in reaching the wall, keeping the brush between ourselves and the town wherever we could. Sergeant Norris had divested himself of his red jacket and his cream-colored shirt was well streaked with mud. My own clothing had reached that state of grey-brown that cannot truly be named as a color, but only as the very definition of grime. Finally, at about an hour before sunset, we neared the spot where the mirror had flashed. We approached the wall with great trepidation. I moved across the last yards of open space as stiffly as a geriatric, heart in throat, sure that a lead ball was going to punch into me at any moment.

The wall here was of less sturdy construction than that which had been throw up along the road. There were overturned kitchen tables, and also stuffed couches and chairs. I recognized one of these as the green velvet chair that had lately graced the sitting room of my home. I also recognized a portion of the old gibbet from Ebo Town and shivered at the sight.

When we were no more than ten feet from the barrier, I realized that eyes were watching from a gap between two high backed chairs. "Are you always so slow?" said a child's voice.

"Alice?" I hurried closer. Through the opening, I could see the small face staring out. "What are you doing?"

Sergeant Norris crept up beside me. "Who's this Alice?" he asked.

"Her mother keeps house for me," I said before turning back to the young girl. "What are you doing?"

"I'm saving everybody," said Alice.

"Yes, but...where's your mother?"

"I had to climb up a tree and over a roof to get here," replied Alice. "Mother couldn't fit."

"I see. And was it you that signaled to us?"

The girl's blue eyes bobbed up and down past the slot as she nodded. "That was Mother's idea. She said you would come. But you took so long."

"Yes," I said. "I'm sorry. Alice, how are you supposed to save us? Can your mother open the wall?"

"No," she said. "Mother says you'll have to do that."

"But there are soldiers," said Sergeant Norris, raising his voice to be heard. "They'll hurt us if we try."

"There aren't too many soldiers. That's the thing Mother wanted you to know."

"How many?" I said.

"There are five that walk around, and five more by the road."

I looked at Sergeant Norris and frowned in puzzlement. There should have been fifty or more soldiers left in St. George, even if Lieutenant Bland and his men had not made a safe return. Why should so few be assigned to guarding the wall?

"Do you know where the rest are?" asked Norris. "The other soldiers."

"Some are the big house," said Alice. "But only a couple."

"Company House," Norris said to me in a low voice. "Haverset is protecting his own scrawny shanks and leaving the rest of the town with nothing but a token."

I nodded, but the situation seemed hardly more hopeful than it had before. "If there are five men at the wall, they can still shoot a good number of us."

Sergeant Norris scowled, but after a moment he nodded in agreement. "And once the first bunch volleys, the others will come at a run. Ten men behind a wall can stand off quite a force."

"There won't be ten," said the little girl beyond the slot.

I leaned down so I could look more directly at Alice. "What?"

"Mother says there'll only be five, if you come at the right time."

"What time is that?"

"After dark, and right when the moon comes up," she said.

Sergeant Norris pushed his head in next to mine so he could look into the girl's eyes. "What's your mother up to, child?"

"She didn't tell me that," said Alice. "She just said to remember after dark, right when the moon comes up."

"Right," said Norris. "We'll remember."

I thought about the antrider groups in the wood and how some of them were starting to move. "If we can wait that long."

Then before I could say anything more, I heard a man call from the other side of the barrier. Alice disappeared from the opening immediately, without a word of good-bye. Sergeant Norris and I waited for a few minutes, hunkered close to the stack of broken boards and furniture, but the girl did not reappear. Finally, the sergeant looked at me and nodded. Together, we hurried across the swath of open space and back into the stunted trees along the river bank.

"Do you have any thought of what this woman intends to do when night comes?" Norris asked when we were out of earshot and making our way down to the water.

"No, not really."

The sergeant shook his head. "I'm afraid your housekeeper is going to get herself killed."

We paddled our tiny coracle back to the other side of the river and rejoined Miss Marlowe and Muley on the road. Private Hadley was off elsewhere, arbitrating in some dispute among the displaced settlers. Muley seemed surprised that we had not gotten shot. Miss Marlowe was more keen to hear what we had learned. We repeated to her our conversation with Alice. Her first response was very nearly the same as that of Sergeant Norris.

"I'm worried for Mrs. Dillworth," Miss Marlowe said. "She shouldn't be getting in the way of these soldiers."

"That's a fact," said Norris, "but it seems she intends to go there, and we've no way to warn her. The only question is, what are we to do about it?"

The prospects for action appeared to be few. We could certainly mount a charge on the wall, and might persuade a hundred men to join us. But to do so would be to risk a number of deaths. We quickly agreed that, should the antriders appear, we would gamble on an assault, but any effort that almost guaranteed death for several of the participants was to be avoided unless there were no other choices. As one of those who might fall in this charge, I heartily agreed with this consensus.

It was Muley that thought of the river. "What about using the water?" he suggested. "We could float right through their wall and come up behind them."

"That would be fine," I said. "But the river and the bridge are right beside the road. All any of the soldiers would have to do is glance toward the water to end our surprise."

For a minute, this seemed to end the possibility of a river-borne attack, then Miss Marlowe spoke up. "What we need to do," she said. "Is to make sure that none of the soldiers are looking at the river."

"And how do we do that?"

By way of response, Miss Marlowe walked briskly away. A few minutes later, she returned with a red garment thrown over her arm. "Here," she said. "Hold this for me."

I took the garment gingerly. It was a dress, deep ruby red in color, with cream lace around the throat. Miss Marlowe placed a hand on my shoulder for balance while she raised her left leg. She removed one boot, then switched feet and removed the other. Then, with no more apparent concern than is attributed to the savages in the wood, she unlaced her britches and pulled them down. I turned away quickly, sure that my face was several degrees warmer than the sun beating down on the road. From the corner of my eye, I saw the trousers hit the ground, followed in moments by her shirt and some white undergarment that I could not quite work out. The red dress was pulled from my fingers.

"You can look now," she said.

The dress was different from any that I had seen on the women at Company House, and more different still than those worn by shopkeeper's wives. There was no whalebone in its construction, or wire hoops. The cloth fit very tight, top to bottom, and did little to hide the curves of Miss Marlowe's form. The garment had clearly been scaled for someone of a shorter stature, as the bottom of the skirt failed to reach even to her knees while the throat was open so wide that only some miracle of design kept it in place. The skin of Miss Marlowe's face was tanned by exposure to the sun, but below the shoulders she was pale as milk.

I stared at her openmouthed, realized I was staring, stammered out an apology and turned away quickly. The sergeant and Muley likewise turned to face the river.

"I'm pleased to find that you are all gentlemen," Miss Marlowe said. "Now, let us hope that the soldiers we're facing are at least somewhat less noble."

"Now, miss, where did you find something like that?" asked Muley.

Miss Marlowe laughed. "There's a woman in Harbridge, a woman alone, who loaned it to me."

Sergeant Norris gave a little grunt. "I thought I recognized that gown. I believe I know the woman who owned it quite...well. No offense, miss, but what will you do it they aren't fixed on you? You'll be at a distance, and it's going to be dark before moonrise. You're charms may not be so easy to make out."

"If need be, I'll move closer," said Miss Marlowe.

"But what if..."

"If that's not enough," she said, "then I'll take off the dress. Do you think that will draw their attention, sergeant?"

From that point, we began to plot the details of our aquatic assault. At nightfall, I found myself in the company of eight men, waiting to pass into the city. We might have drawn more, and certainly had more volunteers among the impatient, frightened settlers waiting along the road, but our numbers were limited by the number of boats we had been able to find along the river.

I found myself squeezed into the coracle again, with a man whose size was beyond the limits that such a craft should bear. The man's name was Brandice, and he spoke to me politely enough, though with little warmth. The uncomfortable situation was made more so when I recognized this man as the one from whom Sergeant Norris had appropriated my horse. We paddled off at full dark, but even as we drifted silently toward the wall, I wondered if my partner might just as soon take out his anger on me as the soldiers we were expecting to engage.

As we floated by the edge of the camp, I saw a torch move away from the cluster of wagons and bed-sheet tents. "There she goes," I whispered.

There was no reply, which was just as well considering how clearly voices carried across the water. I could barely make out a fishing punt at the front of our little flotilla which held Sergeant Norris, Private Hadley, Muley, and a rangy settler with a wild black beard. Behind us, two more men were balanced on a canoe fashioned after the ones made by the natives. From the manner in which it swayed back and forth, this last craft left something to be desired in the way of stability.

I dared dip our paddle into the water only lightly as we neared the wall. I used it once to fend off a drifting log, and again to keep us near the center of the channel. It took at least five minutes of drifting in this slow-moving channel before we reached the wall. The construction had been carried right down to the edge of the water, and I could see bits of wood bobbing at the edge of the stream. It was clear now that the wall involved not only furniture, but wood taken from houses and shops. Some portion of St. George had been disassembled to provide the raw material for this barrier. That such a construction had been planned and executed in less than a day was in some ways quite admirable—had the wall not been fixed between us and our goal. And, of course, had it been of any value against the actual threat.

Now that we were inside the wall, I found my heart beating as fast as it had in any confrontation with the antriders. I followed Sergeant Norris' example in allowing my craft to drift another twenty feet before bringing it to the bank near the foot of the bridge. I picked up a loaded pistol from the floor of the little boat and climbed out. Each sound generated by my exit from the coracle caused me to cringe, but I made it onto the shore without drawing any obvious attention from the soldiers. Brandice followed with admirable grace for such a large man. Sergeant Norris and the other occupants of his craft were already hiding in the deep shadows beneath the bridge footing. Seconds after, the men in the canoe joined us, but not without nearly upset their craft and making such noise that I was sure we were all about to meet our end.

We might have moved then, and done so under the protective cover of the darkness, but the moon had not yet made its appearance. Even if the gloom allowed us to gain advantage over the men at the wall, it was doubtful we could take them all without a shot fired on either side. So we huddled together near the water's edge, swallowing every desire to speak or cough. Waiting.

It seemed an hour, though it was surely scarce minutes, before silver light touched the tops of the trees across the river and flowed swiftly downward to touch the wall. At once, Sergeant Norris raised his pistol and mimed pulling back the hammer. He waited a second while the rest of us followed this action, then he was off, moving up the hill and toward the wall.

If our footfalls made noise on that rapid, shuffling approach to the wall, I did not hear them. There was no room in my ears for anything but the sound of my heart pounding in my chest and the blood rushing through my ears.

As we cleared the riverbank, I got my first look at the inside of the wall. The soldiers had built for themselves a kind of shelf, about five feet above the road, on which they could stand and survey the road beyond. They were there as we approached. Whatever exhibition Miss Marlowe had undertaken, it had not failed to get their attention. Not one of the soldiers so much as turned our way until Private Hadley reached up onto the shelf, took one man by the ankle, and pulled him down.

Then there was chaos.

A soldier turned and fired, catching the black-bearded man, whose name I never learned, straight on in the face. Blood and grey matter sprayed across us. There was an explosion at my hand. I stopped, thinking that I had also been shot, then realized that the explosion was of my own generation. In my nervousness, I had fired my pistol blindly and with no chance of striking home. The weapon was now no more than a club.

Sergeant Norris took one of the soldiers with a knife. Another jumped down from the wall himself and began to grapple with Muley. I charged at the last man still standing on the platform, my empty pistol raised in what I hoped was a threatening manner.

"Surrender!" I shouted. Even in my own ears, my voice was strained and frightened.

The soldier was equally unimpressed. Rather than laying down his rifle, he leveled the weapon toward my chest and brought his cheek down to the barrel.

A crack sounded behind me. I winced as a ball buzzed past my head like an angry hornet. The soldier on the platform fell back across the tumbled mess of the wall. His rifle dropped from his fingers and clattered on the boards.

I looked around behind me and saw Brandice, smoke still rising from his pistol. "Thank you," I said.

He nodded. "I think, sir, that I'll be wanting my horse back now."

"Yes. Certainly."

The number provided us by Alice was precisely accurate. There had been five soldiers at the road, and now all five were on the ground. Three of them were dead outright. From my examination, another would not be far behind. I knelt on the bloody road beside the man and pulled back his jacket to get a better view of the wound. "The shot has gone clean through his kidney," I said. "I'm sorry."

Sergeant Norris nodded and wiped a runnel of blood from his cheek. "I knew every one of these men. Now that we've killed them, I begin to wonder what it was I ever liked about this plan." I had no good answer to that.

Brandice was sent off to watch the road to Company House and warn should any more soldiers sally out to meet us. The other men began to tear open the wall under the direction of Private Hadley. Muley climbed up onto the shelf and waved. "Tell them to come up," he called to Miss Marlowe. "The shooting's over." The American climbed back down with a broad smile on his face. "I can see why those boys weren't looking our way."

I moved to the last of the soldiers. He had been struck insensible by a blow to the head. A flap of scalp had been torn free and there was considerable bleeding, but his heart was strong. "I think this one will recover," I said.

"That's something," replied Sergeant Norris.

Another gunshot sounded. I raised my head. This shot had not come from nearby, but from somewhere on the other side of the town.

I looked at Sergeant Norris. "Mrs. Dillworth." I stood, but the sergeant took me by the arm.

"Get the wall open."

"Mrs. Dillworth may be injured. She could need my help."

"That may be," said Norris, "but you can't help until we can convince those other soldiers to put down their guns. And nothing will be quite so convincing as a hundred men on this side of the wall."

Reluctantly, I joined in breaking through the wall. As the level of the barrier fell, I could see that a large number of men and women and even children were dragging down the obstacle from the other side. In a few minutes, we had made an opening wide enough to bring in a cart. The settlers began to stream into St. George.

While this was going on, Brandice and Private Hadley had watched for any approaching soldiers, but the road remained clear. St. George appeared to be deserted but for the settlers now entering through the wall.

"Where is everyone?" I asked.

Sergeant Norris shook his head. "I don't know, they couldn't have put everyone in Company House. Maybe they're down by the pier."

Miss Marlowe appeared, still barefoot and wearing the red dress. I started to compliment her on the job she had done on distracting the soldiers, but before I could stammer out the words, she delivered more urgent news.

"The antriders are coming," she said. "They're less than a mile away, coming straight down the road."

Sergeant Norris cursed. "Get everyone inside," he said. "We'll start building the wall back as soon as the last in through."

"It won't help," I said.

Both of them turned to look at me. "What?"

I pointed at the wall. "You've seen what these insects can do. They crossed the river on a rope and a few floating logs. They won't stop because there's a wall in their way and they certainly won't be bothered by any rifles we point their way."

Sergeant Norris looked as if he was about to shout something in reply, then the breath went out of him and his shoulders sagged. "God. Why did we work so hard to get in here? We're just as trapped on this side of the wall as we were on the other."

# 16

*St. George*
*19 August 1832*

My home was empty. Not just empty of people, but of most everything that had made it a home. Every stick of furniture was gone from the front room, along with every book from the shelves and even the specimens that had hung on the walls. There was broken glass on the floor, and some dry beetles that had spilled from a case, but little else. I stood for a moment, thinking of the years I had spent assisting Dr. Wilmater in this place, and my brief time there as an acting physician. It was clear enough that my chance to tend shingles and fishing wounds was at an end. St. George itself seemed at an end.

"Mrs. Dillworth?" I called. "Alice?" Neither name brought a reply.

A glass eye—undoubtedly formerly fixed in the face of some taxidermically prepared fox or howler monkey—looked up at me from the floor. A small table had been knocked over and left behind, but the chair where I had spent my last night in St. George was absent.

Through the open window, I could detect the bright, clean scent of the sea, which had always been part of the smell of home, but even that now seemed alien. I sighed and left the room.

Miss Marlowe met me at the door as I was coming out. She was in her travel worn trousers and shirt again. Now that it had served its purpose, the red dress had evidently been retired or returned to its original owner. "Mrs. Dillworth and her daughter?" she said.

I shook my head. "No. No one is here." I rubbed at my tired eyes.

"We have to hurry," said Miss Marlowe. "Sergeant Norris is going up to Company House. There are people in the streets up there. And soldiers."

I nodded. "What about the ships? There were two in the harbor last week. If we can get..."

"I don't know," she said. "I didn't go down Water Street."

I put a tired hand through my damp, grimy hair. "We had best check. If there are ships there, if there's so much as a bum boat or a fish skiff, we can use it."

Together Miss Marlowe and I hurried across the Sarstoon Bridge and up the Kings Highway to the corner of Water Street. The ground was higher here, and the town laid out to see. On the west side the wall of broken homes and furniture was visible in the silver moonlight. The barrier had been constructed in a grand semicircle, starting on the bluffs above the old Spanish fort, hooking north across the main road, a small gap for the river, then resuming on the south bank to curl back toward the harbor. The majority of St. George lay inside the wall, but Ebo Town, including Plunket's uncomfortable accommodations, had been left outside this protection. Evidently, this section of the town was not held in high esteem by those in charge of the construction. Off to the east, the ocean was dark and invisible.

A good number of the displaced settlers of Selvanos still remained near where the road had brought them past the wall. It seemed to me that they milled about in a tight mass of confusion, waiting for someone to direct them to safety. They appeared almost like insects themselves, a hive of bees stirred up at night. Lit by the moon, the town and the people seemed ghostly and the trees of the jungle outside were dark as ink. If the antriders were out there, I could see no sign of them.

We turned the corner and went down slope along Water Street and the docks. The streets of the capital littered with debris from the hasty construction of the wall. No more than a handful of people were in sight as we hiked past closed shops and dark houses. I tried to gain the attention of one, a provisioner who regularly sold pork and oil at Company House. But the man turned in the opposite direction and disappeared along an alley. It was hard to blame him.

Everyone we passed seemed near to violence, and to solidify this impression, there were shouts and the sound of breaking glass in the distance. Some of the settlers, tired of being on the march, had made camp along the street, or broken into shops. There were cries for help, and for the soldiers to come, but no aid was at hand.

We reached the docks, still hopeful that there was some ship hiding in the night. But the hawsers were thrown back across the planks and no ship's boats bobbed alongside the pier. Out on the water, there were no lanterns or candles to be seen.

"There were two ships," I said. I walked out to the end of the dock and peered at the empty bay. "Enough to hold five hundred at least. Twice that if we stayed in the harbor and only waited for the insects to leave."

Miss Marlowe kicked the frayed end of one thick rope and sent it splashing over the edge. "They've gone now," she said. "Gone and left us nothing to do but face these things where we stand."

I clenched my fists in frustration then blew out a long breath. "Very well," I said. "Sergeant Norris is waiting for us, and may have news. Lord Haverset must have ordered the wall built and set the soldiers to guard the road. Those plans we've seen make little sense, but he must have taken other guards. When we get up to Company House, he might—"

"No," said a voice from across the dockyard. "He's not there to tell you anything more."

I strained against the backlight of the distant fires and recognized a familiar figure coming toward us. "Mrs. Dillworth!" I called. "I was afraid you were dead." Miss Marlowe and I hurried back to meet her.

"I thought we all were," she replied. Mrs. Dillworth joined us at the foot of the pier. Even in the dim light, her face looked as exhausted and haggard as those who had made the long walk into town. Miss Marlowe rushed forward to envelop the woman in a hug. "I see you made it in."

"We did," I said. "With your help and with Alice."

"But how did you stop those soldiers without injuring yourself?" asked Miss Marlowe. She stepped back from Mrs. Dillworth. "We had eight men with us, and still got one of them killed."

"Ahh," said the woman, "you had eight men, but I had a rather large bottle of wine and an equally generous supply of laudanum from among your medicinals, Dr. Brown. I presented my gift to the soldiers and they took care of themselves."

I marveled. "They drank themselves insensible?"

"Sleeping sound as stones," she said, hooking her thumb toward the south. "Some hours yet, I'd venture."

"But we heard a gunshot," said Miss Marlowe.

Mrs. Dillworth nodded. "That was among those at the docks, I believe. They were not pleased when they realized the ships didn't mean to come back for them."

"Where is Lord Haverset?" asked Miss Marlowe.

"Gone. Your Lord High Director Haverset was on the first ship, he and most of the landowners that were in town, along with some others that had the luck or waved enough money."

"Why did they build this wall?" I asked. "Did he really think it would stop the antriders?"

"Wasn't meant for your bugs," said Mrs. Dillworth. "The wall was to stop you."

"What?"

The housekeeper pointed out across the empty water. "That fellow Bland got here before dawn yesterday. Soon after that, half the soldiers were packing everything from Company House into the ships. The other half was building the wall."

It took me a moment to credit what I was hearing. "How many men?" I asked. "How many men on each ship."

Mrs. Dillworth rubbed at her chin. "A hundred at most on the first," she said. "Maybe twice that on the second. Them, a like number of chests, a score of horses, and some of the better furniture."

Miss Marlowe seemed for once dumbstruck. "Furniture?" she whispered.

"I saw a bed carried up. Very nice, it was."

"They left us," said Miss Marlow. "They took furniture, but they left us."

I allowed myself to put a hand on her shoulder. "Come on, Genevieve. Let us find Sergeant Norris and see if we can salvage any sort of plan for what we do next."

We met up with Sergeant Norris along the block between Water Street and the brick square outside Company House. The sergeant was surrounded by a hundred or more settlers.

"Have you met any other soldiers?" I asked as our small party drew up.

Norris nodded. "Seen them, yes, but that's all I can claim. There were two lads up there in the square outside the house. They ran off as soon as they saw us near."

I informed the sergeant that Lord Haverset was gone and that the town had apparently been left to its own ends. He scowled so hard at the news, I thought his nose and chin might meet. "That's bloody dark news, Dr. Brown," said the sergeant. "I took Haverset for a fool from the first time I saw him, but I didn't know the man was a coward."

The bold way in which Sergeant Norris spoke against a titled officer of the company gave me some pause. It was as sure a sign as the disarray around us that Selvanos was unraveling.

"Well, doctor," said Norris. "What would you have us do now?"

I looked around, hoping that some other person might spring up to provide an answer, but all of the tired settlers appeared to be looking right back at me. "We should go to the fort."

"Why?" asked Miss Marlow.

"There are provisions there," I said. "Food, and barreled water. Besides, the walls are steep. Even for the antriders, it may be a difficult climb."

Norris snatched a torch from one of the men along the road and stormed off toward the Spanish fort. I followed in behind, along with Miss Marlowe, Mrs. Dillworth, and little Alice who had emerged from the crowd to take her mother's hand. As we passed, the settlers dropped in line until we made a grand parade of battered figures along the street. Considering the light, the condition of the town, and the sorry, sodden state of those in our procession, we might have been enacting some scene from Dante. I am certain I looked as damned as all the rest.

At the bricked square outside of Company House, we at last met two soldiers still at their posts. On sight of us, they raised their rifles, but once they saw how many people were coming along the road, they quickly reversed their actions and fled.

"Calloway!" Sergeant Norris called after one of the men. "Damn it, Calloway, get back here." But the sergeant had no more luck. The two soldiers darted around the corner of Company House and vanished.

"Let them go," I said, before Norris could disappear in pursuit. "We need to see to these people who are following us before we can go after those that don't want to be caught."

Norris nodded, but I could see that his anger had not diminished.

The Spanish fort had a commanding view of the harbor and walls so thick they would guard against thirty-pound guns. There were bluffs that came within a few feet of the walls on the seaward side and which fell down fifty feet and more to the surf. It seemed a sensible enough place to assemble the citizens of St. George in case of most any form of attack. Though the antriders were certainly not the sort of problem for which those thick walls had been built.

When we came up to the fort, I could see that there were several torches along the top of the wall and the shadowy form of men peeking down at the approaching mass. I feared that we might arrive to find the door barred against us, but the gates of the fort were wide and the vicar, Father Samms, stood waiting.

The clergyman's coat was torn along one sleeve, and he looked as haggard as I must have been in the depths of Plunket's jail, but he smiled on seeing me. "Brown! We were told you were dead."

"You were?" I said. "By who?"

"Lieutenant Bland," said the abbot. "He put out that you had been killed by those bugs out near the Qualm."

"It was a near thing, but I'm happy to say that he is wrong in that regard." I looked past Father Samms at the others crowding the door of the fort. "How many are still here?"

"Near enough to four hundred," he said. "It looks like you've doubled our company."

"Doubled, and then some," I replied. "There are more down along the road and in town."

"So many?" the clergyman stepped forward, squinting against the red light of the fires. "We were told there was no one left out there."

"We were lied to," said Mrs. Dillworth. "The soldiers were not holding out the creatures, but good British citizens, even landowners of Selvanos."

Samms frowned, drawing deep creases around his eyes and mouth. "They said...they would return for us."

"I'd not count on that, Father."

Sergeant Norris began to ask questions about the placement of the other soldiers, and Miss Marlowe stepped past to help an ailing settler find some place of rest in the fort. For a while then, I was all but insensible. I sat on stack of stone blocks and saw people coming and going, but had little notion of who or why. Miss Marlowe sat beside me for some of this time, and I thought I felt her hand against my cheek, but that might have been a dream.

It was when my face received attention of a different sort that I snapped back to wakefulness. A sharp pain lanced through my face from a point just below the socket of my left eye. I slapped my hand against the pain immediately and felt something break under the blow.

I lowered my hand and looked at the contents. At first, I could not be sure what I was seeing. The light was poor, and the deliverer of this sting had been well and truly broken. But after a few moments of scrutiny, I knew without doubt that I had been attacked by an antrider. Somehow, they were inside the town.

By torch light, it was hard to be sure, but the carapace of the crushed antrider did not appear red, black, or even yellow like that of the bridge builders. Instead, this insect was a light blue in color, sky blue. A rare color in insects of any kind and, so far as I was aware, unique among the Hymenoptera.

With the tip of one finger, I arranged the fragments of the intruder's body, trying to repair the damage I had done. From what I could tell, the blue antrider was structured more like one of the little knights than their mounts. Its thorax had the same upright posture with forward set head. This blue insect lacked the elongated lance of the riders, having more normally formed forelimbs. Instead, its most remarkable feature was very large eyes that wrapped around both sides of the head in a saddle shape and came close to meeting at both back and front.

One aspect that I could not find in the crushed remains was a stinger, but there was little doubt the antrider had possessed such an instrument. The point on my cheek where it had wounded me began to swell and felt hot, tight, and painful. The sting from this insect was much like that delivered by a Paraponera, the so-called bullet ant whose stings held the pain of receiving a gunshot.

"How did you get here," I said to the dead bug.

Checking the semicircle of jumbled material that shielded St. George on the landward side showed no signs of an approaching horde. In any case, I saw no more in my area. Unlike the swarming riders, it seemed that this aggressive little bug was on its own.

The settlers came up through the town and passed me as they moved over the square toward the fort. As they moved by, I noticed one woman swat at something on her shoulder. This was not unusual behavior. Selvanos was solidly in the tropics, with all that implies about the wealth of stinging and biting insects. But this woman rubbed at the bite as she walked, giving it more attention that I would have expected from the wound of a mosquito. I saw a man a few paces back suddenly start and take a stumble. He bent his arm around awkwardly, reaching for the small of his back. Another man squawked, removed his hat, and slapped it forcefully against his leg. In a moment, the orderly motion of the settlers toward the fort turned into a boil.

Some people darted ahead. Others danced about in pain. While more looked on in confusion.

I hurried forward. It was clear that the settlers were under assault, and I suspected the culprit was the same form of antrider that had stung me only minutes earlier. But how these creatures were getting in was still a mystery.

One of the men in the parade carried an oil lamp. I snatched this away from him before he could protest and moved to where the commotion was at its worst. Most of the afflicted settlers were moving on, with little more than a curse, but one elderly woman was down to her knees with her face red and her eyes bulging. I stooped to help her, but as I did, something was caught in the glow of my lamp. A little spot of blue suspended below a pale streak. Raising the lantern, I saw another and another.

"Sergeant Norris!" I shouted. "Miss Marlowe!"

There was no immediate response to my cries, and I turned my attention to carrying for the unfortunate woman who had been stung. The intruder's sting had apparently taken her very hard, and she was having difficulty in breathing. With the help of some other settlers hurrying past, the woman was carried off toward the fort. As I was seeing her off, another of the blue antriders bit me at the back of the knee. The pain was sharp and unexpected and I joined the others in cursing these insects.

Sergeant Norris arrived while I was searching for the culprit who had savaged this tender spot. "I was told you were calling for me," he said.

"I was." I gave my injury a brief rub and stood. "There are antriders inside the town."

"There are?" The soldier was immediately alarmed. "Bloody hell. I told Hadley to shout if they came in sight along the road."

"They didn't come up the road. Or at least not the way you think." I held my lamp aloft.

"What are you..."

"Just wait a moment." I moved my hand back and forth through the smoky air. "There! There, do you see it?"

Another blue antrider was drifting through the air, suspended below a waving streamer of silk. No sooner had this first insect floated out of view, than a second replaced it. It seemed to me that the dark eyes of the insects were fixed downward, observing every aspect of the ground. I could even catch the reflection of my lamp gleaming in their oversized eyes.

"The bloody things can fly now?" Sergeant Norris waved a hand toward one of the blue riders, but the breeze he stirred only sent the insect on a new course.

"Not fly," I said. "Balloon." I held the lamp close to another antrider as it wafted by. "Many species of spiders practice this skill in their youth. They spin out silk that carries them along with the wind. That allows them to spread out over a great distance."

"So you think..." started Sergeant Norris. His question was interrupted as he slapped at his neck. "They bite!"

"They sting. Ants and bees and wasps are closely related."

Norris rubbed a hand across his neck. "They fly and they sting. That's brilliant. Just brilliant. You think they're trying to spread out, like you said with the spiders?"

I watched another of the blue riders moving in our direction and quickly stepped aside to keep from providing a point of landing. The insect's head quite clearly swiveled to watch me as it went past, its eyes again catching the glitter of the lamp. "No," I said. "I don't think these ants have come to colonize. I rather suspect they're here to spy."

The idea seemed to strike the sergeant nearly as hard as the intruder's sting. "Spy?" he shook his head. "You can't mean that."

"I mean exactly that," I replied. "I've seen these creatures ford a running stream and stage an ambush. You saw for yourself how they behaved at the ferry." I turned to survey the burning barrier around the town. "They'll look for weakness. And when they find it, they'll move against us."

Norris was unconvinced. "It's one thing to run along a rope," he said, "and another thing to plot and plan. These little spies are inside the town with the rest of us. How could they even tell their friends where to bite?"

The answer to that question had been forming in my own mind for some days, though I had not voiced it to anyone as yet. "By smell. You've noticed the odor that lingers around the antriders?"

"Yes," said Sergeant Norris with a nod. "Lemons."

"They can generate other smells, as well. Smells that drive attack. Smells that signal a gathering." I pointed out to the line. "When these floating spies find their weak point, they'll make a smell that brings down the rest."

"Smell." Norris turned the idea for some time, but at last shook his head. "Damn if I know, Doctor Brown. These bugs of yours don't act like anything I've seen. I suppose I wouldn't be too surprised if the bloody things signaled each other with naval flags."

While we were talking, the cloud of drifting blue antriders grew thin, then disappeared. I waved the lamp around, and bent to shine it on the bricks, but could find no more sign of the spies. "It looks as if they've floated past," I said. "Maybe they'll end up in the sea without finding the chink in our armor."

"The devil they will," said Norris. He clamped a hand on my shoulder and directed my face south. "Look there," he said. "Along the river."

It took only a second to see what he meant. Something was moving there, like a spill of oily fluid in the moonlight. "They're doing something, those bloody bugs, and we better go see what."

We passed the last group of fort bound settlers as we trooped back down the Kings Highway to the river. The wall was twenty feet off the bridge. It was the same spot where we had slipped past to make our raid on the soldiers minding the road, and the very point where I had marveled at the thoroughness of the preparations in bringing the debris of the wall right down into the water. But the antriders were clearly less impressed by the structure than I had been. They were massed just across the wall, the gleam from their armored bodies clearly visible in the firelight.

"What are they up to?" asked Norris. "What are they doing?"

I shook my head. The plans of the insects were not clear to me. But we did not have to wait long to see those plans put to action.

Dawn was not far away, and the brightening sky gave us a better view of what was happening on the far side of the wall. As we watched, a group of antriders that could only have numbered in the thousands fetched some object that was floating at the edge of the river. This proved to be a branch, still bearing large green leaves and dripping with water. As they had at the ferry, the antriders soon adopted this bit of wood as a craft to move them across the narrow bit of river.

"We ought to sink them," said Norris. "Drive them back."

It was a good notion, but before we could act on it, the antriders put another portion of their plan to work. The air just across from us was abruptly marked by what seemed to be a cloud of smoke. But as cloud drifted closer we saw the truth. It was not smoke, but a great number of the blue antriders hanging beneath silk banners.

The spies did not wait for the streamers to settle, or chance to bring them near us. Instead, they dropped their hold on the silk and fell. Some of them landed straight on Sergeant Norris. I was missed by this initial fusillade, but my reprieve was brief. Those antriders that hit the ground scuttled toward me rapidly. In a second, my legs and feet were alive with pain. The spies had turned soldiers.

Norris whooped and bellowed. He threw himself to the ground and rolled, only to spring back up slapping at a dozen fresh bites.

I tried to move to aid him, but the attention of the insects was not limited to the sergeant. At every step it seemed I received a new sting. Pain lanced from the tender points near my Achilles heel, and from my shin. The antriders even proved capable of piercing the top of my boot to plant their stinger square in my foot.

"It's no good," I said. "We have to get away."

Sergeant Norris was too busy pounding his hands against his own face and shoulders to reply, but he began running back up along the road. I followed, wincing at the pain inflected by the stings. I imagined that it would feel no worse had my feet been stripped of all flesh and plunged straight away into salt water.

When we were thirty yards or so removed from the wall, the antriders stopped their harassment. Both Norris and I continued on a few steps to be sure that we were away from the stings, and then stopped and wheeled around.

"They'll be on us," said Norris. "Not five more minutes, and they'll be at the fort."

I looked at the sergeant and saw that he had taken several stings in the face. Already his cheek was swollen and bruised, his left eye nearly forced shut. He looked like a man who had taken a long beating from a bare knuckle prizefighter.

"They sent those spies in to attack us," I said. "That was deliberate. If we bring down more men, they'll only send more."

"Bloody hell," was the only answer the sergeant gave.

I watched the antriders for a few seconds more. "We have to move back. We can close up the fort. If we shut ourselves in, maybe we can stop them there." The notion was one without much hope, but the situation at the wall was clearly impossible.

Sergeant Norris nodded slowly. "I'll go you one better," he said. "We can shut ourselves behind more than walls. Come on then, I have the very thing."

We ran back through the heart of St. George, but I saw not a man on the street. The windows of the storefronts reflected the fire and the red dawn, so that sometimes it appeared the whole town was alight. The sound of our footsteps and exhausted breathing was all that could be heard outside the background crackle of the flames.

We reached the square, and Sergeant Norris led me not toward the front door of Company House, but around to the side where the soldier's quarters lay. "There are barrels of oil," he said. "Twenty or better. If we can get them up to the fort, we can soak the outer walls."

The thought was a good one. It might even be that the oil alone would prove sufficient to stop the antriders. If not, then we could always touch a flame and set up a barricade of fire. If we could hold our place long enough, the antriders would have to move on. The people in the fort would be hungry, but so would the insects. A mass the size of the antriders besieging St. George had to equal the weight of fifty jaguars. Perhaps a hundred. And like the jaguar, the antriders were active, aggressive hunters. They would need more meat, and quickly. If we could show them that we would not soon be taken, there was hope the insects would move elsewhere. Or at least, I hoped it was so.

We found the door into the storeroom and traveled down a sloping passage to a cool chamber buried half in the ground. There were fewer barrels of oil than the sergeant had expected. Perhaps some had been used to soak the wall, or even sent off aboard ship with Lord Haverset—lamp oil could be a pricey commodity. Still, an even dozen barrels remained to us.

Working together, we tipped a barrel up on its side and got it aimed toward the door. "Start this one back," said Norris. "I'll see if there's more in the tinker's store." I agreed, and Norris ran off down a hall.

The barrel was heavy and starting it in motion was not easy, but after a few turns the heavy cask of oil picked up some momentum. I pushed faster, gathering speed to make the ramp outside. Upsetting the barrel had evidently loosened its lid, as a thin trickle of yellow oil began to drip along the right. I slipped several times in my efforts to move the heavy cask out of the room.

I had brought the barrel to a level place, and paused to wipe the sweat which was sluicing down my face, when I heard a noise from down the hallways of Company House. I turned, thinking that Norris might have encountered remaining members of the company, still secreted within the many rooms of the house, when the unmistakable sound of a pistol shot boomed along the hallway. Dawn was just breaking outside, and the light that slanted in through the widely-space windows of Company House was wan and shot through with deep red.

At once I ran back the same way that Norris had gone, quickly passing the open door of the storeroom, and the still quite heavily barred door of the powder magazine. Up a short ramp, and then around a quick corner where I nearly collided with Sergeant Norris. The Sergeant was leaning back against the paneled wall of the passage, his right hand pressed hard to the biceps of his left arm. Between his fingers a steady, but thankfully thin, stream of blood dripped onto the hardwood floor.

"What—" I started.

"Bloody bastard shot me," Norris said without turning his head.

Following his gaze across the hall, I saw that he was staring into the open door of an office. From that door the multiple barrels of a pepperbox pistol emerged, held by a trembling hand.

"And I'll do it again, sir," said the reedy voice of the company secretary. "Mark my words." The man stepped out of the office, still training the pistol in the direction of Sergeant Norris.

The secretary had always been very thin, but now the man's face seemed properly skeletal. His stiff wig was askew, and his waistcoat was torn open along one seem and smeared with mud halfway to his chest. His eyes cut my way for an instant, before swiftly focusing again on Norris. He walked just far enough from the office to allow his back to clear the doorway, then began to slide crabwise down the paneled hallway, his shaking arm angling ever more to one side so as to keep the sergeant at the focus of the small, four-barreled gun.

"Sir," I said. "Please, we are not your enemy."

The secretary gave a strangled laugh. "Are you not?" He glanced my way again. "No, Mr. Brown, I believe you have always been my enemy. You have been right from the start of this sorry episode."

"What do you mean?" I started to take another step toward him, but the secretary's aim abruptly shifted in my direction.

"You've never had the wisdom the lord gave a calf," he said, shaking his head slowly. "But then, Wilmater proved equally foolish in this affair."

"Doctor Wilmater?" The mention of my old mentor puzzled me enough that for a moment I almost forgot about the gun in the secretary's hand. "What has Doctor Wilmater to do with this? He left Selvanos months ago."

Again, the secretary gave a bark of laughter. "Everything! He has everything to do with this." His narrow face twisted. "You think you're the discoverer of these bugs, these antriders? Why, Wilmater found them two years ago." The secretary's hand began to sway, the blunt structure of the pepperbox punctuating his words. "He discovered them, described them, studied them..." The secretary gave a sad shake of his head. "The poor man was convinced these creatures would make him crown-head of the Royal Society."

Before I could reply, Sergeant Norris shifted against the wall. "But they didn't, now, did they?"

"They did not." The secretary's wavering arm dropped for a moment. "I'm afraid the poor doctor will gain not even the dog's portion of fame." A thin smile came to his equally thin lips. "Not that you two are likely to fare much better." He shuffled another step, moving into dimmer light as he drew away from the nearest window.

My mind was whirling as I attempted to place some frame around his words. "You... knew about the antriders. Knew they were out there." And I was jolted by a memory from my first trip into the interior with Captain Valamont. Something I had seen just before the antriders appeared—the remains of a sheep tethered in the yard of the deserted Braithwaite estate. I peered into the shadows, trying to see the secretary's eyes. "You lured them in, deliberately brought them out of the forest."

The response was a bit slow to come, but after a moment I saw the secretary's head bob in the shadows. "Not personally, no. But yes, others did as much."

"Others?" I shook my head in confusion. "Surely not Captain Valamont."

The secretary made no reply, but Norris straightened, allowing his bloody hand to come away from the tear in his left sleeve. "No, it wouldn't be Valamont. The man can be hard as a chalk biscuit, and a bit of a stiff-rump, but he's no traitor." Norris tilted his head to the side and eyed the secretary speculatively. "No, I'd say you were in this with Bland and that lot. Men like you, who had a place, but no land in the current order of things. Isn't that right, sir?"

In response, the secretary raised his hand and fired. Despite the brevity of the range, the resulting ball struck neither of us. Instead it created a laceration in the dark wood of the paneling just beyond the Sergeant's head.

It seemed to take the secretary a moment to realize that he had failed to drop either of us, and to raise his hand to rotate the barrels on his pepperbox, but before he could do so, Sergeant Norris produced a spadroon and lunged sharply forward. The point of the infantry blade penetrated the secretary's chest not an inch from the center line, and did so with such force that for a moment the man was actually fastened against the wall as neatly as any insect was ever pinned to a board. Then the pepperbox fell from the secretary's hand, and in the same instant it struck the ground Sergeant Norris withdrew his blade, allowing the secretary himself to slide down the wall. Already the man's eyes seemed glazed over in death.

Though I had moved not a muscle in this action, I found myself panting as though having finished a sprint. I looked up the hallway, half expecting to see more figures approaching at a sprint, but the corridor was empty. "There could be a ship," I said.

Norris drew his spadroon across the knee of the fallen man's breeches to clean the blade. "What's that?"

"If the secretary was still here," I said. "It could mean there's still a ship about."

He thought about for a moment, then shook his head. "I expect they just left him." He gave the dead man a soft kick on the sole of one boot. "Can't be sure everything this lot was about, but they must have been trying to clear off landowners, and take more of the company for themselves."

I had to lean against the nearest wall as I sought to fit this idea with what I already knew. The body of the soldier we had found at Grey's Works. The fire we had seen in the distance after we crossed the ferry. Both might have been results of some plan to use the antriders as a means of moving landowners off their tracts. However, any such plan had surely turned to chaos as the insects proved a good deal less biddable than the plotters might have expected.

"Perhaps..." I started, looked down at the body of the secretary, cleared my throat and tried again. "Perhaps we can look through the offices."

"For what?" asked Norris.

"Information. To find what exactly were the plans and who was involved."

The sergeant scowled. "I doubt there's any letters laying out the case, doctor. And besides, I doubt we have the time to do much searching before your bugs arrive."

Reminded of the impending onslaught, I reluctantly left the secretary's body where it had fallen and accompanied Sergeant Norris back to the point where I had left the barrel on first hearing a shot. Though it was clear to me that the sergeant's arm was causing him considerable pain, and a thin flow of blood resumed as we pushed the barrel along the cobbled street, he did not stint in his efforts. Together we pushed the barrel up to the broad doors of the old fort. As we turned toward Company House for another, the growing light revealed a flood tide about to fall across St. George. The whole of the south end of the town was blanketed under a dark mass of antriders.

They might have advanced quickly and cut us off, but the insects seemed to be moving with deliberation. Sergeant Norris and I exchanged a glance, and dashed back across the square to retrieve a second barrel. The antriders paid us no mind at all as we crossed within five yards of them.

We had to pound to get someone to open the gates at the fort when we returned. Even then, I heard some discussion on the other side of the doors before the metal latched creaked open. Miss Marlowe and Private Hadley were there to see us in.

To my great surprise, Miss Marlowe grabbed me, put her arms around me, and pulled me tight against her. For at least a few moments, I stopped thinking about the antriders.

The doors of the fort slammed shut. Private Hadley shoved cloth against the cracks. We were shut in tight.

There was nowhere left to retreat.

# 17

*St. George*
*20 August 1832*

There were just over a hundred gallons of oil in the fort. Eighty had come with us in the two casks we rolled up from Company House. Another twenty odd gallons were found in jugs among the stores. Sergeant Norris applied the material to the sides of the fort with exceeding stinginess, using a soaked cloth to spread the thinnest layer of oil over the stone. When it was clear that even this mild usage was going to take a full quarter of the supply, a mad search was made to see if there was more oil, or pitch, or lard might be found. We were able to augment our supply of flammables with a few cans of turpentine and a barrel of shellac. In all, it seemed much too small an arsenal compared to the force of our foe.

I went so far as suggesting that we might make another run to Company House. There was much more oil there, as Sergeant Norris could attest, and if we could send a dozen men to retrieve a dozen barrels, our chance of survival would be much enhanced. Unfortunately, one glance into the town showed that it was too late. First on one side, then on another, the antriders pressed close. The fort was surrounded.

Miss Marlowe joined me on the board platform that ran around the inside of the walls. "I never saw them all together before," she said. She looked at the scene for a moment then gave a slight laugh. "Somehow, now that I can see them all, it doesn't seem like so many."

It was an impression that I shared. Though the antriders spread over a space a good two hundred feet on the side, there was some comfort in seeing the bare ground beyond. Before, when they had worked toward us along narrow roads, or through fields and jungle, there had always been that thought of unlimited numbers still out of sight. But here they were, gathered around us. Vast, certainly, but not without limits.

The walls of the fort were only sparsely covered with insects. So far, the antriders seemed to be testing us. Only a few of their horses and riders scrambled up the walls, along with the pale colored engineers and the blue spies. I looked for signs of some other caste, but if they were there, they did not reveal themselves.

"Two men," I said.

"What?" asked Miss Marlowe.

I shook my head. "It's nothing. Only a thought I had about the antriders."

"Tell me," she said. "I'd rather hear your thoughts than go on with ones as dark as my own."

"I'm not sure that mine are any lighter." I explained to her how I had been estimating the size of the antrider army, and compared their mass to that of several jaguars. "It occurred to me just now that, though each of them has no more than a few grains to serve as a mind, together it may be that they carry a brain whose mass is equal to a man. Perhaps two men."

"The mind of two men," she said, "and a million weapons to deliver those thoughts." Though it was still daylight, and warm, I saw a shiver run through her body.

Without thinking, I put a hand on her back. Rather than pulling away, she moved toward me and I soon found my arm draped right round her shoulders. There were others on the planks with us, and several hundred souls packed tight in the yard below. It was certain that we were being watched. But I found myself marveling at the warmth of her skin. Her shoulders were neither so plump nor soft as those recorded in paintings presented as examples of perfect femininity, but they were very pleasant under my arm and I felt no compulsion to move away.

"How much longer?" she said.

"I can't know," I said. "They may move off in hours, or wait us out for days."

She shook her head, and the tumble of her short-cut curls brushed across my sleeve. "I wasn't speaking of the antriders. I was talking about you, Doctor Almost. How much longer must you work for the company to pay your debt?"

I was surprised that such a question should come up in this moment. "How did you even learn I was indebted?"

"You told me."

I turned to her and found that she had given off watching the antriders try their chances on the wall. Instead, her green eyes were fixed on me. "A year," I said. "Or at least, it was to be a year. Now, with all this..." I shrugged. "Who is to say?" I had not yet told Miss Marlowe about the death of the secretary, or what he had revealed before he died.

Miss Marlowe reached up and placed her own hand over mine. "I am. When Lord Haverset returns, I will insist that the rest of your term be forgiven, for services rendered the company."

From the heat I felt on my face, I was sure I presented a countenance as crimson as that of the antrider mounts. "I don't know that I've done anything that deserves reward."

She pulled free of my arm at this and moved round to stand face to face. "It was you that brought the warning of the intruder's advance. Had you not come back from Applewash, we would have had no word."

"That was a matter of survival," I said. "I don't know that I can claim any action more noble that keeping my own flesh away from the mouths of these insects."

Miss Marlowe considered this for a while, her generous lips pressed together in thought. "Well, even if you claim nothing but your own life, then you've showed more cleverness than all those that failed in the same task. You should be proud of that much."

Our conversation was interrupted as Sergeant Norris came stomping along the boards. If he was taken aback by closeness of Miss Marlowe and myself, he did not show it. "There's someone down below as wants to talk to you," he said.

"Where?"

"Inside the wall," he said. "The old commandant's office."

That was the place where the injured had been placed. I went down expecting that I would find that myself summoned by some settler who wanted my attention as patient.

Inside the office, there were several ranks of cots spread, so close that it was barely possible to fit between one and the next. Several of those confined to this place had been injured in conflict with the antriders.

Others had suffered gunshot, or injuries incurred along the road. There was an older man tending a badly burned woman in the corner, but the only real point of motion in the room was one I was surprised to see. Going back and forth among the cots was the small figure of Alice. From somewhere, the girl had found a sailor's ribboned hat and set it on her blonde head. She went from bed to bed, examining bandages and carrying water and food. Apparently, young Alice had taken a fondness for things medical.

I lifted the brim of her hat as she poured out a pitcher of water. "Where did you get this?"

"From him," she said, pointing at a man curled under a worn blanket. "He was sick, and his boat left him here."

"I see." Undoubtedly, some passenger had paid well for the berth that should have been occupied by this unfortunate sailor. "It's a shame we aren't really in the navy ourselves," I said. "You could be a surgeon's mate."

She looked up at me from under the hat, her eyes near the same blue as the ribbons. "Could I?"

The question was asked with such enthusiasm that I avoided the uncomfortable answer by asking a question of my own. "Was it you that called me down here?"

"No," said the man in the corner. "It was I."

I stared at him a moment, and was about to ask his name, when the sharp, haggard features suddenly came clear. "Captain Valamont?"

The soldier nodded and stood. The captain bore little resemblance to the man who had led that first ill-fated expedition out to Applewash. He was no longer wearing his fine braided uniform, and his own illness had carved flesh from his frame as effectively as a butcher paring down a ham. Fortunately, it also seemed that he was missing the madness that had so filled his eyes when he had first returned from that encounter.

"Sir," I said. "Are you sure you should not be in a cot yourself?"

Valamont shook his head quickly. "I've spent far too much time abed." He walked through the maze of cots to come closer. "Since you were out there doing my job in the service of the company, it seemed only appropriate that I aid those who were injured."

"I couldn't do your job, Captain. I am not a military man."

"The job of a soldier is to protect the citizens. It seems to me you've done that task much better than I." I tried to protest, but Captain Valamont gave me no chance.

"Dr. Brown, I asked you down here so that I could express my appreciation for your actions in saving my life."

"Saving you?" I flushed again at this fresh compliment. Everyone seemed prepared to reward me for courage I had never displayed. "At Caney Creek, I saved no one. No one but myself."

"I wasn't speaking of what happened in the west," replied Valamont. "I had in mind events that occurred in this same fort. Had you not come to me, I would have been killed."

"Oh," I said. "It seemed only fair. After I left, I—"

"You did not leave me, Dr. Brown," he said with the same forceful tone with which he had given orders to his men. "I was in command of our expedition, not you. I was responsible for the loss of those men."

I shook my head. "You didn't know, sir. I might have warned you."

"You did so. More than once if I recall." Valamont swayed on his feet. "But I ignored you."

"Sir," I said, "you are not well." I swallowed awkwardly, not sure how to comfort this man. It had been Valamont's delusions about the natives that sent me back out to face the antriders, though clearly he had made these assertions after his wits had left him. However, from what the secretary had said, both I and the captain had been sent into known danger. The false information had likely been provided him only to further the plot of those involved and increase the likelihood that both the soldiers and myself would meet a swift end. "You shouldn't be ashamed. Such a scene as we encountered could affect anyone."

"I am shamed," said Captain Valamont. "Even if I don't end my days on a gibbet, my honor is gone." He stood, nodded to me, and began to cross the room.

"Sir. Captain. It's not you who lacks honor." When he turned back to me, I recounted quickly the last meeting with the secretary and what he had revealed about the plot to draw out the antriders. I might have expected anger, but the captain only seemed more weary at the end of my statement than he had at the beginning. If there were more I could have said to reassure him, I would have done so. Instead, I checked on the patients who seemed most seriously ill then retreated from the room, leaving Captain Valamont to himself.

It was full up noon when I left the commandant's office. Out in the center of the fort, bed sheets and coats had been raised up as makeshift tents against the sun. The colonnade around the fort's perimeter was cooler by some degrees than the open parade ground, but few of the settlers or townspeople availed themselves of this shade. Without asking, I knew why this was so: they wanted as much space from the antriders as they could manage.

I climbed the slanted ladder back up to the boardwalk and looked over the wall. The antriders were still there. If anything, the insects were thicker than before. In some places they clung to the walls of the fort so thickly that it seemed the stones had grown some strange, colorful lichen.

Sergeant Norris went past, spotted a particularly dense mass of the insects, and poured a ladle of oil over the brim. A mostly clean clout had been wound around his wounded arm, and he seemed to be giving the injury little regard. The antriders went dancing out of the way of the sergeant's dollops of oil, but several were soaked. "Go on now," Norris called down. "There's tastier vittles to be had off in the jungle."

"How much oil is left?" I asked.

The sergeant lifted the bucket he carried and considered the contents. "Half a gallon here, still fifty some down below. Not counting that turpentine."

"They haven't tried to cross it?"

"No," he said, "but if we leave it too long in this heat, the stuff dries up, or soaks in, and then your bugs come creeping."

Fifty gallons. At the rate the oil was being consumed, we would be without defense in a matter of two days. Perhaps less, certainly no more. "What about food?" I asked.

Norris shrugged. "There's enough," he said. "Not so much as to have a feast, you understand, but there's bully beef and biscuit that was laid up here for the soldiers. Should hold this lot a week if we ration it out thin."

"Well, that's good then."

"The problem is the water."

I winced. "What about water?"

"In this heat, a man's going to need two quart a day, you can count on it," said the sergeant. "And that's if we ask nothing of him but to rest in the shade. A woman or a child might drink less, I wouldn't know, as I've never had to ration either before. We better hope they're bloody camels, because otherwise we'll be sucking the bottom of the barrels tomorrow night."

The news was bad on two fronts. Either the oil would run out first, and the antriders would scale the walls, or the water would run dry, and we would die of thirst.

"We're going to have to go out," I said.

"Out there?" Norris shook the ladle he carried toward the ground. "Have you looked out there? There's not a patch of ground big as a man's shoe that doesn't have a hundred of those bastards waiting to bite."

"We could rig something," I said. "There must be a way."

Norris shook his head. "Even if there's a way out, how will you get back in, especially if you're lugging a barrel of water or oil?"

I had no immediate response to this quandary. Norris resumed his course around the walls, ladling out oil where the barrier was starting to dry. Even with his attention, it seemed to me that the antriders were getting more daring. They were testing the edge of the oil, and though it was clear they didn't like what they found, I suspected they would soon apply their abilities to overcoming this new obstacle.

One way or another, time was growing short.

For the best part of an hour, while the sun passed its zenith and started down toward the west, I stood sweating on the boardwalk, watching the antriders, and considering everything that had happened in the last weeks. When that hour was over, I knew what I had to do.

Descending to the parade ground, I found Miss Marlowe working to unseal a barrel of biscuits. She looked up at me with a displeased expression. "Weevily," she said. "All of them. And the beef as hard as iron."

"I'm sorry," I said. Then, before I could lose my nerve, I followed up with another statement. "I'm leaving."

She wrestled at the top of the barrel for a moment longer then fixed her green eyes on mine. "Leaving? What in God's name does that mean?"

"Let me find Sergeant Norris and Father Samms," I said. "I'll need some help with this, and there's not time to go through it more than once."

Miss Marlowe followed me while I searched out the two men. Finally, the four of us gathered under the ladder on the north side of the fort.

"It's bad luck to stand under a ladder," said Norris.

"I hope not," I replied, "because I'm going to need my ration of luck and more to see this through." I gathered my breath and held up a sheet that I had liberated from the commandant's office. "I want you to wrap me up in cloth, like an Egyptian mummy."

"What good will that do?" asked Norris. "Those little buggers came right through my boots. No bit of bandage is like to stop them."

"It will," I said, "if it's on fire."

The commotion generated by this statement was loud enough to draw many curious looks from the people camped on the parade ground. I had to wait through many furious objections before I could explain further.

"The ocean is but twenty feet from the side of this fort," I said, keeping my voice pitched in a tone I hoped was calming to both my audience and my own twitching nerves. With every word of the plan, Father Samm's eyes got wider, and Miss Marlowe's narrowed. Sergeant Norris might have been playing at a hand of whist, so stolid was his expression. I plunged on, putting out my plan to its last.

When I was finished, I thought the vicar looked ill. I shared his feeling myself. "It's desperate, I'll grant you," I said, "but I believe it can work."

The clergyman shook his head vehemently. "No. It's far too much a risk. In all likelihood you'll be killing yourself for the barest of chances."

"It's a chance, but I'll lay you a certainty. If we take no action, within a matter of days, every man, woman, and child in this fort will be dead."

Sergeant Norris made a noise that sounded like laughter, but shorn of all amusement. "That's true enough," he said. "But even if this madness works to get you past them bugs going out, what's to get you back in?"

"I've thought of an answer to that, too." I said. "Help me get out, and I'll take care of the rest."

Through this last exchange, Miss Marlowe had remained silent. She stepped forward, her eyes so bright that it made me wonder if they might produce a light of their own. "Can you swim?" she asked.

I nodded. "Yes." Then I thought a bit longer, and amended my position. "But poorly."

"I see," said Miss Marlowe. "From the top of the wall, it's a forty foot fall to the waves, and that at high tide."

"Yes, I suppose that's so."

"And the currents are sharp against the bluffs."

"Probably."

"And you're to be wrapped top to bottom in layers of cloth—flaming cloth at that."

"Yes, though the sea should put out the flames quickly enough." I found the certainty of my voice much reduced. As Miss Marlowe spoke, my plan seemed more ridiculous by the word.

She paused a moment, then gave a nod. "I'm a passing good swimmer," she said.

I had only thought my plan drew active complaint. As soon as these words were out of Miss Marlowe's mouth, both Sergeant Norris and Father Samms came close to explosion. The Sergeant planted himself in front of the young woman and fairly screamed his disapproval. At one point, the vicar vented words I had not thought a clergyman would know, much less use.

Though the original plan was mine, I felt compelled to join in the condemnation of her proposal. "You can't go, miss," I said. "It's far too dangerous."

"You just said everyone here is going to die," replied Miss Marlowe, still calm despite the agitation around her. "What could be more dangerous than the situation in which we currently find ourselves?"

I drew a breath and started another tack. "You're needed here. These people know you."

"These people need a doctor far more than they need me," she said. "If I'm needed, then you're needed."

Father Samms began to offer another reason for her remaining, but Miss Marlowe cut him off at a glance. "Gentlemen, my father was the largest landholder in Selvanos, and by the grace of God and the express order of the director, his lands have been put under my control. With Lord Haverset away from the colony, I think you will find that I am the controlling officer present. If you do not wish to help me voluntarily, then consider this an order from the acting director."

Two hours later, we were both being escorted to the top of the wall.

"Watch your head there," said Sergeant Norris.

I ducked blindly, as watching my head was the one thing I could not do. Thick cloth had been wrapped around my face as well as my arms, body, and legs. I could barely move my feet to gain the next step, and could see nothing of whatever obstacle was there to strike my head. The bindings were so tight, and so thick, that the cloth made my movements extremely stiff. I could bend but little at either elbows or knees and could only walk by leaning first left, then right. I could scarce imagine what the people down on the parade ground must have thought to see myself and Miss Marlowe lurching up the sloping ladder and along the boardwalk.

I leaned right to take another step, and a hand clamped hard on my shoulder. "Careful now," said Sergeant Norris. "You're right at the edge."

I held still, feeling precarious and more than a little ridiculous. "Is Miss Marlowe here?" I had to work against the bandages simply to move my chin.

"I'm here," said her muffled voice from somewhere beyond the screen of bandages.

There was a fumbling at my waist as hands worked to tie a rope around me. "We'll have you ready in a moment."

"Good." My voice came out a squeak. I cleared my throat and tried again. "That's good. Wait until I've made it safely to the bay before you lower Miss Marlowe."

"I should go first," she said. "I'm the better swimmer."

"No," I said. "The antriders might not be stopped by the cloth. I have to go first and see that it's safe."

"But if you reach the water, and you get into trouble—"

"Hush up, the both of you," said Sergeant Norris. "Neither one is likely to live long enough to reach the ground, so I'm sending you both together."

A moment later, the pungent scent of lamp oil was thick in my nose. "Lightly," I said. "Else we'll burn too quick."

The sergeant laughed. "I expect you'll go up like candles."

For several minutes, I could feel hands brushing over me as the oil was applied to the outer coat of bandages. I tried to stand still during this treatment, but I feared the sergeant could feel me trembling.

"There now," said Norris. "Your painted good as a fence. Are you ready to go over?"

"Yes," I said. Beside me, I heard Miss Marlowe answer the same. The rope around my waist grew snug. "Don't—"

"You want to stop this idiocy?"

I shook my head, though I could not turn it far under the wrappings. "Don't light the oil until they come after us. The oil kept them from topping the wall. Maybe it will keep them off us."

"Maybe. But from the way they've piled up to greet you, I think I'll be dropping that torch soon."

I could not see the antriders that had assembled to meet our descent. For that bit of blindness, I was grateful.

The rope grew tighter yet. I slid my feet forward and felt empty space beneath my toes. I might have turned back still, but the oiled wall was slippery beneath my oiled feet. In a moment, I had left the top of the fort and was being lowered down the wall.

My legs and back bumped against the wall. Something crunched beneath me. I kicked my wrapped legs and swung back into the air. In the dark, hot confines of my bandages, the short trip down the wall seemed almost endless. My feet came up against the wall again. This time, there was no sound of crushed insects. Instead, a lancing pain struck at my ankle. Another on my shin. And my thigh. The pain struck again. And again. There were antriders on me, perhaps hundreds, and they were undeterred by the oil.

"Light it!" I cried. "Drop the torch!"

At once there was a dull noise, like a fist pounded into the ground. Heat washed over me. It was much hotter than I had expected, almost as if the oil had been spread on my skin rather than on cloth nearly an inch thick. I tried to breath, and drew in air so hot and saturated in smoke that I coughed again. I felt something under my foot, thought it was an antrider, and tried to pull my leg up. It was the ground. I landed unevenly, stumbled, and fell to my knees. Along my back, I felt the cloth tear and fire licked at my skin.

I struggled back to my feet and began to run. It was only three steps from the bottom of the wall to the top of the bluffs, but I took five steps. Ten. The fire was still tearing at me. My lungs crying for breath. Voices shouted. To my left. I had become turned around somehow, and instead of running to the bluff, had run along it. I turned right, took a single step, and plunged into the sea.

I had time to scream as I fell, but with no breath, could only give the faintest cry. I hit the water on my side, taking a good slap in the process. Then, before I could fill my lungs, I was under the waves.

There was blessed relief from the fire at my back and the heat that had coated me everywhere, but the pain in my chest only intensified and the salt water aggravated the points where I had been lanced by antrider knights. A length of rope was still tied round my waist, and the thick coat of cloth hindered me more in the water than on land. I fumbled at the rope. Tore at the cloth. Went back to the rope. It felt as if I were sinking, going deeper and deeper into the blue sea.

One hand came free of the wrapping. I clawed at the wrappings over my face.

Hands took hold of my arms and pulled. At first, my fear fueled by the fire, and the fall, and the bites of the antriders, I tried to escape this new attack. Then I realized the hands were taking me away from danger rather than adding more. My head emerged from the sea, and I took a great, ragged breath through the damp cloth.

"Hold still," said Miss Marlowe. "Lay back and float. I need to swim a bit if we're to find a safe place to reach land."

I coughed, breathed again, and nodded. "Thank you, Miss Marlowe."

"My name is Genevieve," she said. "You better start using it, or I'm putting you back under the waves." With only a minimal amount of additional assistance, I managed to follow her toward the surf.

She stopped at a point where she was still waist deep in the ocean, stood with her hands on her hips and peered toward the shore. "I don't see them," she said. "But I don't trust them."

We moved south along the shore, keeping to sandbars and shallows so that we did as much walking as swimming. Looking at the muddy shore where the Sarstoon emptied into the bay, we could see the edge of the wall and the homes and shops that had been the southern edge of St. George, but of the antriders there was no sign.

THE NATURALIST ✳ 195

"They've shown no sign of following us into the sea," I said. "Let's get up on shore, and if they come for us, we can always hurry back to the waves and move on."

Genevieve hesitated a moment then nodded and started slogging toward the shore. I stood and watched her. The fire had seared her clothing, leaving black marks along her shirt and darkening her linen trousers. Her hair, already thick with curls, had been tightened still more by the heat, and some of those scorched coils would have to be cut loose. Her torn, damp clothing stuck against her so that I could see every movement of the muscles in her legs and back as she moved toward shore. Again, I was struck by how little she resembled the illustrations that were meant to show womanly charms. And by how unreservedly beautiful she truly was.

We reached the ground at a place just at the Sarstoon's north bank. There were logs snagged against the end of the river, piled up and held in check by the ruins of the bridge, which had fallen into the water in two half-burnt sections. Off to our right, the waterfront inn stood intact, along with the warehouses and pier. They looked so still in the late afternoon light, but it was not impossible to think that the proprietor was still inside, or that tarry seamen might come strolling around the corner at any moment.

Cautiously, I crept up along the bank of the river and wound through the maze of storehouses that fronted the water. At first, I saw no antriders. We reached the open stretch of Kings Highway and looked up the hill toward the fort. I could see the dark horde that hugged the walls of the stronghold. The antriders had not given up their siege.

I had no idea if the antriders were sensitive to sound, but we moved across the road without comment. Genevieve needed no urging to keep quiet. Now that we were on the ground, she was anxious to move along. We passed between the shops on the west side of the street and got a good sight of the wall that been built around St. George. The barricade of furniture and boards was still intact everywhere but the place where we had opened it to the settlers. For the antriders, it had been no barrier at all.

I took a step into the space between the last shop and the start of the brick paving around Company House. "We should go in the west entrance," I said. "That will lead us straight to where the oil is held."

Genevieve did not respond. When I turned to look her way, I saw that her attention was fixed on the clapboard wall beside her.

"Calvin," she whispered. "Look here."

I followed the direction of her gaze and quickly found the source of her concern. A single blue antrider was clinging to the flaking green paint that covered the boards of the shop. Its head was up, and its forelimbs crooked in a way that made it more than ever resemble a mantis. The insect made no move to advance on us, but it's dark eyes tracked me as I stepped back beside Genevieve, the head moving by sudden shifts like that of a hunting bird.

"What is it doing?" asked Genevieve.

I shook my head. "I don't know. It might have become separated from the rest."

A slight odor reached my nose. It was sharp, almost like ammonia. I looked at the antrider and felt increasing anger as I understood what it was about. "They've set pickets."

"What?" asked Genevieve.

I rushed forward and slapped at the antrider. The creature responded with rapidity. It scurried away across the boards, just avoiding my fingers. Then it stopped again, pawing the air with its forelimbs and raising its stinger in a menacing way. I started to swing at its new position, but Genevieve stayed my hand.

"If it stings you, you'll be nursing that hand all day," she said. "You might need it for something else."

That was true enough. My right leg was still swollen and stiff from where the antriders had stung through the wrappings and my knee was hard to bend. "It's a beacon," I said. "They've posted pickets, like an army camped on enemy ground." I waved toward the insect on the wall. "This one has already sent his signal to the rest."

Genevieve scowled at the insect. She snatched a rock from the ground and hurled it at the little spy, but her blow missed by a hair and had no more effect than mine, as the antrider did not even bother to move to avoid the stone. "We should go," she said. "Before this little bastard's warning calls down the rest."

I agreed. Together we resumed our course out of the town.

But we did not slip away unnoticed. When we were still fifty yards shy of Company House, a patch of darkness came gliding toward us along the central street. The antriders were arranged in a square formation, as neatly dressed along the ranks as any Greek phalanx. The size of this group was small when compared to the great army at the fort, near ten feet on a side, but I had no doubt there were enough of the insects to deal with two humans—tired, injured humans at that. The antriders were approaching at the pace of a running man, and neither of us was fresh enough for a long pursuit.

Genevieve snatched at my hand as they approached. "The river," she said. "We should go into the river, or back to the docks."

I hesitated a second, then started dragging her in the other direction. "This way."

"They'll catch us," she said as we moved toward the brick square.

I glanced off to my right. The antriders were coming hard. "No they won't. Keep going."

We reached the door of Company House, still open from when Sergeant Norris and I had made our escape, and hurried down the hall to where the oil was stored. Our hands were still entangled as we plunged along the empty corridor, and my aching leg nearly folded as my foot slipped on some spilled oil, but with Genevieve's help, I remained upright long enough to reach the storeroom.

Genevieve halted beside me and looked back. "They're not ten yards behind us."

"Quick," I said. "Help me turn this over." Together we took hold of the nearest barrel and rocked it forward, back, and then forward with all our combined force. The barrel fell loudly, and the band at the top separated. Oil immediately gushed forth, sending a frothy wave back down the path we had just followed.

Genevieve looked around the room. "That should stop them for now," she said, "but how are we to get out."

"Over there." I indicated a narrow window along the side of the room.

The answer seemed to puzzle her. "We can't get the barrels out that window. It's too small, and besides, they're too heavy to lift."

"I don't intend to move the barrels," I said. I searched among the shelves of the storeroom until I had found rags and wrapped them around two ax handles. Then I crouched and rolled the cloth across the oil soaked floor.

"What are you doing?" asked Jenny.

"Making torches."

"It won't be dark for hours yet. Why do we need torches?"

"Because," I said. "We're going to burn St. George."

# 18

*St. George*
*2 September 1832*

*HMS Admirable,* a second-rater out of Kingston, left from St. George harbor on the afternoon tide, carrying with her most of the surviving colonists of Selvanos. I stood on the ash covered shore and continued to wave long after I could no longer make out the form of Genevieve Marlow among the figures on the deck.

As one of the largest stakeholders in the company, Genevieve might have been expected to protest the idea of setting a torch to everything of value in the town. However, it took her only a moment's thought to agree with my plan. We departed through the window of Company House with the oil already burning merrily behind us. By the time we were a hundred yards away, black smoke was boiling from every window of the structure and yellow flames could be seen escaping at the eaves.

Soon enough, neighboring buildings were also aflame, and when it seemed that the fire might not jump King's Way and make its way to the blocks along Water Street, we used our torches to be sure that it did. Lastly, we retreated to the edge of the city and set fire to the wall of jumbled furniture and boards.

From the top of the old fort, both of us had noted that the numbers of the antriders were not unlimited. More than that, their ranks were all contained in St. George—all pressed into narrow roads between clapboard buildings. All contained within that barricade of wood that had done so little to keep them out. But set alight, it served well enough to keep them in, just as smaller conflagrations had served to halt their movements in my previous encounters.

Several times during that afternoon, the antriders made attempts to stop us. Given time to plan their strangely rational plans, they might have worked out a way around the flame, ash, and smoke. We did not give them time. We spread the fire quickly, barely staying ahead of the flames. That night, Genevieve and I stood together waist-deep in the crashing waves and watched all the homes of St. George, including my own, rise up in a ferment of embers and smoke. Even from where we stood, the heat was so intense that it scorched what little hair had remained unharmed in our escape from the fort. From Company House, great towers of flame burst skyward as barrels of oil and casks of black powder exploded. In the square, the heat was so penetrating that the bricks themselves were shattered.

For those inside the fort, I am told the heat was nearly unbearable. But only nearly so. Everyone in the fort who was not gravely wounded lived through the firestorm.

Afterward, a few of the settlers from the interior regions declared their intent to return to their homes, but only a scant few. Many were afraid that more antriders might still wait in the jungle. Others were merely unsure that they could make a living from their land when there was no company to organize sales and manage the port. Even most of those works which had gone untouched by the passage of the antriders were soon deserted.

Gradually, the story of the secretary's plot had come out, and speculation rose on which of the company officers might have been involved in the affair. Both Sergeant Norris and I were called on repeatedly to recount our story in front of larger and larger groups, but there was no way of settling the thing short of taking the accusations to the men involved.

It was inevitable that Genevieve would have to take leave on the first boat. Haverset, despite everything he had done, was still Lord Haverset, and many of those he had taken away with him had high standing. Genevieve, and Captain Valamont, and Father Samms, and many others besides, would have to press their case in court if they wanted to see any chance of justice when it came to settling the company's accounts.

I might have gone with them, but considering that I was still in debt to the company, no funds recovered were likely to flow my way, and the lands I had hoped so long to inherit were in all likelihood as worthless of those of the others who had abandoned the smoldering ashes of St. George,

I decided there was little value in following after the leaders. Besides, in the days since the fire, an opinion had been growing among many of the survivors that burning the town had not been necessary. More temperate action might have saved both lives and the colony, they said. By the day of the *Admirable's* departure, many of them seemed to hold me as much to blame as the antriders.

Perhaps at some future date, St. George would be rebuilt, and the lumber on my parents' land would again have value. Perhaps the British Central Timber Company would be restored to soundness and my place in it secured. It seemed unlikely. Until then, it seemed best that I stay well away from those who had lost everything in the failed experiment of Selvanos.

Fortunately for me, the captain of the *Admirable* had let me know of a pair of ships beating their way south on a hydrographic survey of the southern end of the continent. One of these was the *Adventure*, the other the little coffin brig, *Beagle*. I was told that one of these ships would surely have use for a ship's doctor. And though it is unlikely, perhaps one of them might even make use of an amateur naturalist.

## About the Author

Mark is the author of a bunch of novels, lots of short stories, and essays. His novel *Devil's Tower* was nominated for the World Fantasy Award, and his *News from the Edge* series was turned into a TV show called *The Chronicle*, which aired on the Syfy Network.

Mark has held nearly every job known to man, including coal miner, USGS cartographer, newspaper photographer, and database architect. He has dug for dinosaurs in South Dakota. He used to know the genus and species of every freshwater fish in the United States. When he isn't writing or working or blogging, Mark enjoys paddling out on the lake in his kayak and watching the resident osprey hunt for his breakfast. The lake used to contain a lake monster, but Mark hasn't spotted him in a while.

## Word Posse Fun Fact

Though I tried my hand at writing several times in high school and college, the results were uniformly awful. It wasn't until I was in my early thirties that I took a creative writing class at Meramec Community College near St. Louis. In that class, I cranked out a story called "Live Bear" which featured an agent from the Bureau of Indian Affairs who was disappointed by the contradictions of his job and the ugliness of the limits he had to impose. The story went on to be featured in a small press magazine and gave me enough of an ego boost to get serious about cranking out words. It was only two years from there to winning the Writers of the Future Award and selling my first novel.

www.ingramcontent.com/pod-product-compliance
Lightning Source LLC
Chambersburg PA
CBHW060056150626
46556CB00017BA/872